# Lured by the Lorelei

**EMILIA ABRAHAM**

"I just have something—"

"I didn't want to bring this up, but you owe me, Slade. I'm calling in your debt. You do this and we'll be square."

I sigh and my chest tightens as magic spears into me. "You're a real asshole, you know that, Holden?"

He chuckles lightly. "Don't I know it. I'd do it myself if I could, Slade. Unfortunately, I have my own saving to do. Can't be there for everyone all at once. You know a thing or two about that, don't you?"

"Yeah, I do," I breathe. "Fine, I'll be there by tonight. You going to have a place for me to stay or do I have to sleep in my car? Again."

"Uh, no. I wouldn't make you do that. I'll…I'm texting you an address. You can stay there."

"You're not sending me to a dog groomer, are you? Because that shit was funny the first time, but a second is pushing it."

He laughs, then hangs up. A minute later, his text comes through. I pull over to the side of the deserted road and plug the address into my GPS. A house pops up, not a dog groomer, but that doesn't mean much. It could be someone working out of their home.

I'd deserve a prank like that. I've participated in my fair share, especially with Holden. Like the time I sent him fifty raw potatoes in the mail, one at a time, from various parts of the country. He kept sending me photos of them covered in stamps, absolutely flabbergasted. Took him way too long to figure out it was me.

I pull onto the road again and make my way toward Hart's Hallow. Towns become sparse until long stretches of woods bracket my car. With the lack of traffic and endless pavement in front of me, my mind wanders all the way back to my childhood home in Moon Cove.

Before I left, Dad was hiding something. He never was very forthcoming, especially with his kids. Mom wasn't talking either, though. I need to call Kira to see if she'll visit them soon. Alissa's still hiding out in the woods north of Moon Cove, and the others aren't answering their phones. If my parents need help, they'll never ask us.

I almost miss the turnoff, my head is so far in the clouds. I slam on the brakes, pebbles pinging off my undercarriage and dust swirling around me. I huff out a deep breath and slowly make the turn. A canopy of leaves overhead has shadows dancing on the gravel. I'd probably think it was idyllic if I was trying not to get lost.

With each curve in the road, my stomach flips, expecting to see a house, a business, hell, even a road sign. Except there's nothing. Nothing save for the fluffy seeds floating through the air and the heavy heat seeping through the windshield. Spring around here doesn't seem to agree half the time. Either it's hella hot with steam coming off the pavement or a lovely May day that turns into a thunderstorm without warning.

"If this shit makes me stuffy, I'm going to lose it," I mutter as I crest a large hill. As the valley opens up, my jaw drops, and I slam on the brakes.

Nestled at the bottom is a quaint town spreading from the main street running down the middle. I've never seen roofs in so many different colors. Everything from rust red to pale blue to sunset orange. Whoever designed this place definitely had a vision. Each of the businesses sports a front porch complete with either rocking chairs or a swing.

I ease my way into town, creeping along to gawk at the hand-painted signs announcing what each building sells. A diner sits next to a post office, butting up to a bookshop. I peer down a side street and find a bed-and-breakfast on the edge of a pond. I glance at my phone, but it tells me to keep going straight.

Following the road, I leave the businesses behind and wind my way around several curves. A small house comes into view. I swear it came straight out of a fairy tale, complete with the fancy swirl edging around the roof. I'm half expecting gumdrops to be stuck to the top and candy canes to make up the little fence lining the front walk.

My phone buzzes, and Holden's text flashes across the screen: *Be nice to my sister.* Well, shit. I'm not surprised he sprung this on me, though.

A woman steps onto the porch and wipes her hands on her frilly apron. She shields her eyes from the setting sun as she tracks my car bobbling its way toward her. Holden's elusive sister.

I hit a particularly deep pothole and wince. I don't know what Kira did to this thing while she was driving halfway across the country, but it drifts now. One wrong move and I'm afraid the tire will go flying toward her. Killing Holden's sister would definitely put a damper on our relationship. I slam on my brakes, and gravel kicks toward her, the dust swirling around me.

She crosses her arms and leans against the porch column. When she pops her hip out, my mouth waters. A very curvy, very delectable hip. If taking her out with parts of my car would be bad, hooking up with her would be worse. I save my flings for strangers I'll never see again. The kind of people who don't care when I blast out of town for the next adventure. Everyone's on the same page. Better than leaving a trail of hurt feelings and broken hearts in my wake. Which means I definitely can't bed Holden's sister. No strings, no threads, no ties. It's worked for me this long. I'm not about to fuck with the system for a woman. Especially this woman.

With those hips and that golden hair and her lush lips, staying away from her might be harder than I thought. I push from the car and plaster on my most charming smile. She narrows her eyes, though that's probably the sun. Unless Holden didn't tell her I was coming. He might have kept that little nugget from her, assuming she'd just roll with this new development.

"Hi there," I call, lifting my hand in greeting.

Her gaze sweeps across my body, and a flash of heat hits me. My foot hits a rock and I stumble. Thankfully, I catch myself before I faceplant in front of her. Not exactly a good first impression.

"I think your car is smokin'," she murmurs. Her voice floats through the air, wraps around me, and settles in my bones. It's both light and dark—secrets hidden within shadows. Ethereal.

Her words filter sluggishly through the dull buzz ringing in my ears. I shake my head, then whip around. She's right. Smoke billows from under the hood, tingeing the air with the smell of burning rubber. I'm not a mechanic, but even I know it's not good. My skills extend slightly beyond basic maintenance. Changing the oil? Easy peasy. Bursting into flames? Not a chance. Hopefully, it's just a belt.

"Uh, yeah. I'll…deal with that later," I mumble as I turn back to her. "I'm Slade, Holden's friend?"

"There something I can help you with?"

"Actually, he said there's something I can help *you* with." I shoot her another smile, and I swear her eye twitches.

"Too bad for you, I don't need anything. I'm just fine how I am. Call someone to get that…thing off my property. Good meetin' ya."

She turns, her hair streaming behind her. Just like that. She didn't even seem fazed. I don't know if I've ever met someone who put me in my place so abruptly without at least a warning. I should let her go. I definitely shouldn't see it as a challenge to at least get a smile out of her. That'd be way too much, especially since we've only just met. I rush forward and she spins around.

"Stop," she snaps as my feet hit the bottom of the steps, and I freeze. "I don't know who you are, mister, but you will leave. Now."

"Sorry, I didn't..." I pinch the bridge of my nose to ease the headache suddenly forming behind my eyes. "Thing is, I can't just leave. Holden called in a debt, and I have to repay him."

She presses her lips together, then points at my feet. "Stay."

With that, she sweeps into the house, the screen door slamming shut behind her. I glance over my shoulder, wishing I had grabbed my phone. She's probably calling Holden, but if she's ringing up the sheriff, I'm going to need an alibi. That's probably not the right word. My head is muddled, though. I've been on the road for too long. I need a bed and no more visits from mysterious dark creatures. Running might help, but shifting right now seems like a lot of work.

The sun streams through the leaves, and I tuck my chin to my chest. It'll be dark soon and I'd rather not be caught out here in the woods at night. Finding a place to stay will be top priority. The woman's raised voice streams through the screen, and I peer inside. I can't see much other than a dark room and a couch. The woman paces toward the back, dragging a long cord behind her. I didn't think people had landlines anymore. I'm pretty sure she's in the kitchen.

"Well, I don't want him here. I don't need help." She pauses, clearly listening for a response. "I'm perfectly capable of fixin' it up myself. I don't want—No, Holden." She rubs her forehead. "I...fine. One week, then he's gone. But if he keeps smiling at me, I'm going to punch him in his pretty face."

She hangs the phone on the receiver, then sucks in a deep breath as she smooths her palms down her apron. She's clearly bracing herself to deal with me.

An unbidden smile lifts my lips, and I wipe it away. No reason to piss her off more than she is already. She stomps back toward me, her bare feet snapping on the hardwood floors. When she spots me, she scowls.

"Ground rules," she snarls through the screen door. "Don't be an asshole. Don't go swimming in the river. Don't go into my bedroom. Showers are to be no more than ten minutes and no using my shampoo. I will not feed you. I will not do your laundry. I will not fix your car. You do as much as you can in a week and then you're gone."

She ticks off each one on her fingers. I don't hear half of what she says. I'm too busy studying her heart-shaped face and pert nose. The shadows hide the color of her eyes, and I'm kicking myself for not paying attention earlier. She clears her throat and glares at me.

"This is important. If it's night and you hear someone whistling, no you didn't. Understood?"

I run my tongue along my bottom lip, and her gaze darts down. "So you think I'm pretty?"

# Chapter 2
## Scarlett

I thought coming out to the middle of nowhere would mean I'd avoid situations like this. For the last five years, it's worked wonderfully. Holden, my brother, had to be a meddling harpy and ruin all my plans. I was perfectly fine plodding along without the extra baggage. I have enough of that to last me a lifetime.

My hand hits the wall and I close my eyes, attempting to catch my breath. This is the last thing I need right now. Footsteps shuffle behind me, and my spine snaps straight. When I glance over my shoulder, Slade doesn't seem to notice. I'm good at hiding how I feel. He seems entirely self-absorbed. The sooner I get him out of my house, the sooner things can go back to normal.

"So, Holden didn't tell me much of anything."

"Probably so you'd agree to come," I mutter as I lead him toward the back of the house.

"Didn't have much choice. I owed him."

I grit my teeth, refusing to engage in any fluffy conversation. I'll just make Holden tell me everything later. Beats making small talk with the interloper.

"We don't have to chitchat. I'm used to being alone, and I'm sure you have better things to do."

"Not really. I don't even know your name. Don't you think that's something I should know?"

I huff, though it's mostly because I can't catch my breath. "It's Scarlett. Holden is my brother. The back of the house is falling down and needs to be renovated. I'm assuming that's why he sent you."

I lead him out the side door and around the back. My place isn't very big, but I'm only one person. A bigger kitchen would be nice, though. With the amount of baking I do, I should add an oven. And a sink. And more countertop. None of which matters since I can't afford to redo the entire layout of the house.

"Do I get more of a tour of the house?" he asks from entirely too close. When I turn around, though, he's several feet behind me. I spin back and continue down the tree-lined lane.

"No. You're staying back here. It's not fancy, but it's got a bed and a toilet. Showering has to happen in the house."

I wouldn't be surprised if he balks when he sees the state of the place. In fact, I'm banking on it. Pretty boy like him prob-ably needs a feather bed and silk sheets, not a rundown shed that's been converted into a one-room shack. I'm gracious enough to let him stay a night instead of sleeping in his car. We reach the end of the path, and I sweep my hand out to present his new home.

"This is…nice." He leans back on his heels, hands tucked in his pockets. "Just a quick question. Does the roof leak? And if yes, then do you have a tarp?"

"A tarp won't help if there's rain. Wind comes through this valley something fierce. It'll be fine, though." It probably won't. May is pretty wet here, and the storms can get pretty bad. If it comes down to it, I won't make him stay here. I don't have to offer, though. At least not yet.

He nods, then tilts his head. "More of a lean-to, huh? Think there's spiders?"

"Can't stay if you've got arachnophobia. I won't judge you for having a phobia, but you really can't—"

"Don't have arachnophobia. Unless I'm in the shower. Close my eyes and I'm afraid they'll come out the showerhead." He shudders, then grins. "You seen that movie?"

"No." I have, but he doesn't need to know that. "Sheets and whatever are in the closet. Do you need anything else?"

He glances at the sky, then at me. "It's early. You telling me I have to sequester myself in here until morning? Because I haven't eaten in a hot minute."

"Rule number five: I'm not feeding you."

He smirks, rocking back on his heels again. "Actually, I thought we'd go out. My treat."

I narrow my eyes. "No."

I slip around him, and his chuckle follows me as I make my way back to the house.

"Doesn't have to be a date, beautiful," he calls.

My feet stutter to a stop, and I swing back to face him. "New rule. Don't call me beautiful."

His eyebrows inch under his dark hair sweeping over his forehead. I've done my best to keep myself from studying him. The minute he stepped from his rust bucket, I knew I was screwed. He's exactly who I would have been drawn to when I was younger. He represents everything I left behind. Minus the smiling, I suppose. Most of my past is filled with assholes and deadbeats. The narcissists were the worst, though. While I haven't gotten that gut feeling when it comes to Slade, I'm not taking any chances. Besides, men like him never stick around.

Slade nods. "Duly noted. My apologies, Scarlett. I was serious, though. I need to eat, and I assume you do, too. We don't even have to talk. We can sit in comfortable silence while we consume food. You might have to drive, though."

He seems genuine, but I still don't trust him. Of course I don't. I just met him and he's invading my life, even if it is only for a week. I trust Holden, though, and if my brother trusts Slade, then I might have to give in just a little. Besides, it's not like Holden hasn't been pushing for this for months now. He warned me he was going to get someone out here. I just didn't believe him.

"I'm making fried bologna for dinner," I say slowly, and his eyes light up. They remind me of dark brown sugar, all crumbly and sweet. This is bad. Very fucking bad.

"Okay?" His tone holds a hint of anticipation. I could back out right now and walk away.

I sigh, my chest tightening as I do. "You can join me. With the silence as a side."

"Great. I love fried bologna. Lead the way, beau—Scarlett."

I pivot again and march to the house. I make the mistake of going through the back door. The hinges scream and I wince. If he gets hurt by putting his foot through a weak floorboard, I'm screwed. Then again, he's probably a shifter. He'll heal quick enough, but he'd still end up on my couch.

I open my mouth to warn him, then snap it shut. If I'm not careful, I'll end up letting him in. He'll burrow deep enough I'll never get him out. His presence will fester with the rest of my mistakes and never leave me be.

"This what I'll be working on, then?" He scans the closed-in porch.

"Sure," I murmur, glancing around.

I'd convinced myself it wasn't as bad as I first thought. Seeing it through his eyes and yeah, it's really bad. Holes litter the floor, all the windows need to be replaced, and the frames are chipping. I can't wait until he sees the rest of the work. We might not even get to dinner.

"Do you have supplies already?"

"Uh, no." I swallow hard, then shuffle my way toward the other door. At least this one doesn't screech at my entrance. Instead, it sticks in the frame, and I yank harder on the handle.

Slade slips next to me, his arm brushing mine, and I jerk away. "May I?"

I step back, and he wiggles the door until it pops open. He steps inside before I can stop him. I didn't expect to be embarrassed. It's not my fault the house is falling apart. And I didn't buy it in this condition.

I lived a long time without having any issues. Then, one of the pipes burst in winter. Next, hail came through and took out some of the windows. The roof didn't fare much better, but I only had enough money to fix one of them. Holden did what he could with some used windows. It wasn't enough. When the raccoons moved into the crawl space under this room, I almost lost it. Part of me wishes I could just demolish everything past the kitchen. I'd be without half the square footage, but whatever.

"Scarlett," Slade calls, and I hurry into the next room. "You know this would take more than a week, right? And I'm not a contractor. Not technically."

"What does that mean?" I plant my fists on my hips.

"I used to be licensed. Ran a crew for a contractor for a while, but that was a long time ago. And not in this state. And I had others who did things like the electrical and plumbing. If I do this, I won't be able to pull permits or get it inspected." He ducks his head and practically sticks it in the defunct fireplace. It hasn't worked in over a year.

"Suppose you should just tell Holden that, then. Or you can do whatever you can without a permit. I'll...hire someone else to do the rest."

I sweep past him through the arched doorway. I pass the half bath and closet, studiously ignoring the closed doors on either side of me. He hasn't followed me, and I fight the urge to tell him to get on with it.

I yank my bedroom door closed and rest my forehead against the white wood. The last thing I want to do is cry in front of this man. I told Holden I didn't want help for this exact reason. He didn't understand, insisting no one would care—no one would judge.

"You know I can—"

"I'm going to make the fried bologna. You want one or two?" I straighten and swipe my sweaty palms on my apron.

I hurry into the kitchen before he can respond. By the time he appears, I've gathered half the ingredients and I'm setting a pan on the stove.

"What type of bread is that?" he asks as he sits on one of the stools by the pass-through to the dining room. My kitchen isn't exactly built for more than one person. Holden said it was ridiculous to put such a large island in this small space, but I needed the extra counter rather than the places to walk.

"Croissant sourdough," I mutter as I cut several slices.

"Looks good. Three." He leans back, his gaze boring into me.

I glance up and instantly regret it. His eyes are fixed on me, or rather, my hands. My mouth waters, and I blame it on the sweet scent of the bread instead of his shirt pulled tight across his chest. Heat flashes through me, and I grab the chain above me to turn on the fan. This room gets hot quickly when I'm using the oven. Not that it's on right now. It has nothing to do with his tight jeans encasing his long legs stretched out in front of him. My own feet dangle when I'm sitting on the stool, and I'm not exactly short.

In my haste to get away from my own thoughts, my hip slams into the corner of the counter. I grimace and rub the spot before grabbing the butter from the fridge.

"Three what?" I choke out, then clear my throat.

"I'll take three sandwiches," he murmurs, and I realize he's right across the island now. Like he jumped up as soon as I hurt myself.

I go through the familiar motions of making the food. He doesn't ask if I'm alright. He doesn't fill the silence with needless chatter. He doesn't pepper me with questions about the renovation. By the time he sits again and I'm ready to cook, most of the tension has drained from me. A band of pressure squeezes my forehead still. It'll get better as soon as I eat.

He takes the plate I hand him and follows me into the small dining table I shoved in the corner of the living room. Holden always thought it was weird to eat at the table when it was just me. For some reason, it makes me feel less lonely. Having someone else here, even a man I don't actually know, isn't as awkward as I expected. He takes his promise seriously, never breaking the quiet. When he's finished, he leans back and folds his hands over his stomach.

"That was the best grilled bologna I've ever had even if it's the first one. But that bread?" He shakes his head as if he doesn't have words.

I fight off a smile. "Fried. And I made it."

He gives me a curious look. "Yeah, beau—Scarlett. I watched you make them."

"No, I mean the bread. That's what I do. I make bread and sell it in town. Among other things."

"I have questions about the other things, but first...you fucking made this?" He leans forward, planting his elbows on the table. "How do you do it? My mom makes buns for Samhain. Now that I think of it, though, that's probably Kira."

"Who's Kira?" As soon as the question pops out, I wish I could stuff it back in. This is exactly what I wanted to avoid—getting to know him.

"One of my sisters. I have a lot of siblings. We're all kind of scattered now."

Anxiety wells up within me. I can't stay here in this small room with him. The walls move, slowly closing in on me. My vision tunnels and I struggle to pull in a full breath. I shove my chair back, and it knocks against the wall. The edges of Slade's form waver as he tips halfway out of his seat. I gather his plate and mine, desperate to get away but needing an excuse.

"I'm going to bed. There's bedding in the closet in the cabin."

I rush from the room, not giving him a chance to respond. I'm sure he can see me through the cutout in the wall. My gaze keeps skipping around, and I drop the dishes into the sink. I'll deal with them tomorrow. It'll put more on my list, but I need to hide. I hurry away and resist the urge to slam my bedroom door.

I lean against the wood and close my eyes. As soon as I get myself together, I'll be fine. Everything will be fine. I just have to remember to keep my distance. One week and my life will go back to normal. Slade will leave and the quiet will seep back in. I'll be alone, but that's just the way I like it.

# Chapter 3

I stare at Scarlett's closed door, weighing the risks of knocking. I don't know what I said or did to make her run. Sighing, I shuffle to the front. I shouldn't snoop while she isn't around, but I can't help noticing things. Each room is an eclectic mishmash of items. It's as if she's traveled all over the world and filled her space with reminders of her adventures. I could spend weeks in here and still not see it all. I'd expect it to feel cluttered and disorganized. Instead, it's cozy and inviting.

The cool night air washes over me as I step outside. I pull in a deep breath, letting the familiar noise of the forest settle me. I leave most of my stuff in the car, taking only what I'll need for tonight. My phone lights up from its mount, and I snatch it up. I'm greeted with a dozen text messages from Holden, plus a few from my various family members. I slip it into my pocket.

I opt to go around the house instead of through it this time. No reason to freak Scarlett out. I get the feeling she's not used to visitors. Ambushing her after she practically sprinted out of the dining room wouldn't put her at ease at all. Besides, I need to remember why I'm here, and it's not to get a woman to like me. Once I fulfill my debt to Holden, I'll be in the wind. I have no idea where I'll go next, and I'm not ready to figure it out.

My head whips around at the shuffling of leaves to my right.

Of course, nothing emerges from the darkness, and I hurry onward. The shack comes into view, and my shoulders slump. Scarlett may have called it a cabin, but it's more of a lean-to. I wouldn't be surprised if it had been used as a shed in the past. The steps sag under my weight, and the door creaks as I push it open. Hopefully it has a lock, or I might end up with a fuzzy friend to cuddle with.

I flip the switch by the door, but nothing happens. I do it a couple more times, just in case. The flashlight on my phone will have to do. The small beam doesn't help much, and I end up tripping over a small stool.

"What are you milking, cows?" I mutter as I shove it away with my foot.

It takes me a couple minutes, but I finally find a string hanging from the ceiling. Blessed light floods the space when I tug on it. I scan the space. A small bed shoved in the corner with a tiny nightstand tucked next to it. Walls jutted out to encase what I assume is the toilet. The world's smallest sink tucked beside it. I'll have to wash my hands one at a time. Closet is a generous word to describe where the bedding is. I drop my bags and take one step, then reach for the blankets in the cubby hanging near the ceiling.

"I'll be lucky to get out of this with only a dozen slivers," I mumble, then glance around. I'm not usually paranoid about talking to myself, but I swear the walls have eyes. Or maybe it's the single window hanging by the front door. Only a thin piece of fabric covers the glass.

Once I finally settle between the sheets, I'm exhausted and it isn't even that late. Today took it out of me. Between running from the night watchers, worrying about my family, and getting bullied into coming here, I need sleep. I have to respond to Holden first, though. The rest can wait until tomorrow.

I only get through two messages before my phone vibrates

and Holden's name flashes across my screen. I brace myself before answering.

"Hey, Holden. Just got to your texts. What's up?" I tuck one arm behind my head and stare at the ceiling.

"What's up? Seriously? The last message I got from you was you were lost. Then you don't answer your phone for hours. What the fuck."

"Uh, sorry?" I'm not used to someone checking on me or caring enough to even try. Most of my family gets caught up in their own lives. My friends assume I'm off on another adventure.

"Seriously, Slade," he snaps, then sighs. "Is she okay?"

I hold back a chuckle as it finally clicks. He's not worried about me at all. I don't blame him for caring about his sister more than me. She's his family. I hide the sting of hurt under humor.

"She's fine. A bit...standoffish. Gave me a whole set of rules to follow. I'll wear her down." Even if I'm not going to pursue her, doesn't mean I don't want her to like me.

A strangled sound echoes through the phone. "Abso-fuck-ing-lutely not."

I scramble to sit up, and my head grazes a shelf hanging above the bed. I rub the spot as I laugh. "No. I just mean she hasn't been charmed by me yet."

"Not helping, asshole."

"Shit. I'm not trying to fu—"

"Shut the fuck up. I knew this was a bad idea."

"Okay. Okay. Just...calm down. I'm just not used to people not liking me. I get the feeling she doesn't want me here, but she definitely needs the help. Have you seen the back of her house? Half the wood is rotted. She only gave me a week—"

"For fuck's sake," he breathes, and I wait. "Listen, I don't want her losing the house. It's the only reason I called you. She's one bad storm away from having the whole damn thing blow away. I'll get her to let you stay longer."

"I don't need you to step in, Holden. I'll figure things out." The minute he calls her, I'm screwed. She'll never trust me, and it'll make my stay incredibly awkward.

"Shit. She got you, didn't she? Fuck. I knew this would… listen. It's not real and it's not her fault. Just go easy on her. And don't get attached. Keep your head down and do the work, then be on your way. Out of anyone, I know you'll be able to handle it. I gotta go." He hangs up before I can ask questions. And I have a lot of questions.

What exactly do I need to be handling? What's not real? I probably wouldn't blame Scarlett regardless of what he said. She doesn't seem the type to be mean on purpose, despite her treatment of me.

I send out a few texts to Holden, but they sit undelivered. I thought Holden was going out of town for work. One of us must be in a dead zone, which is just fucking great. Asking Scarlett wouldn't go over very well.

With a huff, I toss my phone on the nightstand, but it slides off the other side. I'll get it tomorrow. Even after I turn out the light and close my eyes, sleep evades me. I spend a long time coming up with various theories. Chasing after her secrets will only expose my own. And I can't allow that to happen.

# Chapter 4

## Scarlett

Five in the morning comes too soon. I stumble my way into the kitchen and shiver at the chill. Leaving the window cracked last night wasn't my best idea. I should get dressed, then make my tonic. Pajama shorts and a ratty tank top aren't going to keep me warm. Muscle memory takes over after I shut the window and set my kettle on the stove. My eyes flutter shut while I wait for the water to boil.

My mind wanders to yesterday. Slade seems like the type to sleep in, so I don't have to worry about him busting in here. I tip some leaves into the kettle and seal the jar. Steam wafts through the air, and I press a fist to my chest. The cold air helps, but it's not enough. Once my tonic is done, I sip it slowly. Heat seeps into my bones, unravels my muscles, and eases my lungs. The peace won't last long, but it'll get me through the morning.

As soon as my head clears, I set about cleaning up the kitchen from the night before. Thankfully, I put all the food away last night so I just have the dishes. I go through my routine, emptying the dishwasher and filling it again, then setting up my things to make bread. Two dozen loaves and a batch of cookies are on order today. I should have split it up over a couple days. By the time I'm done, my body will probably shut down.

I set my music, then start the dough. I've been doing this for years now and no longer need a recipe for most things. Even though I can eyeball most of the ingredients, I still use a scale.

The next hour flies by and I'm opening the window by the end. I need an extra oven. And a larger dishwasher. And more counter space. Or I just need to get better at spacing out the orders. Either way, I can't keep going like this.

By the time my dough is resting, I'm exhausted. I could go back to bed, sleep for thirty minutes, then deal with my dough. Usually, I do yoga while the sun rises. Most days I have to force myself to go through with the plan and today is no different. It takes me a good ten minutes to change and get my stuff set up by the river.

I glance at the cabin, though I can barely make it out through the trees. I'd go farther away, but this is the only flat space that's not in the middle of the yard. At least here I'm hidden away a bit. Thank the goddess for headphones.

I pull up my playlist and start, yet my gaze keeps being pulled back toward the cabin. When I close my eyes, an image of him last night, legs stretched out, hands folded over his flat stomach, and a smirk playing on his face, pops into my mind. He won't leave me alone, and he's been here less than twenty-four hours.

Eventually, I just go through the motions. I won't be ascending to any meditative states this morning. Then again, I rarely do anyway. Whenever I get done, I feel both better and worse. Muscles like jelly and brittle bones about to crumble to dust. My brain feels like it's breathing again. Like I've scooped it out of my head, unraveled it, and wound it back up before inserting it into place once more.

The music dies out, and chirps from birds in the trees filter in. As the wind whistles through the trees, a small smile lifts my lips. I gather my things and turn to go shower.

Movement by the back of the house catches my eye, and I

freeze. Slade's form comes into view, but he's focused on assessing the damage on the house. I don't think he's seen me, so I crouch. I probably look ridiculous as I run hunched over. Still, I make it to the front without him calling out to me.

I rush into the kitchen and deal with the bread before stumbling into the shower. The hot water eases the ache from my body, and the steam opens up my lungs. It's enough to keep me going. I need a nap and food. Not necessarily in that order.

If I don't hurry, I'll end up feeding Slade again. If I make him food, I'll be forced to talk to him. I didn't exactly give a good impression yesterday. I can't figure out if I'm okay with that or not.

"Scarlett?" Slade's voice echoes through my bedroom door. It's like I summoned him, which is ridiculous. I haven't even spoken to him, much less anything else.

I clear my throat. "Yeah?"

"Sorry, I didn't want to bust in, but I don't want to lose a lot of daylight." He sounds like he's standing in the living room, and I open the door.

"I'll be right there."

My head swims, and I grip the knob to steady myself. Once my vision focuses, I make my way to the kitchen. Slade is nowhere to be found, and I heat my kettle again. He'll wander in before I'm ready, I'm sure. I wonder if he wants coffee. The only reason I have a machine is for when Holden visits. I dig my hands into the dough, then cover the bowls again to rest.

"That's a lot of bread," Slade murmurs from the doorway.

"Large order. Do you need coffee?" I avoid his eyes, but I don't have anything else to do. I end up picking up a bunch of items, then setting them down again.

"I can make my own coffee, beau—Scarlett."

"You going to keep messing that up, aren't you?" I snap, though there's little heat behind my words.

"Probably." He chuckles, pushing off of the doorframe. "Kind of got stuck in my brain."

"It's been less than a day. You telling me you get ridiculous nicknames stuck in your brain that quick?"

"Maybe." He slips around me and gets the coffeepot to fill. "Lots of things get stuck up there without my noticing."

I huff, glancing at the clock. "Good to know your head is as empty as your gas tank."

I glance over my shoulder and find his eyes on me. He's leaning against the counter, arms crossed with a smile playing on his lips. I don't know why he can't just…leave me be. If he keeps this up, he'll get attached. It won't be real and I can't stop it. It happens all the time. Every. Fucking. Time.

"My gas tank is full, thank you very much. Engine might be shot, but at least I have enough go-juice."

"No one says go-juice," I mutter as I turn back around and pull my sourdough starter toward me. I need to feed it, but Slade will probably ask more questions.

"Guess I'm just special like that. We might have a problem, though." He spoons the grounds into the machine, and I wonder if he was poking around in here before I came in. I keep the coffee tucked in the back of the cupboard on the top shelf. No way he'd be able to find it unless…

I spin around. "You're a shifter."

"That a question or an accusation?"

"Both. Definitely both."

He laughs, and the sound fills my lungs in a way my breath never does. "I am a shifter. I assume you know all about them, given you're related to Holden. And I'm also assuming you're not one."

My heart stutters and I gaze at him wide-eyed. I'm probably being ridiculously obvious. Anyone who knows shifters exist would see right through me. Not all of them can sniff out another shifter, but the signs are there. I had my suspicions when he showed up. Smelling the coffee from its hiding place confirmed it. If I had been paying attention, I would have known earlier.

Shifters carry themselves differently, moving through the world like they're connected to the earth. They reveal themselves in the little things. Maybe someone like me is the only one who notices those random bits.

"Why do you say that?" I wheeze.

He taps the side of his nose with a grin. "Goddess gave me a little extra magic."

"Well, don't go shifting around town. They'll freak out and send out a hunting party complete with pitchforks and torches."

"Noted." He spares me from saying anything more by reaching for a mug and pouring himself some coffee.

The last thing I need is him finding out what I am. He may be fine with shifters, but I'm something else. They group us all together yet treat us differently. I want to ask him where he grew up, if it was a shifter community or among humans. I want to ask him how many shifters he comes across. I want to know if there's anyone else in town who's like him. I want to know why he can't sniff my kind out. I want to know more than I should.

My mouth stays shut, and I busy my hands with starting the cookies. He'll interpret my questions as an invitation to ask his own, and I can't afford that. I need to call Holden. He has some explaining to do.

"So, about our problem. I walked around and made a list of all the supplies I need to get started. Don't have a car to get there. Or to haul them back here. I've got my tools, but I might need to get a couple more specialty ones as well."

"Can you do anything right now until later? I need to bake these, then drop them off. Won't be done until the afternoon."

"What exactly are you doing with them? They look...fine." He sidles up next to me and leans over one of the bowls.

I snort and put some distance between us. One brush of his arm against mine shouldn't have such an effect on me. For some reason he doesn't react, which is strange for me. I avoid accidental touches for a reason. Not that he needs to know that. Whenever I brought it up, people would act weird or make jokes at my expense. I'm not about to fall into that trap again.

"You don't know the first thing about baking. How would you know it's fine?"

"Guess I wouldn't. Maybe I just trust you know what you're doing." He glances at me, and his hair flops over his forehead. If I didn't know any better, I'd think he did it on purpose. He raises an eyebrow.

"I suppose this is the point where I say I trust you to fix my house," I murmur.

"I get the feeling you don't take people at their word. You're more of a put your money where your mouth is kind of woman. I wouldn't dream of asking you to trust me."

"What an odd thing to say," I mutter. "Go take a shower. There's more towels in the closet in the hall."

"That bad, huh?" he laughs as I circle the island.

He walks away and I relax a little. It's strange having someone else in the house. Even when Holden visits, he doesn't usually sleep here. He's not here first thing in the morning or sticking around past sunset.

I'm sure our sibling relationship seems strange to others. Sometimes I wish we could be closer, like Slade seems to be with his family. Unfortunately, that's wishful thinking. I can't change who I am or force Holden to accept me for my differences. He does what he can, and I know he loves me. That's enough.

I spend the next couple hours baking bread and making cookies. It's a good thing I've made all this so many times or I would have messed up a million times. My ears keep straining to pinpoint where Slade is. From singing in the shower to the creaking of the floorboards in the back to his phone sending out a jaunty tune, I'm hyperaware of his presence. I wonder if he's doing it on purpose.

As I pull the last loaf from the oven, I wince. I need an oven in the wall instead of having to bend over again and again. I add it to the mental list of all the things I'd love to upgrade. Writing them down will only make me sad, so I keep them tucked away in a forgotten corner of my mind.

My bottom lip slips between my teeth, and I drop the oven mitts on the island. Ten minutes later, I have a scrap piece of paper filled with priorities for Slade. I probably should have done this before I sent him off to do whatever he could. A week isn't enough time to get even a fourth of these things done, and I refuse to extend his stay. Hopefully, he'll be able to get the most urgent projects done first. I'll deal with everything else later.

My head whips up as Slade clears his throat. He slaps a pair of leather gloves on his jeans. A man, shifter or not, should not look that good after riffling around in a demolition zone. The goddess gave him more than just the ability to recognize other shifters. She went overboard with him, and it makes me irrationally angry.

"Can I help you?" I snap, immediately regretting it.

His dark eyes harden and he sighs. "Holden said you're not answering your phone, which apparently is a common occurrence. Wanted me to tell you to call Jude. He's worried about you."

"Who's worried about me?" I swear his lip curls as he straightens.

"Your boyfriend."

# Chapter 5

## Slade

I stomp away before she can make excuses. Not that she owes me anything. Within a day, she's made it pretty clear where I stand with her. I should have known a woman like her would be attached in some way. Besides, I vowed to keep my damn pants on.

It doesn't make sense why I'm so upset about Holden's revelation. He made it pretty clear who Jude was to Scarlett. He was also pretty fucking vague about his cryptic warning last night. He kept dodging my questions, then practically hung up on me.

"Oh, no you don't," Scarlett snarls from behind me.

I shut the door to the back porch. It won't keep her out, but it feels good at least. I need to get my shit together and remind myself why I'm here before I talk to her. If Holden called me right now and relieved me of my debt, I'd be gone. I'd have to walk, but that's the least of my worries. He won't do it. He's weirdly obsessed with my doing this job for his sister.

"Seriously, Slade?"

A shiver rolls through me at my name on her lips. Even with the annoyance in her tone, I wasn't expecting an ache to bloom in my chest or my breathing to hitch. I catch her reflection in the busted window. Even in the cracked glass, she's ethereal.

None of which helps or erases the irrational anger at her having a boyfriend.

"Listen," I snap as I spin around. "I don't care. It doesn't matter to me. I just don't like being stuck here when you have someone who might be a better fit for this job."

She plants her fists on her hips and glares at me. "Jude ain't my boyfriend, he's Holden's. And I don't know why you want to be here, anyway. I am perfectly capable of taking care of all this by myself. Why don't you just focus on getting your car running and then you can go, hmm?"

"I...whatever. I can't leave." I shouldn't be hurt Holden didn't tell me he was seeing someone. Maybe our relationship doesn't go as deep as I thought it did. I wouldn't be surprised if most of my relationships are similar.

"You said that before," she says, narrowing her eyes. "Why not?"

"Figured you'd understand. I owe Holden a life debt. Shifter thing. He called it in, and if I try to skirt that duty, I'll spend the next year as a wolf. I'd rather not deal with that."

"I know what a life debt is. My question is why. Wait, you're a wolf shifter?" Her annoyance slips away.

"Yes. There a problem with that?" I cross my arms as she has the good grace to look ashamed.

"No, I just...it's nothing to do with you. Or shifters. Or wolves. It's...nothing." She shakes her head and digs her thumbs into her temples. "What the hell just happened? You should be the one... Never mind. I'll talk to Holden, get you out of here."

She stumbles back through the door, and I take a step before I realize what I'm doing. When my phone rings, she trips over her own feet. She holds up her hand and waves me off, even though I didn't move. My phone rings again, and I fish it from my pocket to glance at the screen. By the time I look up, Scarlett has disappeared into the house.

"What's up, Jake?" I answer, my gaze fixed on where Scarlett vanished.

"Hey Slade, you talk to your dad lately?" Jake's gruff voice seems even gruffer than usual. I'm sure he's gearing up for another summer with his camp. I've helped him a couple times and it's organized chaos, plus incredibly tiring.

"Couple days ago. Why?" Every time I think about my dad, my gut tightens and a sense of foreboding floods my senses. I shove the feeling away.

"Your mom said he went to visit Alissa, but he hasn't been back in a few days. Gemma's worried. Figured I'd check with you before she demanded we drive cross-country to check up on him." He sighs and I wonder if both Gemma and Kira are on his ass about this.

"Talked to him before I headed out a few days ago. He was slower than normal, but he's not as young as he used to be. He did mention he needed to spend some time in the woods. I got the feeling it's been a while since he shifted." It's the only explanation I have. All the alternatives either don't fit or are too painful to examine.

He sighs again, and I wonder how much this has weighed on Gemma. Jake may be my best friend, but Gemma is my sister. I wanted them to get together. Didn't expect them to be fated mates, but I wasn't questioning the goddess. I merely opened the door for them to meet. It led to Chase, Jake's best friend, meeting my sister Kira. Like one domino plunking into the next, my siblings are finding their destinies. I can't lie, I've been beating back jealousy over it.

"Jake, I can call him, then talk to Gemma. Alissa might answer Kira's calls. She's dodging mine right now." It's all I can do right now. It's not like I can drop what I'm doing to check on my parents. Dad would kick my ass if I did. He'd tell me he's a grown-ass man who can take care of himself. It wouldn't be the first time he's put me in my place.

"What'd you do to Alissa?" Jake asks gruffly.

"I may have suggested she come out of the woods every once in a while to help with the general store."

Jake's booming laugh echoes down the line. "Bet that went down well."

"Well, she's not talking to me, so yeah. It was great. Just… don't tell Kira. I don't want her to slip into whatever."

"An existential crisis about leaving her parents to run their business alone?"

I huff, running a hand through my hair. "Exactly. She'll take it as a slight, think I'm talking behind her back and all that. I'll deal with her later."

"Maybe don't use those words. I've learned saying you'll 'deal' with them doesn't go over well. Especially since they're perfect and amazing and, most of the time, right."

"Gemma just walked in, didn't she?"

"Sure did."

Gemma's voice echoes in the background, demanding to know where I am. I swear her voice is lighter than the last time we spoke. An unbidden smile tugs at my lips all while an ache builds in my chest. I'll blame it on my interaction with Scarlett, which I'll have to deal with sooner rather than later.

"Gemma wants to know where you are this time," Jake grumbles. He hates being on the phone and hates it even more when Gemma talks through him.

"Hart's Hallow."

"Where the fuck is that?"

"South of you guys. I'm, uh, helping out a friend."

"Friend, huh? Don't tell me anything you don't want your sister to know. Even if I wanted to keep secrets from her, I can't."

I let out a light chuckle and lean against the window frame. The wood creaks under my weight and I straighten, eyeing it.

I'm going to demo it anyway, but I'd rather not create a hole in Scarlett's house I can't cover.

"Is that a mate thing?"

"Nope. That's a Gemma thing. Woman gives me a look, and I cave. Listen, I gotta go, but let us know how Ben is." A door slams on his end, and I imagine he's hiding behind his cabin. "Between you and me, I'm worried. When we were out there for spring equinox, he looked...different. Gemma didn't seem to notice, but seeing as how it was the first time she's been back in years, I'm not surprised."

"How did you notice then?" My eyes pop up at a creak in the floorboards, and I find Scarlett hovering in the hallway. "You've never met the man."

"We've been doing the computer thing at Chase's. There was something in his eyes when I met him. I could chalk it up to weird lighting or getting older, but I don't know. I downplayed it with Gemma."

"And she took it and went down the rabbit hole. Let me guess, she's been talking to Kira a lot more, too."

Scarlett wrings her hands in front of her, pacing back and forth. Every once in a while she glances toward me, never quite meeting my gaze. It's distracting in the best way possible. Which only leads me to remind myself I need to stay as far away as possible. With the house being so small, I doubt I'll succeed. I don't even know if I want to.

"I don't think it's Kira. I mean, it is, but it isn't. I'm just worried. Your dad. Slade, he's one of the good ones."

"Don't worry about it. I'll call him and get this cleared up. Bet he broke his leg again or one of his friends beat him at cards. He does this every once in a while. Mom knows how to deal with him." It took me a long time, but I finally saw how alike Dad and Kira are. It's probably why they're so close and why it was so hard for my sister to leave home.

"Convince Gemma of that," he mutters. "Listen, I gotta go before she finds me."

"Uh, you live in a one-bedroom cabin. I'm pretty sure she knows where you are, man."

Scarlett finally plucks up the courage to walk down the hallway. She trips to a stop when she sees I'm on the phone. I hold up a finger as Jake gives me some shit, then says goodbye.

"What do you need, Scarlett?" I pause before I say her name, and a look of annoyance flashes across her face.

"I need to drop the bread off to the cafe and the general store. If you want to tag along for...whatever you need, you can."

"How gracious of you," I murmur, and she scowls.

"What's that supposed to mean?"

I slip my phone into my pocket and put my hammer away before turning to her. "I figured after our little tiff you'd make me find my own way."

She rolls her eyes. "It's like five miles. I wouldn't make you walk that far."

"You forget, beautiful. I'm a wolf shifter. I would run." I smirk, though I'm not entirely sure whether we're still fighting or just needed some space.

Her lips purse and she spins. I'm pretty sure she mutters something about galloping. For a split second, I think about calling her out, then think better of it. I follow her through the house and almost run into her when she stops by the kitchen. When she attempts to sling the canvas tote bag over her shoulder, I snatch it from her.

"I can carry it," she snarls, though she lets go.

"Just because you can, doesn't mean you have to."

I march out the front door, then down the porch stairs. It isn't until I'm halfway to my car, I remember it won't go anywhere. I spin around and find Scarlett loitering at the top of the stairs. She glances between me and some spot in the forest, then back to me.

"Want to tell me where your vehicle is?" I call.

She huffs and stomps toward me. She veers off, heading for the woods, and I hurry after her. I don't know why she's hiding her car in the trees. We're in the middle of nowhere. I doubt someone would try to steal it. Maybe she just doesn't want people poking around.

She ducks under a low branch and holds it up for me to pass through, revealing a truck. A nice one. Not that I know what type it is or even whether it's actually nice. It's old, though. Her gaze keeps darting to me.

"Guessing you don't want this in the back?" I ask as I round the bed.

"Uh, no. I usually put it on the seat, so you'll have to keep it on your lap." She opens the driver's door. "You really don't care, do you?"

I haul myself inside as she settles in the seat. "Care about what? The truck? Nope. As evidenced by my own rust bucket, I don't know much about cars. Or trucks, in this instance. Is that why you put rule number seven on the list?"

She backs out of her hiding spot like she's done it a thousand times and heads toward town. "What? No, it doesn't matter. Just don't squish the bread. No one likes smashed bread. Potatoes, sure, but not bread."

"I promise not to smash the bread," I murmur as I stare at her.

A blush spreads across her cheeks, and I wonder what she's thinking. It certainly isn't about bread. I pull in a deep breath, letting her scent fill me. As the wind from the cracked window sends her hair floating, I suppress a shudder. I swing my gaze around and stare out the window.

After only a day, she's got me on a rollercoaster of emotions, none of which I particularly want to examine. I vow to get through this week, maybe convince her to let me stay until the job is done, then go back to searching for something worth living for.

# Chapter 6

I don't know how I'm going to drive all the way into town with this man sitting next to me. Slade doesn't seem to notice my discomfort. He smells…different. Not from how he usually does. No, I don't know how he usually smells because I don't really know him. I do know his scent, though, and being trapped in this small space has him infiltrating my space. I refuse to admit it's my fault.

At any point, I could have stopped all this. I could have pushed harder against him staying. Fighting with my brother isn't my favorite thing, but if I had put my foot down, he would have listened. At least, I think he would have.

Holden has a tendency of thinking he knows better than me. He's accused me more than once of not taking care of myself. He doesn't understand, though. Few do. I'm doing the best I can with what I have. I may not possess as much as other people, but the goddess gave me what she could. That's what I tell myself. The lie doesn't always work.

"Question," Slade murmurs, and I glance at him from the corner of my eye.

"What?" I snap, then press my lips together.

"How much is the bread?"

"Sorry," I sigh. "I just don't like going into town. A loaf is ten and the cookies are…actually, I don't know. I just bake them by the dozen, and Naomi wraps them up. I'm sure she sells them for whatever makes sense."

"You don't get a cut? Seems like bad business."

I grit my teeth, reminding myself not to bite his head off. "She pays me a base price. If she wants to mark them up more, what do I care? That's not bad business. Not in a tiny-ass town like Hart's Hallow. If it weren't for her and the town fairs, I wouldn't be able to do this. I'd have to go back to…well, I'd have to find other work."

"You know, nothing bad will happen if you share things with me. Not like I'm going to use the information against you." He says it with an air of amusement, which only rankles me more.

"Most people think they won't. Then suddenly there's an argument or an opportunity and that sentiment becomes dust in the wind. Everyone turns on you eventually. Maybe not everyone, but a fair few for sure. A person's instinct is to lash out when they're backed into a corner." I swallow hard, refusing to pull my eyes away from the road, no matter how much I want to.

"Scarlett, most people don't think like that. Not unless…I'm not going to use whatever job you did however many years ago against you. Not really my style."

"Then what is your style?"

Immediately I regret the question, yet I desperately want to know. For some reason, I need to know more about him. I've been fighting against the feeling since he bumped his way down my driveway. If I hold out a bit longer, the need will disappear. Life will go back to normal. The closer I get to him, the harder it will be to remember how to be alone.

"I'm more of a live and let live. Unless someone threatens the people I love. Then all bets are off, I suppose. Sometimes I don't always get it right."

We pull into town, saving me from asking him about when

he didn't get it right. It's late enough in the afternoon for the sidewalks to be full of townsfolk, or at least full for a small town like Hart's Hallow.

The entire village is basically self-sustaining. It's the only way a place like this can survive. We're too far from a city to supplement with supplies or provide jobs. Most of the families have lived here for generations. I'm the stranger—the interloper. It puts me on the outside looking in most of the time, which is just how I like it. That's what I tell myself whenever someone shuts me out.

I pull in front of the cafe and slam the truck into park. I swear Slade chuckles, but I'm already out the door. I swing around the bed, then stop short when Slade swings his own door open and hops out.

When I try to take the tote from him, he scowls and holds it out of my reach. I'm not about to fight with him in the middle of the street. We're already getting strange looks from the couple passing by on the sidewalk. Not to mention the people with their noses pressed against the glass of the cafe.

Slade has the audacity of opening the door and shooing me inside. Normally, I'd think it was a nice gesture, but all his actions put me on edge. People aren't nice for no reason. They get something out of it, whether it's merely a good feeling in their gut or an expectation of repayment later. Hell, he's even here because of a life debt to Holden. If his friend had asked him to help out the little sister in over her head as a favor, Slade probably would've declined.

Maybe he just has good manners or grew up in a small town where holding the door open was expected. I remind myself he's not the bad guy. He hasn't given me any reason to be a bitch to him. It's not his fault he's here, and I shouldn't take it out on him.

Keeping him at arm's length while remembering that he's not the enemy won't be easy. Not because of him. No, this is squarely on me. It's my default mechanism in most situations. It's kept me safe for the last five years.

"Ms. Redd you're a little late," Bernice Clemson quips.

From what I've heard, she's been the proud owner of the Sunrise Cafe for ten years. A staple of Hart Hallow and one of the only places to eat. Which means Bernice has a big ole head and thinks she can call the shots. I much prefer dealing with Naomi down the street. She at least treats me like a person rather than just an object with the bread.

"Bread does what it wants, Miss Bernice. Can't make it rise any faster than it's supposed to."

I grab half a dozen loaves and place them on the long counter lining two walls. It looks like every other soda shop I imagined from way back when. Not that I spent much time thinking about what they were like, but I watched movies like everyone else. I like to think I was a typical kid. Typical adult? Not so much.

"Well, since I've already had people complaining about the backup loaf I have, I suppose I can't complain about it, hmm?"

"Suppose you can't. Just need the paperwork and I'll be on my way." I force a smile despite her sharp words and the ache in my lower back.

Her gaze keeps darting to Slade, probably expecting me to introduce him. The last thing I want is for her to set her sights on him. I'd love to say it's because then he'll stick around longer than a week. That's what I'm going to keep telling myself. The alternative is jealousy, and it's definitely not that.

Then again, it's not like I could stop them. If he wants to hook up with Bernice Clemson, then so be it. I'll just have to live with it. Perhaps I can make a rule of no nighttime visitors. From the smirk on Bernice's face, maybe no daytime visitors either.

"Hi, I'm Bernice. I own the Sunrise Cafe. First meal's free if you're interested," she says coyly.

"Hello, Bernice. Fortunately, I get all my meals for free, but this place looks lugubrious." He may be speaking to Bernice, yet he's not meeting her eye. I'm pretty sure he's fixated on her shoulder.

"We need to get these to Naomi. Let me know what you'll need next week," I say, cutting her off when she opens her mouth. I slip my hand into the crook of Slade's arm and guide him away.

As soon as we're outside, I try to pull away from him. He squeezes his arm closer to his body and traps me. I'm not about to cause a scene in the middle of the street. If he wants to align himself with me, he's digging his own grave. Except he doesn't know that.

"You shouldn't be too friendly with me," I mutter from the corner of my mouth.

He glances at me, then forward again. "We're just walking together. Don't know what you'd define as friendly, but this is far from it, beautiful. Sorry. Scarlett."

I nod to an older man who shuffles past us. He doesn't acknowledge us. "And how would you define lugubrious?"

Slade's lips twitch. "Is she always like that? Or am I just special?"

"Don't flatter yourself. She'll flirt with anyone with legs. Except me, of course. You realize she's going to look up the word and find out you insulted her business, right?"

"Think she'll be able to spell it? Half the time I forget what vowel goes in the middle."

"If she finds out you called her cafe morose and gloomy, she'll ban you. Which means her best friend Clark will ban you. You do not want that if you like pie."

I yank open the door to Naomi's bakery, finally tugging my hand away from Slade. It may have only been a few minutes, but I had a normal conversation with him. Maybe I can keep him at a distance without insulting him.

"Scarlett, I was beginning to worry," Naomi says in way of greeting. "Oh, you brought company."

"Bread just took a little longer today. I made those cookies you mentioned last time, too." I gesture to Slade, and he sets the cloth tote on the small counter. Most of her space is taken up with display cases and racks. She has a full kitchen in the back that would make a baker swoon. I certainly did when she gave me a tour.

"You're a lifesaver. You know I hate sourdough. Who's your friend?"

Slade steps forward with a disarming grin and holds out his hand. "Slade Livia, ma'am."

"Nice to meet you." Naomi's cheeks redden, and she drops his hold quickly. "So, Scarlett, I know you just brought these, but the Tates are throwing their annual summer roundup. They requested a bunch of those strawberry shortbread cakes."

"What's a bunch?" At least strawberries are in season, and they're fairly easy to make. Unless they want them tomorrow, and then I'm fucked. "And when is it?"

Naomi grabs the loaves and sets them on her back counter. "I think Gunner said fifty. He'll need them in a week. I told him we might not be able to swing that on such short notice, but he did say Clark will provide the strawberries. He could probably drop them off if you're not going to be in town before then. Then again, I'll probably need more of these cinnamon sugar loaves. They sell out within a day no matter how many you make, I swear."

"I should be able to swing the cakes. I'll make a couple more loaves for you later in the week and pick up the strawberries then. No reason Clark needs to go out of his way." *Or be at my house in any way, shape, or form.*

"Well, here's your receipt. I'll email you the exact numbers after I talk to Gunner." She hands over the paper and smiles. "Nice to meet you, Mr. Livia."

She disappears into the back after I wish her a good day. Slade doesn't say anything, just stares at me with a contemplative look on his face. It's probably the most he's heard me talk in the day he's been here. I don't blame him for being freaked out. These interactions are about all I can take most days. Between Bernice's attitude and the random gawking I get, I'm tapped out by the time I get to Naomi's.

I pivot and make my way out the door, Slade following me a second later. "Do you need to go to the shop? Or to Whitakers for wood or whatever?"

Slade grabs my arm and pulls me to a stop. He glances around the street, then tugs me down a side alley toward a small park with a gazebo. I always thought it was a strange addition to a town this tiny. His fingers lace with mine, and he leads me across the manicured space and into the grove of trees dividing the grass from a small stream.

"We go much farther and we'll be in the thick of it. What is going on?"

"Did you know about Naomi?" He spits it out like an accusation.

"Of course I know Naomi. I've been supplying her bread for three years now." I shrug off his hold, and he begins to pace back and forth. There isn't much room between the trees, though. The result is a little comical—four steps one way, pivot, four steps back.

"So, what kind is she? Because after the whole Chase thing, I'm not making assumptions."

"Who's Chase? What the hell are you talking about?"

He stops in front of me and glares. "What kind of shifter is Naomi?"

"Naomi isn't a shifter. If she was..." I shake my head, not willing to admit to him what I am. "I'd know. Your gift must be faulty or something."

His mouth drops open. "Faulty? No, that doesn't happen. She's a shifter. Maybe she just didn't tell you."

"That wouldn't be surprising. It's not like we're friends. Except I would know if she was or not. What does it even matter? *You're* a shifter. My *brother* is a shifter. From what I understand, your entire *family* are shifters. You can't tell me you have some weird prejudice against shifters."

He rears back as if I've slapped him. "That's not what I meant."

"Well, it sure as shit sounded like that. Whatever. The only way you'd know for sure is if you asked her. And if you ask her, then you risk exposing us. Since I actually have to live here, I'd appreciate it if you kept your theories to yourself. Now, do you need to go get supplies or not?"

I cross my arms and wait while he stares at me stupefied. I don't know what he thought would come of his little tirade. And I really want to ask him again who Chase is. What kind of assumptions did he make? Is that why he decided to come here? Is he running from something or someone?

"Fine, but if she…just…" He sighs, running his hand through his hair. "I need to order some windows and flooring. Plus, the drywall needs to be replaced. Let's just get this over with. I'd rather get this done as quickly as possible."

He stomps past me, and I swallow hard, a familiar ache burning in my chest. As I trod after him, I concentrate on building another layer of bricks around my emotions. The sooner we get this done, the sooner he can leave.

# Chapter 7

Scarlett didn't fill the silence as we went to the hardware store. Nor did she speak when we picked up lumber. Not enough, but it'll work for now. She had no opinions on the windows or the flooring or the stain. She merely gestured me in the right direction when I got lost.

In such a small town, I didn't think it was possible to get turned around, yet I accomplished it. When we got home, she disappeared into the house, her head hanging lower than when we left.

Thankfully, I got food when we were in town. Snacks won't hold me over for long, but at least I didn't have to beg Scarlett to feed me. Her words keep turning over in my mind.

*Accusations.*

I'm not surprised by her reaction. From the outside looking in, it sounds like I hate other shifters. I wasn't about to explain everything that happened in Moon Cove, especially in the middle of a grove of trees. What happened with Chase has everything and nothing to do with Naomi. I just don't want to make the same mistakes twice.

I spent the rest of the night avoiding the main house. I thought about shifting and going for a run, but I didn't want to leave without telling Scarlett. Except I didn't want to talk to her.

She clearly doesn't want to know anything about me, nor I about her. I'm not used to people shutting me out, and it's grating on my nerves. It took me forever to fall asleep.

Now, I'm stuck in her back room, tearing shit apart and wondering how I got myself into this mess. Blaming Holden isn't fair, but I'm going to do it anyway. It's his name I've been cursing all day. As I rip another piece of drywall from the frame, I mutter under my breath. They're nonsensical words, but none of them are pretty.

"Fucker," I spit, tossing the piece onto the pile.

"Bad time?" Just the sound of her voice sends a shiver down my spine.

"What do you need, Scarlett?" I sigh, glancing at her. "Sorry. I'm just tired."

Her eyes widen for a split second, then her calm, beautiful mask slips over her features. "It's like three in the afternoon."

"Yeah, well, I've been working on this since five so…" I tear off another section, silently cursing whoever used these old square nails. I didn't even think they made them anymore.

"No, I mean it's three in the afternoon and you haven't eaten. And you didn't eat last night, which isn't smart, by the way. Especially with how much you're working, you need to eat. So I thought if you wanted to eat, I could…make you something to eat." She tips her chin to her chest, and her golden hair slips over her shoulders.

"You just said eat like seven times. You alright?"

"Yeah, I just…I didn't mean to bite your head off yesterday."

I level her with a look. "You didn't."

"I know I snapped at you and probably insulted you—"

"No, I mean you didn't bite my head off. I chose the wrong words and made myself sound like an ass. I deserved to be called out." I cross my arms, then drop them to my sides. "I recently judged someone prematurely based on nothing more than what they shifted into. I stand by my wariness, but not the way I went about it. I just wanted a heads up about Naomi so I didn't jump to conclusions again."

"It's fine," she whispers, her eyes taking on a faraway look.

"Are you going to tell me what Naomi is? Or should I ask her?"

Her head snaps up. "I'd rather you didn't. Like I said yesterday, I wasn't aware she was a shifter. If you ask her, she'll ask *me,* and it'll open up a whole can of worms I'd rather not deal with. Especially since you'll just drop that bomb and then scoot out of town. It wouldn't be fair to me. And while I haven't been the nicest to you, I'm really hoping you won't."

"You know, she might know about you."

Fear flashes in her eyes, then she blinks and it's gone. "What would she know about me?"

"How about the fact your brother is a shifter? Have they met?"

Her shoulders droop the slightest bit, and my gut tightens. She's hiding something. Obviously, I don't know her well enough to figure out what it is. She plays her cards exceptionally close to her chest. This seems like something I should know, though. Unless she's keeping Naomi's secrets.

Scarlett sighs, shaking his head. "I don't know. Probably, but neither of them said anything. It's not like Holden just blurts out that he's a shifter. I doubt Naomi does either. From what I know, most shifters keep that shit to themselves."

"I won't say anything unless she does first. Might be why she was so hesitant around me," I murmur, kicking a piece of drywall closer to the pile.

She snorts, smoothing her hands down her apron. "Doubt it."

"Excuse me? I am very charming, Scarlett."

"Yup, just the goddess's gift to us mere mortals," she mumbles.

My mouth drops open, and she grins as she turns away. "I'm making grilled cheese if you want some."

She flounces down the hall, her hips swaying an excessive amount. Or maybe I've just fallen under her spell. Might be loneliness. I never thought of myself as alone. The friends I've met through my travels are scattered around the world. Which doesn't mean anything. I spend most of my time in my car or at some random motel on my way to the next stop. As Scarlett disappears into the kitchen, I adjust myself in my jeans. This woman is going to be the death of me, and she doesn't even know it. She has no idea how close to the edge I am. I need to shift and run.

A sizzle fills the air as I step into the kitchen. Suddenly, a song starts up through a speaker somewhere I can't find. Scarlett doesn't seem to notice me as she sways to the melody. She moves with a grace I've rarely seen. Enchanting, ethereal, and utterly intoxicating. I watch her from the doorway, waiting for her to start singing. She's already mouthing the words.

She flips the sandwich onto the plate, then drops another piece of bread into the hot pan. More sizzling drowns out the music. When she reaches into the pan, I rush toward her with a cry stuck in the back of my throat.

She doesn't even react, just flips the bread calmly and grabs a grater and a block of cheese. "Settle down, wolfy. I've made a lot of grilled cheese in my life."

"You scared the shit out of me," I growl. I let out a nervous chuckle as I lean against the counter and drop my face in my hands.

"Honestly," she mutters. "You probably would have started a fire if I'd actually burned myself."

"How the hell would a fire start? Not like the oven will burst into flames once the pan leaves the stove."

My mouth waters when she hands me a plate with a golden grilled cheese on it. She grabs her own plate and sets herself up at the island. She has to shove several jars out of the way. I circle around and sit next to her.

Seconds later, she hops up and makes her way to the fridge. I focus on my sandwich. One bite and my eyes close while an involuntary moan leaves me.

"This is the best fucking grilled cheese I've ever had," I say through a mouthful.

"Chew, swallow, then speak," she murmurs, setting a glass of water by my plate.

Before I know it, I've devoured the entire thing. "What the hell did you do to this?"

She chuckles lightly, the sound filling me up. "It's crescent sourdough bread like the other night. And I butter both sides before I put it in the pan. Shredding the cheese doesn't hurt either. I used sharp cheddar in this one. Little bit of garlic powder and a lot of butter and boom—perfect grilled cheese. There's another one on the counter."

I leap from my chair, almost knocking over my stool in my haste. She clears her throat when I hover over the counter about to take a bite. Reluctantly, I trudge back to my seat. I'm already coming up with a plan to coerce her into making me another one. I don't know if it's the bread or the cheese or the butter, but I could eat this every day for the rest of my life.

"How much of this bread can you make?" I say between bites. I want to savor every morsel.

"Um, a lot? I've got my starter built up for tomorrow. Except you'll get sick of it after a while."

"Doubt it," I mumble. "Why are you being nice to me?"

"I'm nice," she snaps.

"I didn't say you weren't nice. I asked why you were being nice *to me*. Difference, beautiful." I glance at her from the corner of my eye. "Scarlett. Sorry."

She sighs heavily, and I wonder if I should apologize again. "You don't have to do that. I don't actually care what you call me. We're going to be around each other for a bit, might as well feed you. Especially since I can't really pay you."

Her cheeks flush as she mumbles the last part. I wasn't expecting to get paid for the work, anyway. If anything, I'd assume Holden was taking care of it. He's the one who asked me to come, plus I'm paying back a debt. I would have died without him. The least I can do is use my construction skills to fix up her house.

"You can pay me in grilled cheese. More than I expected."

Her jaw twitches, and I run through what I said again. I don't think it was wrong. I truly didn't expect her to pay me, and if grilled cheese is too much, that's fine. When I open my mouth to say so, and she holds up her hand.

"I'm not talking to you about my finances."

"Wasn't asking you to," I mumble and shove the last bite into my mouth.

Another sigh leaves her. "I didn't mean to…that is, I shouldn't have jumped to conclusions. I've dealt with my fair share of passive-aggressiveness, and I tend to see it in everything."

"You don't have to explain, Scarlett. I'm paying off a debt. Why would I get money for that? Doesn't make sense. We've got a lot of things I need to do, at least to get you to a place where it shouldn't be hard for someone else to finish."

Her nose wrinkles, and I resist the urge to grin. "What do you mean?"

"You and I both know I can't complete all those projects by myself in a week. Leaves only two options. Either you hire someone after I'm gone or I get someone in here to help me, and even then I probably wouldn't get it done. I get the feeling you don't want more people rambling around. And I'd rather they not eat any grilled cheese you make for me."

She snorts, then sobers. "I could help."

I raise an eyebrow and murmur, "Is that so?"

"What? You don't think I'm capable? Because—"

I hold up a hand and she sputters. "Before you go accusing me of being sexist or maligning your abilities, let me just say it's because you're busy. And short, which may seem irrelevant, but in this case it isn't."

"I have a ladder. And I'm not that short."

"Where exactly is this mysterious ladder? Unless you hid it under my mattress and I think I would have felt that."

She presses her lips together, indecision resting in her eyes. "It's in the other shed."

"Did you bury gold there?"

Her head snaps around. "Excuse me?"

"You're acting cagey about a shed. Add in how you hide your truck, and I assume you're hiding massive amounts of gold around your property. Am I going to find a rope buried in the banks of the river with a lockbox attached to the other end? Do you have dead bodies somewhere?" I grin, but she gives me a deadpan look. "What's it going to take to learn all your secrets, beautiful?"

# Chapter 8

## Scarlett

I've been avoiding Slade for three days. This is why I don't let people in. They dig and they dig and they dig until I have no secrets left. Slade will keep searching until he unearths them. I can't afford for him to figure out what I am—*who* I am. As soon as shifters find out, they treat me differently. No one seems to realize I'm still me.

I punch my fist into the proofed dough and watch it sink slowly. My phone buzzes for the millionth time this morning, and I glance at the screen. Of course it's Holden. He's the only one in my life who actually calls me. Naomi only texts, and no one else has my number. I wipe my knuckles on a towel and finally answer.

"What do you want, Holden?" I snap as I put it on speaker.

"Scarlett?" Holden's voice crackles down the line, and I snatch up my phone.

"Holden? Where are you?" There's a rustle and the sound clears.

"Scarlett," he whispers. "I need you to let him in."

My brows knit together, and I glance over my shoulder. Slade is nowhere to be seen. He's kept to the back room with me sneaking sandwiches in there when he leaves. It's not the most mature thing, but it's worked so far. He stays in his lane, and I…

keep away from the track. I roll my eyes at my own failed metaphor.

"Who exactly am I letting in?" I whisper back.

"I don't have time to explain, Scarlett. You're fighting against your instincts, and I need you to stop."

I tilt my head. "Where the hell is this coming from, Holden?"

"I can't…I just need you to listen. I'm going off-grid, and you won't be able to get ahold of me. Keep Slade with you. Stay with him. Do not let him leave," he breathes.

"What? No. Not until you—"

"Just do it for me, Scarlett. Remember, I'm always here for you." He hangs up before I can respond. Not that I could through the tightness in my throat.

I double over and rest my forehead on the cool counter. Holden's words repeat in my head on a loop. *Keep Slade. I'm always here for you. Let him in. Do it for me. Stay with him.* None of it makes sense. I knew he was going out of town—something about helping a friend. I kick myself for not asking who he was helping or where he was going. If he's in trouble, I won't be able to get to him. I won't even know where to look or who to call. My mind overloads, and I concentrate on pulling in steady breaths.

"Scarlett?" Slade's panicked voice washes over me, and I straighten too quickly. "What's wrong?"

His hand lands on my lower back, and I curse myself for not changing after my yoga session. Heat seeps into my skin from the contact, and a shiver rolls through me. He's murmuring something I can't hear through the roaring in my head.

"I'm fine," I wheeze as I attempt to convince my body to move. It doesn't listen to my brain's good sense. It's perfectly comfortable being coddled by him.

"You don't look fine. You're pale and shaking." He turns me toward him and slides his hands to my jaw. In any other circumstance, I'd be swooning or running. Except he's got fear in his dark eyes and I can't seem to move.

"It's nothing," I whisper.

"Did someone call you? Did you hurt yourself? What is it?" His gaze scans my face as his thumbs brush my cheeks.

I swear if he doesn't move, I'm going to lose it. My heart will beat out of my chest. My lungs will seize. My body will cease to exist. I'll wrap myself up in this space and never want to leave. I'll lose myself in him, forgetting who I am and why I vowed to stay away from everyone. Then he really will dig up all my secrets. My last thought has me stepping away, and he drops his hands to his sides.

"Holden called. He's, uh, going off-grid." I huff, then mumble, "Whatever that means. I just didn't expect him to be gone so long."

"Why?"

I glance at him, then turn back to my dough. "Why what? Why is he going off-grid? I don't know. He wasn't very forth-coming. Never is."

"No, why are you so upset over him being gone? I didn't think he lived in Hart's Hallow. Did he move here?"

"You're asking a lot of questions."

"He's my friend, Scarlett," he growls.

I nod, though I don't really understand. Do friends often share where they're going and how long they'll be gone? And why does he care that I'm upset? He doesn't know me. We've been actively ignoring each other lately.

"I told you, I didn't think he'd be gone as long as he will be. He was planning on coming here to help me with the rest of the renovations when he was done. Took extra time off for it." The dough spills from the bowl, and I spread it out methodically. Anything to keep my hands busy.

"And now?" he murmurs, closer than I expected.

"What do you mean?"

"Well, he took off time to help you finish. He's not able to be here, so what do you plan on doing?"

I shrug as I spread out the dough, then fold it into a loaf. Tears blur my vision, and I beg the goddess to take them away. The last thing I want to do is cry in front of him. I focus on the silky dough as I shape it. The scraper slides easily underneath it, and I slip it into the pan. His hand brushes my arm as I reach for the next ball, and I freeze.

"I'll figure it out." My brother's words whisper in the back of my mind—*stay with him.* "I can't...I don't want to hire someone."

"I'll stay. Just until we know when he's coming back."

I nod, though I doubt he notices. He's too busy walking away. Part of me wants to call him back. Whether to yell at him or change his mind or ask him to hold me, I don't know. Some part of me wants to be comforted even if it is from Slade. Despite pushing him away, I trust him not to take advantage of the situation. At least until I mess it up. Then I'd be fucked. He'd be fucked. Everything would be fucked.

I shake my head and finish my loaves. Naomi will need more soon for her shop, and I need to get going on Gunner's order. The man refuses to speak to me, but he'll take my baking. For a forty-something-year-old man, he's feisty and kind of an asshole. Only to me, though.

I always wondered if he sensed I was different. Maybe he's a shifter like Slade and that's why he treats me like shit. It's pretty easy to ignore Gunner since he spends most of the time on his farm.

As I brew myself some tea, I make a list in my head of the things I'll need for the cakes. It keeps me from spiraling about Holden. Slade creeps into my thoughts more than once. I should tell him he doesn't need to stay. Just because my brother isn't coming back anytime soon doesn't mean I need a babysitter. I do perfectly fine on my own. Renovations kept for this long, a little while longer won't matter.

"Okay, so now that I've got some more time, we should go over the list again." Slade shuffles into the kitchen, his eyes fixed on a wrinkled piece of paper. He sets it on the island and smooths it out. I glance at it and realize it's my list of priorities for him I thought I'd thrown away.

"You don't have to stay. I just didn't have time to—"

"Mask your true feelings? Yeah, I got that. Too bad, though. You're stuck with me now." He shoots me a grin before he stares at the paper again. "I'm going to finish the floors by tomorrow if I work through the night, and then I'll be able to reframe everything. Once that's done, I'll tackle the windows. We'll have to go back to town and get some more supplies for the bathroom, though. I don't know if they'll have everything we need."

I busy myself with pouring the tonic into my mug as he continues to plan. From the sound of it, he expects to be here for months. I lean against the counter and stare at his lips as they form each word. Every once in a while the corner of his mouth twitches slightly, like his muscles can't help but pull into a smile. His broad shoulders are relaxed, none of the stress he was carrying around for the last three days present. His forearms flex as he taps the counter in a steady rhythm. Heat gathers in my gut, and I sip my tea to hide my expression.

"Scarlett," Slade says sharply as if it isn't the first time, and I jolt.

"What?" I snap.

His lips twitch, sending another bolt of heat through me. "I asked if I could have a cup. You were a little distracted objectifying my body, though, so I doubt you heard me."

"I was not."

I spin around, almost spilling my drink, and set it down. His laughter stabs at my senses, worming its way into my body and filling holes I didn't know existed. I reach for the coffee still tucked away on the top shelf. For some reason, Slade keeps putting it back instead of leaving it on the counter. I jolt when his hand lands on my waist and he grabs the container instead.

"For the record, I was asking for some of your tea, not this," he murmurs, his lips dangerously close to my ear. "If you don't want to share, though, I can make my own coffee." He steps back, and I can breathe again.

"Oh, you don't want any of this. I promise it doesn't taste good."

The lie rolls off my tongue with a nervous laugh. His eyebrows disappear under the flop of hair, and my fingers itch to brush it away. He's still too close, but I'm not about to banish him to the back room. That'd be a bitch move. Still, I don't think he'll appreciate my tonic. It takes getting used to even with the sweetener I put in it.

"Smells good so it probably tastes good too. Besides, why would you drink it if it was shit?"

"Fine," I grumble as I pour him a cup.

I shove the mug into his hand, and he grins. He plops back on the stool and inhales deeply, his nose practically touching the tea. I sniff my own and wonder what he smells. There's a ton of herbs steeped in here, and none of them stand out. Or maybe I'm just used to it.

When I first discovered the recipe, I had to choke it down. I have no idea whether or not it actually tasted bad or I just convinced myself it would be horrid. Now, I'm used to it and it makes me feel better, so I don't complain.

He takes a huge gulp, and his eyes bug out. I hide my smirk behind the rim of my mug and glance away. By the time I look back, he's crumpled the paper once more. I straighten from my spot on the counter. He stretches his neck, eyes squeezed shut as he shudders.

"I told you it doesn't taste good," I mutter. I'm not entirely convinced his problem is the drink. Alarm bells ring in my mind when he doesn't respond.

His throat bobs as he grits his teeth. When his gaze finally meets mine, I'm greeted with yellow eyes and black slits. I've seen this before, and it never ends well for my furniture. Holden has a hard time keeping his human form when he's worked up. Oftentimes, I have to lock myself away while he transitions. It's part of the reason the ceiling in the back room is destroyed.

"Slade?" I whisper, hoping he can hear me.

He tilts his head, an animalistic move if I've ever seen one. "What did you put in this?"

"Turmeric, ginger, some sage…" I swallow hard, then whisper, "Peony."

He nods slowly, glancing at his cup, then back at me. "Well, that explains a lot."

I really hope he doesn't question me more or figure out why I put peonies in my tonic. It's not unheard of to put them in tea. Shifters react differently to them, though.

"Are you about to shift? Because I'd rather you didn't do it in the house."

He pushes slowly to his feet, and I tense. "Don't worry, beautiful. I'd never hurt you."

# Chapter 9
## Slade

Fear flashes to life in Scarlett's eyes, and I realize how my words probably sounded to her. A safe person wouldn't say they're not going to hurt her. Especially when they're so close to the edge.

"I've been putting off shifting. Whatever you put in this tea makes it harder to resist the change," I say, pushing the cup away gently. My wolf sits right under the surface, straining against the bonds holding him back.

"Why the hell would you do that? I don't want a feral wolf in my kitchen," she cries, then huffs. "Please go outside and do what you need to do."

I grin as I round the counter. "I've been shifting since I was a teen. I've got a pretty good idea how to deal with my wolf. Then again, the new moon is tomorrow so I should probably—"

"It's tonight."

I freeze and try to figure out the date. Usually, I shift several times during the month and don't have to worry about the new moon forcing me. I've been putting it off for various reasons, always making excuses why I couldn't. In actuality, I'm afraid shifting will send out some type of signal. The dark watchers will be on my tail, and I'll have to outrun them. Not that I can.

"I…I have to shift. Now." I circle the island, giving her a wide berth, then stop at the doorway. "Are you going to be okay on your own?"

She snorts, a smile playing on her lips. "I'm perfectly capable of being by myself. I prefer it normally. Unless you need help…"

"No. No, I definitely don't need help. Again, I've been doing this a while. I have to go farther than I normally would, though."

"Uh, okay." She grabs her cup and takes another sip.

I don't want to worry her with legends and guesses. She'll either know about the dark watchers and freak out or she won't and I'll have to explain them. No one wants to have a bedtime story that involves hooded figures following around and bringing about omens of death. At least not when they're most definitely real.

Alissa, my sister, was supposed to be researching them for me. She didn't believe I had anything to do with them popping up in Moon Cove. Except I saw them before I went home. I kept the information to myself until my other sister, Kira, mentioned seeing them. Any way you slice and dice it, I'm fucked.

"Do you want me to let you know when I'm back?"

Her head snaps up, confusion in her eyes. "Actually, I would. I'll leave the back door open. Just…don't come in while shifted."

"Wouldn't dream of it, beautiful."

I knock twice on the doorframe, though I don't know why. Suppose I need something to do with my hands since all they want to do is touch her. I'm playing with fire, yet it's almost like I want to get burned. Or my wolf does. Either way, it isn't a good idea. Not that she's interested. Not truly. Her body may respond to me, but that doesn't mean much. Being isolated here probably doesn't help. I'm not the one to show her a good time, though.

I leave her staring into her mug, a contemplative look on her face. As much as I want to stay, the need to shift is eating away at me. I'm barely out the back door when my wolf batters against the defenses I've built up. We're usually in sync, yet now he's tearing me apart. I won't make it far at this rate. My gaze darts around, though I can't see much with dusk settling over the landscape.

As I hit the tree line, magic rips through me. I barely feel the sting as I transform from two legs to four. In a blink, my eyes adjust to the twilight. The smell of the forest wraps around me as my paws pound against the ground. I need to get as far away from the house as I can. I swing my head back and forth as I dodge trees and jump over logs. There's no sign of the dark watchers yet, but that doesn't mean much.

They've been plaguing me for months now. We always thought they were a myth, a legend passed down through the generations to keep kids in line. All Alissa could find on them were fables about them being omens and harbingers of death. None of it was good and sent me into a bit of a spiral. I wish I could blame them for how I treated my family when I was home last. Instead, all I have is my own ignorance.

I let my wolf take over, content to scan my surroundings from afar. There's no sign of the dark watchers, but they always seem to show up when I least expect it. The wind rushes through my fur and we slow, then he shakes us out. We stop by a stream and lap at the cold water. The trees overhead rustle as the breeze sends the leaves skittering across the ground.

A shiver rolls down my spine, and a low growl erupts into the night. When nothing emerges, my wolf paws at the ground.

His movements are separate from my own. Usually, I barely notice it, like breathing. Now, we feel disconnected after waiting so long to shift. I can't put it off as much in the future, which might prove difficult with me sticking around Hart's Hallow. I don't know what would be worse—leaving Scarlett alone with dark watchers lurking about while I shift or taking the risk of transforming in the middle of her kitchen. Neither is particularly appealing.

I end up running for an hour, then turn to head back. It probably isn't long enough for the goddess's taste. She might not punish me, but it won't be fun to deal with. The new moon forces me into this state.

Spending time in my wolf form is more than just that, though. It's a bond we can never fully break. Strain, maybe, but never break. It's that strain I worry about. I watched Chase deal with that while navigating a relationship with my sister. The history I have with my wolf will help in the short term. If I don't maintain that bond, he'll revolt, and it'll fucking suck.

Light filters through the trees long before Scarlett's house comes into view. My wolf whines, and the sound echoes through my head. He pushes us faster all while I attempt to hold him back. The last thing I want is to bust through the back door as a wolf. Scarlett was very clear she didn't want a shifter in her home.

I don't blame her. Some shifters can't handle themselves. I should ask her what type Holden is. Though we've known each other for five years, we've never shifted at the same time. Looking back, it seems strange, but I didn't think about it at the time.

I shove my wolf aside and pull the magic within me. Thank fuck the goddess had the foresight to have us keep our clothes intact when we take human form again. Alissa said it wasn't always that way. I can't imagine the types of jams I would have been in when I was a teenager if magic hadn't evolved. Shifting for the first time is awkward enough without adding nudity to the mix.

"Scarlett?" I call as I step through the back door.

Silence greets me and my muscles tense. There's no reason to think she's in danger. Just because the dark watchers didn't trail me doesn't mean they were here. I doubt anyone would kidnap a human, and she isn't the type to run off. At least I don't think she is. Plus, I've never seen the dark watchers come close to anyone. They linger on the fringes. The logical answer is she fell asleep. My body doesn't run on logic, though.

"Scarlett, I'm back," I say a little louder.

My footsteps echo through the stillness, and I kick off my boots, then race toward the kitchen. I go through all the possible reasons she's not answering that don't include death or dismemberment.

The counters are spotless as if Scarlett spent the last couple hours deep cleaning every surface. Baskets full of half-proofed bread line the island. More containers fill the space, and I wonder if they're the cakes for the party Naomi was talking about. The sweet scent of strawberries fills me as I inhale deeply. I wonder if she'll give me some before she ships them off.

I search the living room, then retrace my steps. The bathroom door hangs open and I jolt, a strangled cry leaving me before I realize I'm staring at my own reflection.

"Goddess help me," I wheeze, pressing a fist against my chest. "Scarlett, you'd better come out before I have a heart attack."

Once I've caught my breath, I make my way to her bedroom door. Soft light peeks out the crack, and I knock lightly. She probably went to bed, forgetting she wanted me to tell her when I was back. When there's no answer, no rustle of covers, no breathing at all, I nudge the thick wood open.

In the week I've been here, I've never seen this space. I learned pretty quickly growing up not to mess with my sisters' stuff. I might be older than most of them, but I steered clear of their wrath at all costs.

Scarlett's room is larger than I expected with a massive canopy bed taking up most of the far wall. A desk sits in one corner and a vanity table in the other. It's filled with clothes and knickknacks and color.

So. Much. Color.

Her house is eclectic—a mishmash of cultures and treasures. I assumed it depicted her travels, the world outside of her own. This seems like it's a representation of her memories. Dozens of pictures line the mirror over the vanity. More are tacked onto a corkboard, interspersed with concert tickets. I can't even take it all in.

"Where are you, beautiful?" I whisper as I take a single step into the room.

My foot sinks into the thick carpet and wetness soaks into my sock. My nose wrinkles as I hop away. Scarlett's mug with moons engraved around the rim lies on its side, a bit of tea left inside. Fear flares to life inside of me, and I frantically search for her. A mumbled curse falls from my lips as I spot her unmoving body next to her bed.

I rush to her side and crouch. Gently, I brush her hair aside, the soft silvery strands sliding through my fingers. My knuckles brush against her cheek, and she sighs. At least she's breathing. I search around for a reason she fainted, but nothing jumps out at me.

It doesn't matter right now. I probably shouldn't move her. Isn't that what they say? Regardless, I gather her up and set her on the bed. It takes everything in me to let her go. My palms tingle as I release her.

She groans, throwing her arm over her eyes. My muscles relax, and a wave of lightheadedness washes over me. I didn't realize how tense I was. I don't know what to do with my hands, and they end up hovering between us. Touching her seems like a bad idea. When I notice them trembling, I tuck them in my pockets, then immediately take them out.

"Scarlett?"

She groans again and peeks at me from under her arm. "Rule number three."

"You did tell me to let you know when I was back. I found

you on the floor, Scarlett." I jolt toward her when she tries to sit up. "Don't get up."

"It's fine. I'm…fine." She struggles upright and swings her legs over the side.

"You don't look fine. You look pale and flushed all at once." I run my fingers through my hair. "I think I should call someone."

She shakes her head, then winces. "No. Absolutely not. I promise I'm fine. This is normal."

"Passing out is normal?" My brows pull low, and she sighs.

"I need a shower," she mutters and pushes to her feet. "Don't worry about it."

She staggers, and my hand shoots out to steady her. I expect her to bat me away, but she doesn't. Instead, she leans into me, and I wrap my arm around her waist.

Having her this close, even while she's ill, does something to me. I can't describe it and shove the feeling down deep to be examined later. Or not at all.

"Why don't I just put you to bed and you can shower in the morning?" I murmur and rest my chin on the top of her head.

She tenses, then nods. Whatever's going on with her, she's not in the headspace to explain it. The goddess will have to intervene to get answers out of her, I'm pretty sure.

As I ease her down, she sways in my arms. Whatever's wrong with her, it's not over. I tuck her under the covers, and her body relaxes. I switch off the light, plunging the room into darkness. The sheets rustle as I straighten, and she grabs my hand.

"Thank you," she whispers, her voice hitching a bit.

Her shallow breathing echoes through the air. I expect her to let go or fall asleep quickly, but she doesn't do either. I should leave. Once she wakes up, she'll probably ream me out if I stay.

Yet I can't get my feet to move. I reach for the desk chair and tug it closer, keeping hold of her hand. As I sit, she sighs. My eyes finally adjust to the darkness, and I can make out her silhouette, her chest rising and falling evenly.

I snatch the blanket off the end of the bed and drape it over my lap. At least my wolf has settled, content to watch over her. Tomorrow, I'll get answers. It's not until sleep infiltrates my mind that a thought sneaks through. Maybe the dark watchers found her after all. Maybe they're no longer content with just observing. Maybe they hurt her because of me.

# Chapter 10
## Scarlett

Birdsong filters through the cracked window in the kitchen, and I close my eyes to better listen to their conversations. I should be out there with them doing my yoga or taking a walk through the woods. I've been avoiding leaving the house while Slade was here other than that first day. It's not the smartest decision I've made recently. He probably wouldn't care if I kept up my normal routine. Actually, he'd probably insist on going with me. I doubt I'd be able to relax then.

I hum a tune softly as I shape the dough I set out last night. I wasn't about to put music on with Slade asleep in my bedroom. It was hard enough to sneak from the room without waking him.

I didn't expect him to stay all night. My cheeks blaze just remembering how I grabbed his hand. I'm blaming my latest episode for my lapse in judgment. Now I'm going to have to explain things to him whether I want to or not. So much for keeping my distance from him.

The last loaf plops in the basket when I hear Slade shuffling from the bedroom. I glance from the corner of my eye as he fills the doorway. He rubs his face, his hair going every which way. If I was interested in him, which I'm not, I would say it's adorable—*he's* adorable. Except I'm not. Interested, that is. At all. His presence may not be annoying anymore, but that doesn't mean we're going to hop into bed together. Or be friends, which is a much more likely scenario.

I shake my head, then wince from the pain shooting from my shoulder. Holding hands all night wasn't the greatest for my muscles. Slade stumbles into the kitchen and collapses onto his stool. *No, not his stool.* I focus on flouring my dough to keep my gaze from him. Coffee gurgles into a mug and the machine hisses. I set the cup in front of him, then go back to my baking.

"Thanks," he says huskily, wrapping his hands around it. His head drops and he rolls his neck around. I'm sure his muscles are tight from sleeping upright all night.

"You didn't have to stay last night. I mean, it was fine, but it wasn't necessary." I can't force my voice any louder.

Slade lets out a breathless chuckle. "Fine?"

I wave my hand, still avoiding his gaze. "You know what I mean."

"No, I actually don't. I don't know much of anything when it comes to you."

I bite my cheek to keep my shit together. I knew he'd want an explanation for last night, but I thought he'd wait until after caffeine. If I was blessed by the goddess, he wouldn't ask at all. Too bad she abandoned me long ago. I never could figure out why. Holden never agreed with me, so I stopped bringing it up. It's not like I could ask the goddess myself.

My hands tremble, and I turn to hide the movements. Thankfully, my kettle chooses that exact moment to whistle, and I busy myself with turning it off. I'll deal with turning the hot water into tonic later. By the time I face him again, I've wiped my expression clean and I'm ready to deal with his questions.

"You don't need to know details. I just fainted, and I appreciate you helping me even though I would have been fine." I clear my throat, then take a sip. "Thank you for not shifting in the house."

His mug hits the island with a clanging thump, and I tense.

"Cut the bullshit, Scarlett. I don't need you to divulge your deepest, darkest secrets. I'm not going to badger you about never opening up to me."

"You sure about that? Because your tone suggests otherwise." I thought my cold words would deter him, but he merely lifts an eyebrow. "Listen, I get you deserve...something. You're right, sort of. I'm not going to divulge anything, really. Just know that I fainted last night. It's happened before. It will happen again. To you, it was probably freaky and I understand that, but I'm fine. Really."

He leans back and crosses his arms. I don't like how much he sees. Like he's studying me, delving deep into my mind to root out all my secrets. Everything I've kept hidden from others, he'll find. He'll keep digging, just like I suspected. From the look on his face, he doesn't have a clue what I've been through—what I'm *suffering* from.

"Have you seen a doctor?"

I drop my gaze to my cup. "I'm not entirely sure you can ask me that."

"This isn't a job interview, Scarlett."

My eyes snap to his. "No, it's not. It feels like you're prying into my personal life, which I'm pretty sure violates one of the rules."

"It doesn't. I checked."

I let out a humorless laugh. "You write them down or something?"

"Nope. Got it all up here." He taps his temple. "Now, have you seen a doctor? Or are you raw-dogging this whole thing?"

I choke on my lukewarm tea. "I don't think that means what you think it does."

His lips twitch, but he fights the smirk I'm sure he's dying to let through. "Answer the question, beautiful."

"Weird time to use that nickname," I mutter, then clear my throat. "I've seen a doctor."

He narrows his eyes, then pushes to his feet. I tuck my cup close to my chest as he approaches. I'm not afraid per se. *Slade* isn't a threat to me.

Whatever he wants from me isn't malicious. *He* isn't malicious. What he represents, though, is another story. In the ten seconds it takes him to cross the kitchen, I've played out the next few months in my mind.

I'll open up, tell him about my illness. He'll open up and tell me about his family. We'll become friends or more. Then I'll let it slip I'm a lorelei. He'll question me on what that means, and I'll once again have to explain everything. He still won't understand, and I'll resort to likening my shifter status to that of the Sirens in Greek mythology.

That's when the shift will happen. A slight realization in his eyes. A familiar coldness radiating from him. Then one morning I'll wake up and he'll be gone. No note. No apologies. No explanations. Because they won't be needed. The only other way it could go is he'd fall under the spell the goddess bestowed upon my kind. I'll never know whether he's here for me or because he can't leave.

When he stops in front of me, I banish the thoughts.

"I'm going to ask one more time. Have you been to a doctor?"

"Yes."

He leans close, and his lips brush my ear as he whispers, "Liar."

His phone vibrates, making me tense. He doesn't move other than his hand at his side squeezing into a fist, then releasing. I focus on the movement as he does it over and over. When his phone vibrates again, he sighs.

I swallow hard as he pulls away and slips the device from his pocket. Before I know it, he's gone, the faint rumble of his voice as he answers the call trailing back to me.

Mentally, I shake myself, then set my mug down. My tea went cold a long time ago, and I don't feel like going through the motions of making more. Even with the water already heated. Half a cup will have to get me through the next few hours.

I busy myself with cleaning up the kitchen. Except my eyes keep glancing where Slade disappeared. No matter how many times I scold myself, I can't seem to stop. If I had made friends here, I would have called one of them. Naomi and I have a working relationship and not much else. I've isolated myself too well, cut off any possibility of a support system. Never thought it would bite me in the ass, yet here we are.

In my desperation, I dial Holden's number. It doesn't even ring, just goes straight to voicemail. I hang up without leaving a message. Of course he'd disappear when I need him. He may have been the one who put me in this position in the first place, but I still could use his advice.

Except I know what he'd say. He'd tell me to be honest, to open myself up to others. My brother doesn't grasp the concept of failure. Which is what has happened every time I've taken his suggestion of making friends. I've failed. Or the goddess failed when she made me.

Other lorelei seem to embrace their gifts. They don't think the goddess made a mistake. They see nothing wrong with taking advantage of other people—humans or shifters. I met one who came through town when I was young. She clocked me right away and gave me a knowing smile. I didn't realize it then, but she had been waiting for the right moment to approach me. When she finally did, she took it upon herself to give me advice. Her words have stayed with me all these years.

*You're going to grow and become more powerful. Your mere words will make men drop to their knees. Women will worship you. Others will revere you. All you need to do is use it to your advantage. Play your cards right, and you'll live a very comfortable life like me.*

When I'd innocently asked about love, she'd scoffed. Apparently falling in love was for fools and mortals. I don't know why she assumed we couldn't die. There's nothing to suggest I don't have the same life span as other shifters, which isn't much longer than the average human. I didn't know enough to question her at the time.

I cried myself to sleep for weeks after, wondering if I would have to watch everyone I love die. That was about the time Holden took it upon himself at the ripe old age of twelve to educate himself on all things lorelei. Our parents thought it was adorable, but they were pretty busy keeping our family afloat. Most of their efforts were spent on keeping the lights on and some food in the fridge. It left Holden and me to look out for each other.

I'm too lost in my memories to notice Slade until he collapses onto the stool again. His phone clatters across the hard surface, and he grabs his coffee. Exhaustion pulls at his features. Gone are the familiar smile and the twinkle in his eye. Whatever his call was about, it doesn't seem like good news.

"Do you want more coffee?" I ask after I have everything clean.

"No. I'm going to get to work. I need to go back into town and get some more supplies since I'll be staying. I can knock out some more projects on the list." He stares at the liquid as he sloshes it around, not bothering to drink.

"If you need to go, I can get your car running again," I murmur. For once, I'm not trying to get rid of him. Having him around might be a temptation I don't need, but something's clearly going on with him. I'm not heartless.

His mug hits the quartz counter, and I jump. "Why don't you just fucking ask, Scarlett. Instead of dancing around, pretending you're not as nosy as the rest of us or that you don't give two shits, you should just ask the damn question."

When I don't say anything, he makes a sound in the back of his throat and stomps out of the kitchen once more. After a minute, hammering reverberates down the hall. I'm pretty sure he's attacking the wood. I wonder if he's imagining it's my face.

If he had stuck around, I would have explained why I don't pry into other's business. There's nothing more awkward than putting someone on the spot, expecting them to share when they're not ready. Then again, maybe I wouldn't have told him a damn thing.

The longer he's here, the more we wander into this grey space. Not quite friends, definitely not lovers, but not quite sure where that line is. I've been playing this whole thing by ear, and I'm clearly failing. Last night shouldn't have changed a thing between us, yet here I am, completely and utterly unsure of where to go from here.

# Chapter 11
## Slade

S weat pours down my forehead and gathers in my lashes. I grab the shirt I discarded hours ago and swipe at my eyes. As soon as I stop working, the doubt and anxiety creep back in. And the guilt.

So much fucking guilt.

Each layer stacks on top of the last until I can no longer shove it down. It'll suffocate me if I don't do something soon. Talking to someone, *anyone*, might help, but I don't have that luxury.

Gemma and Jake have enough on their plate with running the summer camps. Plus, Kira's probably helping them. Alissa doesn't have service half the time and won't answer the phone the other half. I still think of Eli as the baby, though he's in college. No way I'm bothering him. The thought of calling Sloane, or hell, Alister is worse than the guilt itself. My brother always thinks he needs to act like Dad instead of my older brother. Mom's busy taking care of the general store, and I'm afraid to talk to Dad since I've been putting off calling him. I'm not close enough to anyone else to unload my problems onto them.

And then there's Scarlett. Even if I opened up to her, I doubt

I'd get the response I was looking for. I'd either get the cold and aloof version of her, the one who doesn't want any human interaction, or the other side of her who doesn't know how to respond.

Besides, I was an asshole to her yet again. I doubt she'd want to have an in-depth conversation about all the shit going wrong in my life. She'd probably call me a baby and tell me to suck it up. It's what I would say to me if I were in her shoes.

My shoulders tense as a familiar scent lingers in the air. A second later there's a scuffle behind me and I close my eyes. I could pretend I didn't hear her leaving lunch for me at the doorway. It's what I've been doing for the past couple days while she cooled off. I can't take another week of this, though.

I pivot on my heel and cross my arms as our gazes collide. Her mouth makes a perfect O, and my cock hardens at the images bombarding me. With her bent over, hand still extended toward the plate, I'm given a perfect view down the front of her dress. If I wasn't such a gentleman, I'd already be crowding her space and devouring those plump lips. I grit my teeth to rein myself in.

"Thank you," I say, my voice gruffer than I intended.

She straightens and her throat bobs. "I…I don't pry."

"What?"

She twists her fingers together, her eyes bouncing around the room. "You wanted me to ask the question—"

I hold up my hand, not willing to have this conversation now. "You don't owe me an explanation. I'm sorry I snapped at you. It had nothing to do with you."

She lets out a humorless snort. "Oh, I'm aware. Regardless, I'm going to explain anyway. We're not friends."

"Great way to start," I breathe, and she glares at me.

"I don't know how to…I'm not used to—" She takes a deep breath. "My point is, I'm not going to pry into your personal life. You demanded I ask questions, but there's nothing I need to know. If you wanted to vent, then go right ahead, but I'm not about to put both of us in an awkward situation where I ask and then you feel like you have to answer."

She opens her mouth, probably intent to overexplain even more. One step toward her is all it takes to get her to snap her jaw shut.

"I shouldn't have snapped at you," I say.

"Listen…wait. What?"

"I'm apologizing."

Her eyes narrow and she drops her hands to her sides. "You apologize a lot."

"Well, if I fuck up, I should own up to it and say I'm sorry."

She studies me as if I spoke another language she learned long ago and can't quite remember. Part of me wants to ask what her childhood was like. Did she have loving parents like I did? Was Holden her friend and protector growing up? Is the concept of an apology that ludicrous to her? Maybe a past boyfriend made her feel like she didn't deserve apologies.

"You had good parents, didn't you?" she whispers.

I clear my throat. "Have. I *have* good parents. I grew up with a lot of siblings. We had to learn how to apologize or we'd live in chaos. It was still chaotic, but get half a dozen teenagers in a room and it's bound to be, I suppose."

She nods, but I doubt she understands. "Names?"

"Alister, Sloane, me, Kira, Gemma, Alissa, and Eli." I fight a smile at her incredulous look. "Most of them have scattered now that Gemma's found her mate. I suppose it woke up something inside them."

"But not you." She says it more like a statement than a question.

"I was always more of a free spirit. My mom says I'm a wanderer, which is not a compliment coming from her."

Silence stretches between us, and I wish I could dig into her mind. It isn't the first time I've wanted those cartoon bubbles to pop up above someone's head. Usually I enjoy the process. Learning someone's quirks, getting to know what makes them tick, creating inside jokes, those are the basis of most of my relationships.

With Scarlett, I feel like I have to pry every piece of information from her. If I prod too hard, she'll shut down. I don't know why I care so much. Even if we become friends, it's not like I'm staying here. This isn't home. Then again, I don't really have a home anymore. Moon Cove is part of my past. I just haven't figured out my future yet.

"You said you needed to go into town?" she finally says.

"Uh, yeah. I've got most of this room done except for the drywall. You didn't have the electrical on here." I pull the list from my pocket and glance at it even though I've memorized it. "I don't think it needs to be redone and if you did do it, you'd have to pull for the entire house. The HVAC looks fine." I glance up and find her wide-eyed. "The duct work. These things?"

I slap my hand on the metal running through the wall next to me. Her eyes narrow, and I wonder what the fuck I did wrong this time. It doesn't seem to matter what I say or how I say it, either way, she's going to take it poorly. I may be to blame for some of our issues, but not all. Probably half.

"There's no possible way that's called duck work." She crosses her arms, and this time I can't beat back my grin.

"*Duct.* The last letter is a T, not a K. No harming of ducks. In fact, I haven't even seen any ducks around here."

"Animals don't really like to come this close to my place. Whatever. I can take you into town when you're ready." She pivots on her heel, and it takes me a good twenty seconds to move. This isn't the first time she's shut down a conversation by walking away. I don't know what it is about ducks or animals in general that makes her run.

I prowl after her, intent on asking about the wildlife around here. She's halfway down the hall when she stumbles and thunks into the wall. I rush forward and wrap my arm around her waist to keep her upright. When her knees give out, I swing her into my arms. She protests weakly, and I grit my teeth to keep from snapping at her. It's not her fault she's sick. I'm more pissed at myself.

"Slade, stop," she wheezes.

"No. I'm taking you to the hospital. Something's not right and I'm not waiting around for you to die. Not only would that royally suck, but your brother would kill me. Then we'd both be in front of the goddess and I haven't finished my business down here." I stomp toward the front door, wishing I'd brought my phone. I left it somewhere back in the mess of renovations.

She tenses, and I hold her closer to me. "Oh no. You can't take me to the hospital. It's like two hours away."

"Then the doctor," I growl.

She holds out her hand as if she can block our way out. I could kick the door down, but it would just end up with one more thing for me to fix. I stop short and glare down at her.

"Doctors can't do anything," she chokes out.

"Are you dying? Is that what this is?" A vise squeezes around my heart, and I struggle to breathe.

She rolls her eyes. "Put me down."

"Not until I get some answers. I'm not about to sit around and watch you slowly waste away. Or come in and find you passed out on the damn floor again. I can't do it, Scarlett." My voice trembles and I snap my mouth shut.

Her jaw twitches, and she refuses to meet my gaze. "Fine. I'll tell you, but I'm not doing it while being hauled around like a fucking damsel."

I pivot on my heel and march over to the couch. Despite the fear and rage bubbling within me, I set her gently on the cushions and step back. No way am I sitting down. The nervous energy zinging through my body won't let me.

She pushes herself upright and tucks her chin to her chest. She's probably trying to hide her wince, as if she could hide anything from a shifter. I can practically smell her pain.

"Yeah, sure, just hover over me, that'll get me to be open and honest." She huffs, and I take one step back. It's as much as I can give her right now. "Doctors can't help me."

"You've said that." I cross my arms as I track the tiny movements on her face. They'll give her away more than her words.

"I mean…" She clears her throat. "*Human* doctors can't help me. And, uh, supernatural ones aren't exactly readily available. I know what I have to do to keep myself in line. I just haven't been on my routine. The tonics help. So does the yoga. I don't know if you've noticed."

I definitely had, but the memory can't take hold. Her words repeat in my mind over and over—*human, supernatural, routine, supernatural, tonic, human, supernatural, supernatural.*

"Supernatural," I whisper.

Pain and possibly disappointment flash in her eyes before she drops her gaze to her lap. "Technically, I'm a shifter. Just a different kind."

"Holden tell you about one of my best friends?" I wait until she shakes her head. "He's a bigfoot. And his friend Chase, who is mated to my sister, is a sliver cat. So, I'm pretty sure I can handle whatever it is you are." Still, I brace myself for her answer.

She lets out a mirthless laugh. "I'd give almost anything to be a bigfoot shifter. Not that I've ever met one, but yeah."

She falls quiet, and I give her a minute. Clearly, this isn't something she tells a lot of people, if anyone. I assume her brother knows. After spending the last week with her, I doubt she has a lot of friends. In fact, she told me she didn't like people. If she shifts into something misunderstood, like Jake, or something with a bad history, like Chase, I can understand her hesitancy.

"Bite the bullet, beautiful."

Her gaze darts up to me, and she gives me a sardonic smirk. "Nice alliteration. Have you heard of a siren?"

Instantly, my muscles tense. Sirens aren't part of our history. Anyone who's paid even the slightest bit of attention to Greek mythology knows what a siren is. It's become ingrained in mainstream media, even though humans don't know they used to actually exist. The equivalent for us shifters, though, is fairly similar.

"Lorelei," I whisper, and she sighs.

My eyes glaze over as my mind skips back to the last lorelei I met. I was a shitty teenager with raging hormones and only a couple years of shifting under my belt. Kids these days are shifting earlier than we did, not having to wait for puberty to set in. Back then, though, I could barely control myself.

Having a lorelei come through town wasn't the best for me and my friends. Sure, we thought the goddess had blessed us at the time. Looking back, I'm ashamed of how we tripped over ourselves to gain her attention.

It wasn't until she disappeared as quickly as she came that the fog lifted and I realized what a fool I'd made of myself. I haven't met one since, which I always thought was strange. I've traveled all over several countries at this point. Chances are I'd have run into one of them.

Now, it's as if the goddess shoved me right in Scarlett's path. Whether to test me or to punish me, I don't know. I've heard the stories of manipulation and destruction the lorelei leaves trailing in their wake. Tales of their ability to bring entire communities to their knees are abundant in shifter lore. And while Scarlett doesn't seem to want anything to do with *anyone*, I doubt I'd ever know her true intentions. It's the way of the lorelei.

My body sways away from her unconsciously. My vision focuses on her once more, and devastation clouds her eyes a split second before she ducks her head again. Even if I decide to stick around, she'll never trust me. I've destroyed any chance I ever had with her with one move.

# Chapter 12


A familiar ache settles in my chest as I glance toward the house for the seventh time in the last hour. I've tried to give Slade his space. At least he didn't run off. Actually, he might have shifted and just left his car here to rot.

I'll be pretty pissed if that's the case since I've been trying to get it going since he walked off. If I can't fix it, I'll have to pay someone to haul off the piece of junk, if I can get anyone to come out in the first place. The only person I could call doesn't like me very much.

I thought if I attempted to fix his car, my mind would focus on that instead of whatever Slade is doing.

And thinking.

And feeling.

I have no idea what the hell he did to this thing, though. If I can't get it running, he'll be stuck here. Or he'll shift and take off, and I'll have to explain to Holden how I chased away his friend because I told him a secret I haven't revealed in at least a decade. That'll go over real well.

I huff as I plant my hands on my hips, staring at the mess of an engine. I glance over my shoulder at the house again, then give myself a scolding. This is what I wanted—Slade gone, my solitude back, my secret safe. So why do I feel like shit?

Somehow he weaseled his way in after only a week. Keeping him at arm's length was a fool's dream. Slade seems to make it his life's mission to befriend others. It's no wonder he attempted to do the same to me.

"Bet he regrets that now," I mutter to the empty yard.

"There are very few things in life I regret, Scarlett."

A heavy sigh leaves me. As much as I hated the nickname he gave me, it hurts that he isn't using it. Like he's sending a clear message of where I stand now. I've put all of my energy into trying to get him to leave, I didn't think about what it would be like when he actually did.

A week couldn't possibly be enough time to get attached. I chalk it up to the break in my solitude. I remembered what it felt like to not be lonely. It happens every time my brother comes to visit. My mind gets used to having someone else around, and then I have to adjust when he leaves. So really, this has nothing to do with Slade. It's me, not him.

"Your oil's overdue, the belts need replaced, and I'm pretty sure you need a new alternator. I'll have to go into the city to get the part, but you should be able to get out of here by tomorrow morning." I avoid his gaze, though I can feel it boring into me. We're not going to have some grand heart-to-heart and find common ground.

"Tire is flat, too. And the hose was on its last leg, per the last mechanic," he murmurs as he leans his hip against the side panel and crosses his arms.

"You took this thing to an actual mechanic? Or was it Rando Joe who helps fix cars on the side out of his carport and his only experience is he changed a tire once?" I give him a sardonic look, hoping he won't bring up the reasons he's leaving.

"I mean, he's a shifter, but I'm pretty sure he knows what he's doing. He said it'd get me around. I may have failed to mention I was taking it across the country," he murmurs.

I drop my gaze back to the engine. "Well, regardless, I can

get it going. It'll limp you home at least. Unless you do drag races or some shit, which I highly suggest you don't."

The rod sticks when I try to lower the hood, and I grumble under my breath. Rust flakes off as I yank it out and drop the heavy metal into place. Slade jumps back like I threw the thing at him.

"I'm not too concerned with my car, Scarlett."

"Stop saying my name," I growl. Wiping my hands on the rag in my back pocket, I grit my teeth.

"Would you rather me go back to calling you beautiful? Because I would very much—"

"Rule number six," I snarl.

I stomp away from him. It would be a glorious exit if my ankle didn't seize this particular moment to roll for no other reason than it forgot how to behave like an ankle. It has one fucking job and it can't even do that. Slade grabs my elbow and hauls me upright.

"You know, if I didn't know any better, I'd say you're doing this on purpose. Also, pretty sure rule six is you won't do my laundry."

A disgusted noise leaves me and I shove him away. "Do not think for one damn second I'm trying to lure you in. Just go…do something else."

I hurry away, thankfully on ankles that do their actual job. When I finally get back inside, I let out a heavy breath. The longer he's here, the more nervous I get. I knew he'd get around to accusing me of using my powers on him. I may not be able to shift into another form, but I have magic coursing through me just like them.

"Scarlett, you can't just run away every time you hear something you don't like," Slade calls as he slams the front door shut.

"I most certainly can," I yell back. I don't really have anything to distract me. My dough isn't ready. I could clean, which is my go-to when I have excess anxiety battering my body. I can't just drive off without him. He'd probably chase after me. In wolf form, no less.

Slade steps into the kitchen and I slip around the island, putting the slab between us. The physical distance might not do any good, but it's the best I've got.

He leans his fists on the counter and glares at me. "In almost any other situation, I'd agree with you. This particular one I don't. Nothing gets resolved if you don't talk about it."

"There's nothing to talk about. I shouldn't have told you anyways."

"Does Holden know?"

I snort before I can stop myself. "Of course he knows. We grew up together. He knows better than to spread my business around. Do you?"

His nostrils flare, and a flash of heat hits me in the gut. Getting under his skin gets me hot and bothered for some reason. I hate it.

*Liar,* a voice in my head whispers. It sounds suspiciously like Slade's, and I hate that too.

"I have one question, and then we can move on." He waits until I wave him on, and he pulls in a deep breath. "Do you know when you're using your…abilities?"

My mouth parts, then I snap it shut. My first instinct is to cuss him out. This type of accusation comes up all too often. We're vilified for magic the goddess gave us. No one seems to realize our *abilities* come from the same place their own do. Except Slade didn't accuse me of anything. He asked a perfectly legitimate question.

"Depends on what you're talking about," I murmur, attempting to keep emotions in check.

"It's not a hard question, Scarlett." He raises an eyebrow like that'll get me to open up.

"Actually, *Slade,* it is. When do you shift? And are there any extenuating circumstances that make you shift? Perhaps you're—"

"Okay, I get it. Just…what do you mean?"

I cross my arms and glance away. "Subtle things slip through without my noticing sometimes. When I'm tired or not paying attention, I don't pick up on it until later. Nothing big, obviously, but half the time I can't tell whether it was me or *me.* Anything more intense and yeah, I have to do it on purpose. Because that's what you really want to know, right? Whether or not I make the choice? And whether or not I've used it on you."

He sighs heavily and straightens. "Scarlett, you have pushed me away at every opportunity you've had. I watched you interact with the townspeople. No one would assume you used your abilities to sway them or put them under your spell. You live in the middle of fucking nowhere, for fuck's sake."

"Obviously. I've been called a manipulative bitch enough for a lifetime. Now I'm just a bitch and I'm fine with that. We don't have to be friends. I don't need you to save me. I'm perfectly content with my life. We both know the only reason you're here is because of your debt to my brother, which, whatever, I don't care. You've done your obligation and I'm sure you won't have to spend the next year as a wolf, so…why don't I just go get the parts for your car and we can call this?"

He tilts his head and his eyes narrow. Maybe I laid it on too thick. Not that I was trying to. I'm content, or at least I was until he crashed into my life with his shitty car and sardonic smirk. I'd never admit it, but I actually enjoy having someone around some of the time. Eating alone isn't fun, and it's really hard to figure out meals for just one person.

"Wait," Slade says, breaking me out of my thoughts. "What does you being a lorelei have to do with your medical issues?"

I thought he would have forgotten about it in the wake of my revelation. "I just have a problem with my blood, that's all.

Was told it offsets my 'abilities,' as you called them. It's fine and it probably won't kill me."

"Probably?" His voice can't seem to figure out whether it wants to drop into a growl or shoot into squeaky range. "Probably? What the fuck does *that* mean?"

"You're more likely to blow up in that crap car than I am to keel over from leplexia," I snap. "Why don't we just forget I ever told you...anything. No lorelei, no illness. This is just business."

He chuckles breathlessly, shaking his head. "This is much more than business, beautiful. I just haven't figured out what we are yet."

I sputter as he pivots and makes his way out the front door. My mind instantly rejects what he's implying, but my body doesn't care. A flush spreads across my skin, leaving me hot and bothered.

"Business," I yell after his retreating back. His laughter floats behind him. He doesn't even bother closing the door, merely lets the screen slam into place.

I don't care where he's going or what he plans on doing. It's clear he's decided to stay here for now. Doesn't mean I have to cater to him and his delicate sensibilities. He's free to go about his life without worrying about me and what I'm doing.

I'll fix his car, and eventually he'll realize I'm not giving in to whatever his plans are. Then he'll leave and my life will go back to normal, just like I imagined this morning.

Am I delusional? Perhaps, but I don't have anything else to cling to. If I give in to him, it'd be amazing. I'd remember what it was like to open up and be friends with someone. Maybe I'd finally get an orgasm from something other than a toy, though I'm not holding my breath. Mostly because I doubt he'd ever get in bed with me. Since he knows I'm a lorelei, he'll probably stay as far away from my bedroom as possible. If that didn't deter him, my illness will.

He'll probably start treating me like a wounded animal or a

piece of glass. No more random touches or sly grins. My body grows heavy as the weight of my new reality hits me. I shove the disappointment down deep, next to my shattered hopes and dreams for a normal life.

I take a deep breath, hoping to center myself enough not to need to rest. If I keep getting worked up, my body will shut down, and I don't have time for that. I need to make more cakes and doughs, fix Slade's car, pull weeds in the garden, call Holden for the hundredth time, and deal with the renovations Slade can't get to. Adding whatever he meant would tip me over the edge.

As I grab my keys and head out the door, I search for my shifter among the trees. *Not my shifter.* From what I can tell, he's disappeared. I swear, if I get his car running and he's already in the wind, I'm going to lose it. Then again, it's the least I can do with all the work he's done. I'm impressed with how much he's accomplished in less than a week. Which is something I should have told him. Saying thank you doesn't seem like enough, and baked goods feel pedantic. I definitely can't repay him with grilled cheese. No matter what he said.

I'll have to think about it later. My emotions have been on a rollercoaster today—all this week, really. Everything can wait until after I get my shit together. Or I've shoved all my feelings down deep enough that I don't have to think about them anymore.

# Chapter 13

## Slade

The light fades as I stare at the sky while leaning against Scarlett's truck. I figure the best thing to do is let her get her shit together. Hanging around while she analyzes my statement wouldn't end well for either of us.

I can't explain what changed between us, but something did. A force I've never felt before hit me square in the chest when she revealed what she is. I tried to push it away, sever the tie, and focus on not freaking out. It didn't work.

The last thing I wanted to do was react like I did with Chase. When he morphed into a long-forgotten cryptid, I zeroed in on the possible threat to my family—to my sister. Kira had already fallen under his spell, and I was afraid she'd get hurt. And while I stand by my reservations, I handled everything all wrong. I pushed her away and pissed off a lot of people. Chase ended up being a pretty good guy, perfect for Kira, and I almost fucked it all up. I wasn't about to make the same mistake twice.

Except I've been on edge ever since. I met three shifters on my way down here randomly, and I never approached them. That's not like me. I've prided myself on making connections and friends in all my travels. Meeting other shifters keeps me grounded and helps me help them. Most of them are just happy to have found someone else who's like them. When I felt other shifters around lately, though, I couldn't talk to them. I rushed out of gas stations and away from hotels like I was being chased, which I suppose I was. The dark watchers have been dogging my steps across the country.

"Fucking bastards," I mutter, then sigh.

"Who's a bastard? And don't lean on my truck. You'll scratch the paint." Scarlett's lilting voice fills my lungs. I inhale deeply, hoping to hold on to her essence for as long as possible despite her words.

My eyes fly open as she smacks me, and a grin spreads across my face. "No buttons, beautiful. I won't be scratching anything. Unless…"

She scowls, then shoves me away from the door. "We're not doing this."

"What exactly aren't we doing?" I ask as I step around her and pull open her door. She doesn't answer as she crawls in or when I shut it behind her. I lean into the open window on crossed arms. "I'm very persistent, Scarlett. Eventually, I'll get it out of you. Best to just give in now."

"You're insufferable. Get off my truck," she snaps, though the corner of her mouth tilts up.

I straighten and hold up my hands. "Never said I wasn't a good listener."

I round the hood, more to make sure she doesn't take off without me than anything. Her gaze tracks me the entire time, and I can't keep the smile off my face. Nor can I ignore the swooping sensation in my gut.

Whatever clicked between us, I'm not going to ignore it. I *can't*. The goddess led me here for a reason, and I'd be a fool not to listen. Even if we aren't meant to be anything other than friends, I have to stick with it. I've already got Holden's debt hanging over my head. The last thing I need is another threat from the goddess.

"Buckle up," Scarlett says as the engine rumbles to life.

She doesn't wait for me to listen before she takes off through the trees. We bump along the path until we hit the gravel road and she turns away from town. I wait until we're on pavement, then roll my own window down and stick my arm into the wind. I let the breeze roll over my skin.

"What are you doing?" At least this time Scarlett isn't snapping at me. Maybe she's settling into the idea of us being more than at each other's throats.

"Airplane," I murmur. "Did you ever do this when you were a kid?"

She glances at me, then back to the road. "No. I wasn't really allowed to go anywhere."

My head snaps around. "Excuse me?"

She rolls her eyes, though her fingers tighten on the steering wheel. "Not exactly easy for my parents to take me out in public. I used to convince people to give me things for free. Random people on the street would give me money just because I asked."

"Didn't your parents have anyone to teach you how to control it?" I don't know how much I can question her before she shuts down again. I wish I could call Alissa. She'd have some insight into how this all works.

"Lorelei aren't super common. The ones we did come across were...living their lives differently." She sighs as she turns onto a highway. "Most of them *wanted* to use their powers to get what they wanted. At least the ones I met were like that. They didn't care about how others would feel afterwards or how it would impact their lives. They take and take and then move on. My parents weren't about to let me live like that."

"So, you could compel me to leave if you wanted?"

Her lips pressed into a thin line. "Yes, but I wouldn't."

"Didn't say you would, beautiful. Just trying to figure you out." I smirk, but she doesn't see it. Probably for the best.

"Well stop. I don't need more friends."

"What's wrong with more friends? I've got loads and more than a couple of them have gotten me out of some tight jams."

She glances at me from the corner of her eye. "So you only keep people around when they're useful? Doesn't seem like much of a friendship."

"Didn't say that. It's more like, having people around makes me happy. At least for a bit. I get pretty restless. Haven't found a place to settle down yet."

I'm probably not making sense. Or she's going to take things the wrong way again. She seems to do that a lot. I wonder how often she's been misunderstood, deliberately or otherwise.

The silence stretches between us, and I wonder if I've lost her completely. Just when I'm about to blurt out something foolish, she sighs heavily.

"Must be hard being so isolated out here," she says, a note of bitterness in her voice.

"Not even a little bit. Though I was a bit worried about how the hell I was going to get you to a hospital." I tap a rhythm on the side of the truck, contemplating whether or not I should keep going. "It actually kind of reminds me of my hometown. Surrounded by the forest and all that."

She takes an exit, a lone gas station the only thing around indicating we're close to a town. It looks like every other small town I've been to over the years—a place stuck in time. Houses next to cafes next to a tiny post office on one block. On the next is a general store next to a bar next to a feed store.

"Holden said you lived in a shifter community."

"Was that a question, beautiful?" I grin at her, but she merely shakes her head. "Yeah, Moon Cove is a shifter community. Tourists come through, thinking they'll spot some cryptids up there. We oblige them with some shifters and the like."

She screws up her nose. "Isn't that exhausting?"

I shrug, glancing out the window again. "Sometimes. When I was a teenager, we thought it was fun, especially when we'd prank the younger ones. Used to be you wouldn't shift until puberty. Now there're kids running around in their shifter forms. The adults warded most of the town so a random human wouldn't wander in."

"How?" she asks sharply.

"Dunno. I could ask my dad, though. Wanting to guard your little slice of paradise against people?" At the thought of my father, my gut tightens. I still need to force him on the phone, but the signal's been spotty out here. At this point, I think he's fucking with us.

"That's my definition of utopia, honestly. No one randomly stopping by. Door-to-door salesmen would skip my place. I'd have one less broken-down car in my driveway." Her lips twitch as she fights a smile.

"Was that a joke? Told you you'd warm up to me."

"One joke and some questions doesn't mean anything, Slade. Don't get your hopes up."

I chuckle, a warmth invading my chest. "Too late. You've lured me in."

She flinches, and I realize I've gone too far. I lean toward her, intent on explaining, and she waves her hand through the air as if shooing me away.

"Don't bother. I know you didn't mean it like that. Just…let it go." She pulls into the parking lot of a lumberyard, though giving it that name doesn't really encompass everything this store holds.

The engine cuts out, and we stare out the windshield, neither moving. I clear my throat, grasping at words that won't come. I have no idea how to erase the last two minutes and get back to bantering. We were finally getting somewhere.

Maybe I should figure out what I'm striving for when it comes to her before I push it. Friends might be the most we could ever be. The thought has another ache building in my chest.

"You got a budget for this trip?" I finally ask.

"Um, no. Let's just see how it goes." She pushes from the truck before I can argue. Because of course I'd argue. Winging it isn't the best idea for these type of projects. Supplies for renovations can add up, and she won't even notice until we're at the registers.

She's halfway across the parking lot, and I scramble from the truck. She scowls over her shoulder as I shut the door. I didn't even slam it, though. I hurry after her and grab her hand when she steps into the driveway in front of the store.

"We're not holding hands, Slade," she hisses.

"Got it. But I'd also like for you not to become a splatter on the asphalt, beautiful."

She opens her mouth, then snaps it shut when a truck drives by, then turns down the row next to us. The man behind the wheel waves, and I lift my hand in response.

I pull her after me and into the cool air conditioning, breathing a sigh of relief. It's only going to get hotter the deeper into summer we get. If I'm going to be here for a while, I'll have to get some more clothes to deal with the heat. From the look on Scarlett's face, I might have to put off that particular trip for another time.

Despite her earlier statement, she doesn't let go of me. I lace our fingers together as we search for a cart. Reluctantly, I release her when we find one. It doesn't take long to find the few small things we need. When we get to the lumber, Scarlett finally seems to understand why I asked about a budget. She hems and haws, refusing to admit I was right.

"Scarlett, the store's going to close soon," I say, leaning against the shelves.

"It's only like four," she mutters. "They close in like three hours."

"Exactly."

She scowls at me, then turns back to the piles. "Which one of these do we need?"

I point right in front of her. We've been over this, but if it makes her feel better, I'll answer all her questions again. And again. And again. Besides, with us stuck here, she can't disappear on me.

"If you tell me how much—"

She throws up her hands and paces away only to turn back with a thunderous expression. She pokes me in the chest as she growls. I fight a grin, knowing it won't help one bit. She'd probably smack me and I'd deserve it. With her scrunched nose and a flush across her cheeks, she looks adorable. I don't have a death wish, though. Scarlett stomps away again, then marches straight back to me.

"I'm not poor," she snarls.

My grin dies. "I didn't say you were."

"I just can't buy a bunch of shit willy-nilly. I've got a lot on my plate and—" She exhales heavily as my hands drop on her shoulders.

"Stop. Breathe. We don't have to spend a shitload. I can figure out how to work within your budget. You don't have to spend your entire savings."

Her muscles relax under my grip. "This is just going to cost me a fortune."

"Doesn't have to. Remember, I'm staying longer now, which means you don't have to pay for labor. Just keep making that bread and I'll be good." I lean down and catch her eyes. "We'll figure this out together."

"Okay," she breathes. "Okay."

She steps out of my hold, and I have the irrational urge to reel her back in. Just for a little bit longer. My palms tingle and I swallow hard. Telling her I was going to pursue whatever this was between us was the right decision. There's something there I can't quite define. And I can't wait to figure it out.

# Chapter 14
## Scarlett

I keep sneaking glances at Slade. He doesn't seem any different from normal, but something's changed. Whether it's him or me or us, I don't know. Mentally, I shy away from it, too worried about the consequences. I doubt I'll be able to keep him at arm's length anymore.

With the lumber bouncing around in the back of my truck, I can't gun it like I want. Still, I push it to the limit. Anything to get away from this feeling clawing its way through me.

"Better slow down, beautiful, or we're going to lose the entire load." Laughter tinges his voice.

"Roll up your window," I snap. It takes him a minute, but he listens, thank fuck. The last thing I want is to eat a mouthful of dirt.

"You feeling okay?" he asks as I take a curve a touch too fast.

I huff, shaking my head. "Don't do that."

"Do what? Pretend I care?"

"Everyone who gets even the slightest hint I might be sick goes down one of two paths. Either they ignore everything and pretend things are perfectly fine or they end up only seeing the illness. Every question has a double meaning. 'How are you' takes on a whole new context. So, don't start with that shit." My nose flares and my knuckles whiten on the steering wheel.

"Okay. Have you told a lot of people?" he asks.

I glance at him from the corner of my eye. Getting into this isn't going to end well. That's true for most things we talk about these days. I keep trying to figure out how he's going to use these tidbits of conversation against me. Even the people who say they won't throw things in my face in the middle of an argument end up doing it in the end. Every relationship, romantic or not, has failed spectacularly in the same way.

"Enough to know the pattern. I'm more than my illness."

He nods, but I don't think he fully gets it. It's hard to explain to someone not living through it. I haven't met anyone who has the same issues as me. Humans have similar symptoms, but they can't really relate to most of mine. Being a shifter makes my illness manifest differently.

"I wasn't trying to—"

"When I was younger, a teenager, my parents let me get a job. There was a girl, a human, I worked with who had cancer." I let out a little laugh. "She had to take a nap at two in the afternoon every single day. I don't know why I remember that. Anyways, she was the only one who understood it. One day she walked in, pissy mood, didn't want to talk to anyone. We went to take out the trash, and she just unloaded."

"Did she know about your…stuff?" he asks gruffly.

I ease around the curve in the road before answering. "Yeah, I'd told her a couple weeks before. That day she'd had to go to a family thing. She kept saying no one actually saw her. They'd ask all the right questions, but they don't really care."

"How did she know?"

I give him a look, then turn back. "She knew. We always know. It's the slight pity in their eyes, the downturn of their mouth, and the soft voice. They don't see anything other than the disease. It's…lonely. That's what she said."

"And you agree." He says it more like a statement than a question.

"I mean, yeah. To an extent. Even Holden does it. Every time I'm tired or don't want to get up in the morning, he makes a comment. It's annoying."

"And lonely."

I shake my head, wishing I had kept that part to myself. "I'm not lonely. I like being by myself. I told you that."

As we pull onto the hidden road, he grunts. I don't know if it's a response or because we're hitting ruts in the gravel. He hasn't said anything about me stashing my truck in a copse of trees. With how he finagles information from me, I doubt I'll keep it from him.

"Shouldn't park here," he says.

"And there it is," I whisper as I pull into my usual spot.

"No idea what that means, but you shouldn't park here with the load in the back. I don't want to haul everything out of the woods, across the lawn, around the house, and to the back porch. Doubt you do either."

I let out a soft curse and throw the truck in reverse. My hand lands on the back of his headrest as I glare over my shoulder. I shouldn't be whipping between the trees with a bunch of lumber in the bed of the truck, but whatever. I've driven this way thousands of times, and I could do it with my eyes closed.

I expect Slade to be pissed and possibly yell at me. Instead, he's got a look in his eyes I can't quite place.

"What?" I snap as I face forward.

"That was…incredibly hot," he breathes.

I don't know what to say, so I keep my mouth shut. We end up bumping down a side path, then across the lawn before stopping by the back door. He mutters something else as I hop out and make my way to the hatch.

It takes a lot longer to unload everything, especially with Slade trying to get me to rest every five minutes. I'm gritting my teeth more because of him than the exertion of hauling things onto the porch. If he keeps it up, I'm liable to swing this board into his gut. He must sense how close I am to the edge because he shuts up and we work in silence.

"I've got the rest," he murmurs when I try to slip past him out the door.

"I can help."

He steps in my way and sets the boards down, then crosses his arms. "There's like one more load. I'm not going to tell you again, Scarlett. Go take a shower. Or make some food. Or just fucking rest. You're no good to me if you run yourself into the ground."

I try to hide my surprise, but I'm not sure I succeed. He spins me around and gently pushes me toward the hallway. I don't have it in me to resist and end up walking away.

My kitchen comes into view and I stop, whispering, "What the hell just happened?"

I don't like being bossed around. At least, I didn't think I did. It's not like our interaction was anything spectacular, yet heat gathers in my gut. Goosebumps erupt along my arms, a direct contradiction with the warmth spreading through me. A physical manifestation of the push and pull within me when it comes to Slade Livia.

I end up puttering around the kitchen, not really committing to anything. I'm desperately trying not to listen for him. He probably won't even come in here when he's done. It feels just like when he first got here. I didn't want anything to do with him then.

Slade was a needless complication—*is* a needless complication. A shifter like him doesn't belong in my life. It's why I shouldn't be letting him get any closer. I shouldn't be letting him stay. I shouldn't be letting him lull me into a sense of calm.

"Should I go into town for dinner?" Slade says from behind me, making me jump.

I let out a muffled curse. "I forgot to get the parts for your car."

He drops onto the stool across from me. "Don't bite my head off, but I could—"

"No. You're not driving my truck."

He grins. "Worth a shot. Why don't I cook?"

My eyes snap to his. "Excuse me?"

"I'm capable of cooking. In fact, I'm pretty damn good at it. You've fed me enough, so let me feed you." He pushes to his feet and rounds the island.

His hands land on my waist, and he shuffles me to the side. It's not until I'm seated on his abandoned stool that I realize he's taken over yet again. And I didn't put up a fight at all. It's like every time he shows up, all the arguments I made up in my head go up in smoke. I'm so confident in my path and then *poof*. Gone.

I clear my throat. "I'm not saying you can't cook, but—"

"You might be the baker, beautiful, but you have no idea how amazing I am at feeding myself."

"Would you stop interrupting me?" I grumble, crossing my arms and glancing away.

"My bad. Continue," he says as he rummages through my fridge.

"I, uh, never mind." I didn't really have anything to say.

Cooking for myself every day over and over isn't something I look forward to. I hate having to figure shit out on my own. And there aren't recipes for only one person. It's either pairs or a group. I end up eating stew for days in the winter merely because I hate to throw anything out.

He hums as he stacks random things on the counter. I can't even begin to imagine what he's making. A twinge hits my back, and I reach around to rub at the spot. I shouldn't have hauled all that wood today. This pain will only get worse the longer I sit, but I can't force myself to get up.

I prop my chin on my folded arms and gaze at Slade glides through the kitchen. I swallow a groan as I arch my back, trying to stretch the ache. It doesn't work. Instead, a spasm runs down my nerves to my knees. I rarely sit on these stools, and I'm suddenly reminded why.

"You good?" Slade asks, and I straighten.

"Of course," I wheeze.

His brows pull low as he glances over his shoulder. I plaster on a tight smile. My shoulders sag when he faces the oven once more. I drop my forehead onto my folded arms. He'll probably catch me napping, but whatever. I'm too tired to keep up the charade. I should probably make my tonic. It'll help me sleep, though the pain won't completely go away.

I doze as the clinking of pots and pans floats around me. Slade's warm hand on my shoulder jolts me awake. He points to a mug by my elbow, then goes back to the stove.

"What's this?" I rasp, sleep heavy in my voice.

"Your tea. Drink it. Supper's almost done."

I eye the liquid suspiciously. He probably found some random tea bag tucked away by the coffee. Except it smells like the tonic I make. There's no way he knew what to put in it, though.

"What kind is it?"

"Same kind you make, Scarlett," he says with a chuckle. "Just drink it."

"There's no way you made it the same. Not to say I don't appreciate it, I do. It's just that it's not easy. There's a lot of ingredients. Not even Holden can get it right." I don't want to taste it and have it exacerbate my symptoms. I can't tell him that, though, since I don't want to sound ungrateful.

He reaches out and opens the cupboard without turning around. His finger hits the piece of paper taped to the inside, and I groan.

"Forgot you wrote it down, beautiful?"

"Shut up," I mumble, tugging the mug closer.

As the tea slides down my throat, warmth spreads through me. Whether it's the tonic or Slade's actions, I don't know. I'm not about to examine the feeling any closer. Except it's been a long time since anyone has taken care of me. Is this what other people feel like all the time? Are they going around with others anticipating their needs and actually following through? Even Holden doesn't do this type of thing for me.

*It's just a cup of tea, Scarlett. Don't start reading more into it.*

My pep talk doesn't extinguish the heat building in my gut. It's probably just from the tonic. I spend the next few minutes reordering my mind into some semblance of normalcy. Except my brain keeps jumping from one theory to the next. Theories about Slade's intentions, my brother's disappearance, my place in the world. None of them feels plausible.

"Bon appétit." Slade drops a plate in front of me, and I flinch.

"What…wait. Is this chicken parmesan?" I tilt my head as my mouth waters. I inhale the scent of melted cheese and tomato sauce.

"Yup. My mom taught me how to make it a long time ago."

I nod, wondering how she taught him. Did she stand in the kitchen with him, showing him each step? Did he read it from a recipe card? I keep the questions inside.

My own mother was too busy with her job to cook most nights. My father did when he was home. Mostly, it was Holden figuring shit out when we were young. We basically taught ourselves from watching reruns of cooking shows.

I've learned more since I started living alone. I needed something to fill my time other than friends and hobbies that involved people.

"Thank you," I murmur and pull the plate closer. I wiggle on my stool, trying to find a more comfortable position, then wince as pain shoots up the back of my legs.

A low growl erupts from Slade, and he yanks my food away.

As he stomps toward the front room, I mourn the loss of a perfectly good meal. Bastard probably did it on purpose—shows me what I could have if I accepted his presence, then cruelly snatches it away.

"Rule one, asshole."

# Chapter 15

Slade

"**G**et in here, Scarlett," I call from the living room, then lean so I can see her. "Or do you need me to carry you?"

She scowls as I smirk. When she slides from the stool, she turns her head and wipes her face on her sleeve. By the time she's hit the archway, she's fixed her face into some semblance of normalcy. Except I notice the redness around her eyes and the slight flush on her cheeks. I doubt she'd answer me if I asked why she's crying.

"There's no place to sit in here," she says, reaching for her plate as she completely ignores the small dining table. I doubt her back will handle the wood chair, though.

"Despite the plethora of seats in here, we're not actually eating in the living room. Open up, will ya?" I maneuver her plate away and gesture toward the front door.

She mutters something about no seating outside either, but at least she listens. She steps back and sweeps her hand out.

I slip by her and lean down as I pass, whispering, "Attitude, beautiful."

I grin at the noise she makes. The porch isn't super big, but it's enough for a small table and two wrought-iron chairs. They'd be uncomfortable if it wasn't for the thick pads on the seat and back. I have no idea what they're called. My mom would know. She's got dozens of outdoor chairs with these types of cushions on them.

I need to call her, but I've been putting it off. I don't have much to tell her since she brushed off our concerns. When I finally got Dad on the phone, he acted like I was making shit up about him pulling away from everyone. He muttered an excuse about inventory to get me off the phone. When I tried to call back, I didn't have a signal, so I gave up.

"Sit." I point at her seat.

"Isn't it too dark?" Still, she drops into the chair as if her legs can't hold her weight anymore.

I reach inside and flip on the porch light, then settle across from her. The soft glow has her hair shimmering. I resist the urge to tuck the strands that escaped her ponytail behind her ear. She's busy cutting up her food, and I hold my breath when she takes a bite. Her eyes flutter closed and she exhales heavily. If she let herself, I bet she'd be moaning right now.

I can't help myself. "Good?"

Her eyes fly open and she nods. We eat, letting the sounds of the night fill the silence. It's been a while since I've been surrounded by the singing of crickets. Most of the time I hear frogs talking to each other through my wolf's ears. I haven't done a ton of research, but I've figured out I can hear a lot more when I'm in wolf form—something about the frequency. I always meant to ask Alissa but never got around to it.

"What's it like?" she asks softly, her voice barely reaching me.

"Going to have to be more specific." I lean back in the chair and fold my hands on my stomach.

She presses her lips together. "Growing up with so many siblings. It was just Holden and me."

"You ever have a best friend? Not like a regular best friend, like a *best* best friend. One who you got pissed at or would call you out on shit?"

Grooves appear between her eyes. "Not really. I had friends, obviously, but there was always this wall between us. I couldn't exactly tell them what I was, and we moved around quite a bit when I was younger. At least until I got my manipulations under control."

"We'll have to talk about *that* later," I mutter, and she gives me a confused look. "Anyways, it's mostly loud."

"But having all those kids around, you must have always had someone to talk to."

"I'm sure they did. With six siblings running around, someone always had a problem, and someone else would be willing to listen. Most of the time, anyway."

Her nose wrinkles. "That makes it seem like you didn't have that."

I chew on the inside of my cheek, wondering how open I should be. "I was the class clown. Popular, yet part of every group. Didn't make for very meaningful relationships. Everything was pretty surface level."

She raises a single eyebrow. "Except I didn't ask about school."

I clear my throat and glance away from her prying eyes. "Suppose you didn't."

"If you don't want to talk about it, that's fine. I didn't mean to—"

"My siblings didn't take me seriously, but I was the one they called when they needed help. When Gemma needed a ride to college, against our parent's wishes, I was the one to drive her. When Eli got caught stealing at a store in town when he was nine, he called me. When Alissa wanted to run away to the woods, she asked me to help." I wave my hand around. "There's more shit, but you get the gist of it. I'm the reliable one while also being hilarious and devastatingly handsome."

I smirk and run my hand through my hair. She doesn't laugh, even with the ridiculous look I'm giving her. I let out a ruthless chuckle. When I mutter about it being a joke, she sighs.

"You still didn't answer my question."

"Yes, I did. You asked if my siblings and I were close. We all have different roles. Mine's just a little different."

"No, I asked if having siblings meant…" She huffs, then closes her eyes. "This wasn't supposed to be a therapy session. I just didn't know what it was like. I'm sorry. I shouldn't have asked."

She pushes to her feet and gathers our plates before I realize what just happened. I grab her wrist, and she freezes. She doesn't want to give up the dishes, but I take them anyway and set them down. She doesn't resist when I guide her back to her seat.

"First of all, I don't mind you asking questions. I *like* it. Second, stop apologizing for being curious. In fact, stop apologizing to me period. I'm not the type of person to be easily offended. Also, I've never been to therapy, whole shifter thing kind of makes it hard. If I *did* go to therapy, though, I wouldn't go to you."

She yanks her wrist away. "That was unnecessarily rude. You're breaking rule num—"

"Yeah, rule number one: don't be an asshole. However, I can't be close to my therapist. Not like we are."

She scoffs. "We're not close."

"Closer than I'd be with a therapist. Now, ask your question again." I track the indecision building in her eyes. We've had a rollercoaster of a time together, yet I feel like we're standing on a precipice. If she doesn't jump, I'll be left dangling off this cliff.

"If you're always doing all these things for others, who does things for you?"

"I do. It's not as bad as it seems." I don't have more explanations than that.

I rely on myself to get me through things. It's not like I'm hiding some deep-seated trauma. I don't feel the need to go off-grid like Alissa. Or find myself on the ocean like Alister. I'm not searching for my fated mate, despite Kira and Gemma finding theirs. I'm not about to drop off the face of the planet like Sloane.

She nods, staring out at the forest. Cicadas fill the silence between us. We don't have them in Moon Cove, though I wish we did. They may be loud, but they're peaceful, in their own way.

She rises again, her movements fluid. "I'll take these in and clean up. Oh, and I'll get your car parts tomorrow."

"Dismissing me?"

She winces, then tries to cover it with a slight smile. "I need a shower."

"Leave the dishes. I'll do them."

She opens her mouth as if she'll protest, then exhales heavily. She murmurs a thanks as she makes her way inside. I stare at the ever-darkening night to give her time to settle in her room.

I don't know where we go from here. Sure, she asked questions, but she didn't open up. It's like she's leaving tidbits of her life for me to gather together. I doubt she even knows she's doing it. With each crumb, I'm sucked further into her orbit. I wonder if it's part of being a lorelei. I make another mental note to call Alissa. Scarlett certainly isn't going to tell me much about them. Her experience doesn't seem very typical of the way lorelei are raised.

Usually, there's at least one parent who is that type of shifter. Unless they're goddess-made like Chase, the ability is passed down from parent to child. Sure, every once in a while there's a fluke, but the goddess doesn't make mistakes. At least, that's what we're taught. My father always had a different opinion. I haven't quite figured out what I believe, and I doubt it matters much. Whether or not I believe the goddess is infallible doesn't affect my life much.

After a good twenty minutes, I push to my feet and make my way to the kitchen. It's quiet inside, only the ticking of a grandfather clock piercing the silence. Scarlett must be done with her shower since the bathroom door sits open.

Once I finish loading the dishwasher and cleaning up my mess, I make my way to my shed. I can't think of it any other way. It's not comfortable, but at least no one can hide inside. An ambush wouldn't be likely regardless, but for some reason it makes me feel better.

I'm halfway across the lawn when my feet stutter to a stop. I stare at the ground, the crescent moon barely lighting the path. A whistle echoes above the crickets, which quickly fall silent. Rule number nine rolls through my mind.

*If you hear someone whistling after dark, no you didn't.*

I didn't question her silly rules before. Most of them made sense and by the time she got to the last one, I wasn't really paying attention. I'd blame her for distracting me, except I know it was my horniness. I can't remember if she said anything after that. Were there instructions beyond "no you didn't" or did she leave me nothing? Maybe she assumed I knew what the hell it meant.

Another whistle, farther away, has me exhaling heavily. My muscles remain tense, my hackles raised. I pivot without really thinking and hurry back to the main house. As soon as I'm inside, I slam the door shut and lean against it. My heart hammers in my chest, and my breath comes in short gasps. Desperately, I try to infuse some logic into my thoughts. I slide down until my ass hits the worn floorboards. I prop my elbows on my knees and grip my hair tightly, trying to center myself.

"Slade? What's wrong?" Scarlett drops in front of me, and her soft hands wrap around my wrists. Her touch grounds me and my head snaps up.

"I—" Staring at her, I realize how ridiculous the whole thing is. What am I supposed to tell her, that I heard a noise in the woods and it freaked me out? So much for sticking around to make her feel safer.

"Was it a bobcat? Bear? Another shifter?"

I shake my head and tangle our fingers together. "Don't laugh."

She narrows her gaze. "I won't."

"Uh, you remember rule nine?"

She tugs away from my grip. "Seriously? What did you do?"

I struggle to my feet, my stomach rolling. "Doesn't matter."

She crawls to the window and peeks out. "Oh, no. It definitely does. Did you lead them here?"

As soon as I start feeling better, she dashes all my hopes.

"Who's them? And why would they follow me?"

She huffs, still searching the darkness for *them*. "The rules are important, Slade. No one knows who they are. Evil spirits, pretty much. Different cultures, different legends. They'd follow you because you didn't follow the damn rules."

Now that the adrenaline has worn off, I'm painfully aware of what she's wearing. My mouth waters as I take in her light pink pajama shorts riding up her thighs and her white tank top molding to her body. It's not even the fact that she's lurking. With her crawling around, she's putting images in my head of things I can't act on.

"Would you get away from the window?" I growl, and she makes a noise in the back of her throat.

I stomp over to her and grab her waist. She squeals as I lift her up but doesn't fight me as I carry her into the hallway. I probably shouldn't break rule number nine and three all in a matter of minutes. Still, I step into her room and set her down.

I expect her to push away from me, maybe shove me out. Instead, she leans into me. My hand twitches at my side, and I fight the urge to hold her. Her head turns and she inhales, her back pressing into my chest.

"Did you just smell me?" I ask with a chuckle.

She finally shoves away. "No. Of course not." She spins around. "So, what did you do after the whistle?"

My cheeks heat and I run a hand through my hair. "Froze. Remembered the rule. Came back to the house."

"Did you hear it more than once?"

"Why exactly does it matter?"

Annoyance flashes across her face. "Listen, I get you're probably embarrassed, but this whole back and forth is irritating. Just answer the damn question, Slade."

"Fine," I snap, crossing my arms. "I heard it and got real freaked out. My body wouldn't move. Then it happened again and I hurried back into the house. Then you found me."

"Closer or farther away?" She shakes her head. "The second time, was it closer or farther?"

"Uh, farther. Why?"

She doesn't answer me, just stomps by. I lean against the doorframe and watch her. She rips open the closet and pulls out a sheet. I don't know what she's doing. Maybe she's going to throw it over her head and pretend to be a ghost. The image of her roaming around outside while trying to scare off an entity she can't name has a grin spreading across my face. I sober when she snatches a blanket as well.

I clear my throat. "I don't need to stay in here, Scarlett. Unless you need me to keep a lookout."

"You don't get it. You can't stay in the shed, so you'll have to stay in here. At least for tonight. Stay away from the windows. Don't answer the door. And for goddess sake, don't go out there. No matter what." She hefts everything in her arms and reaches high above her head. I straighten as her tank top rides up, exposing a strip of skin.

The next thing I know, I'm behind her and wrapping my arm around her waist. I shuffle her to the side and grab the pillow on the top shelf.

"You realize I can't sleep on your couch, right?" I gather everything in my arms.

"What? Why not?" She walks into the living room and stares

at the glorified loveseat. "It's perfectly comfortable. I've slept on it plenty of times."

I dump the supplies on the floor and flop onto the couch. My body barely fits on the cushions, and my feet hang off at least a foot. I smile tightly up at her as she scowls.

She rolls her eyes. "Fine. You can sleep on the floor in my room. But if you hear more whistles, you'd better not go out the window. And remember rule number ten."

She gathers the blankets and marches to her room. I scramble off the couch and follow her. She's busy fluffing out blankets and arranging the pillow when I walk in.

"There were only nine rules," I say as I lean against the door frame.

"I can add more at any time. You should have read the fine print."

"And what exactly is rule number ten, then?" I ask with a grin.

She finally meets my gaze with a serious expression. "Don't climb into my bed in the middle of the night. No matter what."

# Chapter 16
## Scarlett

In a rare move, Slade doesn't question my addition to the rules. Half of them have been thrown out the window, anyway. He hasn't mentioned anything weird that happened. Still, I hid away in my kitchen the day after, and the day after that.

I finally have all the strawberries for the cakes, and I've been making them all day. Slade hasn't come out of the back room. Or maybe he's working on the bathroom. I was too chickenshit to go check. We've barely spoken, and for some reason I feel like I did something wrong.

I shouldn't have pried into his personal life. He clearly uses humor as a shield, and I attempted to blast right through it. I tried to apologize, yet I couldn't get the words out. It was as if something deep inside was stopping me from uttering a single syllable.

Forces beyond us are rife in the air and I don't like it. If the goddess is fucking with me, I'm not going to be happy about it.

Which means my shorts are dusted with flour and strands of hair float around my face, fallen from the bun affixed atop my head. I blow a piece away, only for it to flop back in front of my eye. I should have grabbed some bobby pins to keep it in place. Too late now.

"Scarlett, we need to talk," Slade says by way of greeting.

"About what?" I keep my gaze on the stand mixer as I wait for the ingredients to combine.

"The swimming rule. Are there too many rapids or alligators?"

I snort, fighting a grin. "There aren't any alligators this far north. Figured you'd know that. The river floods quickly. Add in the random rapids and you're in for a surprise. Plus, there's the legends."

"What legends?"

"Do I detect a bit of panic, Mr. Shifter? It's a silly one. Something about wraiths or mermaids. I didn't get the full story. I stay out because of the current. I didn't know if you were a strong swimmer, and I wasn't about to save your ass. And I didn't feel like explaining it at that point. You were an interloper." That's not the only reason I'm careful around water, but I don't want to freak him out more.

"And now?"

I pull in a deep breath. "Now, you're just...you, I suppose. Are you coming with to drop these cakes off?"

"Do you want me to?"

"That's not what I asked. Don't answer a question with a question," I snap.

"Calm down, beautiful," he says with a chuckle, and my blood instantly boils.

I spin around and jab my finger at him. "Don't fucking do that. Don't tell me to calm down when I'm not even angry. Even if I was angry, you have no right to demand I calm down as if I'm some emotional creature who needs you to regulate me."

He holds up his hands, eyes wide, and I know exactly where this will go. Holden does the same thing. He'll backtrack, tell me it wasn't that big of a deal, and I shouldn't fly off the handle over something so insignificant. I don't know if it's gaslighting or just ingrained in males, but it's annoying as fuck. None of it even really matters. I just wanted to know if he was coming with me, and now I don't even care.

"Sorry."

I blink at him, waiting for more. He just stares at me, then runs his hand through his hair. Emotions flash across his face too quickly for me to decipher.

"Did you need something?"

"It's hotter than balls back there, and I wanted to cool off. It's fine," he says gruffly, and I turn off my mixer. "I wasn't trying to control your emotions."

I wave away his explanation. "Doesn't matter. Sorry I snapped at you. I'm just tired from baking. I shouldn't have taken it out on you."

I'm not tired, but I don't want to get into a full-blown conversation about it. Especially since if he pushes, I'll end up revealing things he doesn't need to bother with. Going to the Tates' party to drop these off isn't going to be fun. It's always awkward, and people stare at me like they're waiting for me to ask to stay. I won't.

"Don't diminish yourself because I fucked up, Scarlett."

My head snaps up at his harsh tone. He's glaring, not at me, but at the finished cakes cooling on the island. I don't know what they did to him. They look perfect with a golden crust on top and a few strawberries poking through. Once the whipped cream is added, they'll be delicious.

"It's not that big of a deal," I mutter.

"No, you asked me a question, and I reacted defensively. Or insecurely. I don't want to intrude and make you feel like you have to take me with. I do want to go if only so you don't have to deal with the assholes in town."

My mouth parts as our eyes meet. "Who the hell are you? No, really."

He gives me a lopsided grin. "I'm Slade. I believe we've met."

"Very funny. I mean, I've never heard someone just…say shit

out loud like that. I mean, we all think it, but most people don't just blurt it out."

He sighs, shaking his head. "I hate to tell you this, Scarlett, but most people don't think like that. They don't worry what others are doing unless it impacts them. They also don't apologize for calling out bad behavior."

"Actually, I think that's more of a woman thing," I mutter.

"Yeah, in my family, we take up space. We set boundaries and call people out when they cross them. And then we apologize for our actions."

"Well, goody for you and your perfect little family."

I dump the ingredients for whipped cream into another mixer. It's always amazing to me how it goes from liquid goo to fluffy goodness. I keep my gaze on it instead of Slade, who's wandered closer. His frown doesn't help. He's about to call me out for bashing his family, as he should. Except I can't seem to keep my emotions in check. Or my words, clearly.

"Did you eat lunch?" he asks.

"What?"

"When was the last time you ate?" He opens the fridge and starts rifling around. He pulls out a tub of pasta salad and hands it to me, then grabs a fork before guiding me to the stool. "I'll watch the stuff and you eat."

"I'm not hungry." Even so, I open the container.

"Might not fix everything, but it'll help. What exactly am I supposed to do with this?"

"Nothing. Just wait. Making whipped cream is really easy." I shove another bite into my mouth, and my muscles relax. I hate that he was right. It's not that I didn't eat, but it's been a while.

He leans against the counter, facing me. "You nervous about tonight?"

I choke on a noodle and he curses, scrambling to get a glass of water. I end up gulping it down when he hands it over. I don't know if I was being obvious about not wanting to go or if he's just perceptive.

"Why would I be nervous? I've done this a dozen times."

He presses his lips together into a thin line, and his nostrils flare. I brace myself, but he just glances at the mixer. I have no idea why he's upset. The party isn't a big deal. Do I like going? No. Do I get paid on time? Sometimes. Do I enjoy making cakes? Yes. The second two answers outweigh the first. At least in my mind.

"You know what I don't like? I don't like when you answer me while purposefully being obtuse."

"I wasn't being obtuse. I'm not nervous."

"And I wasn't talking about the whipped cream," he snaps, glaring at me.

"I wasn't either," I cry, throwing my hands up. The noodle on the end of my fork goes flying straight for his head. I wince, anticipating the impact. Instead, he snatches it out of the air, then pops it in his mouth.

"Good salad." His smirk seems forced and his shoulders droop. "You're really not nervous about going tonight?"

I blink at him, trying to figure out how to word things for him to understand. "I'm...it's just...Slade, I'm not *going* to the party. I drop off these cakes and then leave."

His finger taps against the counter. He nods, though I doubt he actually agrees. If he comes with me, he'll see why I don't hang around. Mostly it's because I'm not welcome or invited, yet it's more than that. There's a vibe that shifts when I walk in. If I tell him all those things, though, then suddenly people will be overly nice and beg me to stay. I'll end up seeming like a liar.

"How many times have you done this?"

I shrug, picking at the noodles. "Five years, give or take. It's not a big deal. I don't want to hang out with them. Or anyone."

"They've never asked you to stay?"

"Just leave it, Slade. You'll probably have a different reception so if you want to stay, you're more than welcome to. I'm sure someone will bring you ho—back. I can come get you, too. There's usually a lot of food and a band and I think fireworks, but sometimes they're not able to. I've heard it's actually a good time."

His jaw tics and I swear his eyes flash yellow, but by the time he blinks, it's gone. He doesn't look happy, though. Maybe I should have mentioned I wouldn't be mad if he stayed. I make a note to tell him when we get there. Once he's welcomed with open arms and sees what they have to offer, he'll understand. I'm not about to stop him from making friends. It's clearly important to him.

Which is probably why we'd never work long term. Short term might not be so bad. I swallow a chuckle at how ridiculous the thought is. *Not so bad* isn't exactly a glowing review. It's also a lie. If there'd be no repercussions, I'd jump him. It'd probably be hot and heavy and life-altering, an experience I'd never forget. I'd be an old woman on my deathbed, reliving the nights I spent with him.

"What else do I need to do for this?" he finally says, gesturing to the mixer.

"Nothing. I've got it."

I push to my feet and turn off the machine. He doesn't move, which makes things awkward. Trying to avoid brushing against him isn't easy when he's six inches from me. I'm methodical as I go through the motions of putting the whipped cream into containers and carefully labeling it. No one will notice, but I do it anyway.

The rest of the cakes are done, ready and waiting to be packed up. Without my even asking, Slade grabs a large box and puts them in. Once he's done, I stack my containers on top. He hip checks me when I attempt to lift the box.

If I let myself, I could see this as my future. Slade keeping me company in the kitchen, then helping me drop off my orders.

We'd come back here and make food, eat dinner, and sit on the porch. We'd listen to the night come to life while chatting about things that don't seem to matter, but they do to us. Then we'd eventually end up falling into bed, only to wake up the next day and do it all over again.

And it would all fall apart. I'd get sick, unable to get out of bed, and he'd take care of me. Then it would happen again. And again. And again. Eventually, he'd get resentful. Doubts would creep in. He'd wonder if I used my powers and he was ensorcelled and bewitched. Then he'd leave in the middle of the night, leaving me to worry where he was. No note. No text. No future.

I grit my teeth and stomp toward my bedroom. I close the door before he can follow me. Not that he would. There's something beneath the surface, though. Maybe his wolf side makes him act differently. I've caught a glimpse of it after he met Naomi, each time he's upset, or when he thought I needed to go to the hospital. A shiver rolls through me at the thought of him going full wolf on me.

"Nope. Not going there," I mutter as I pull on a sundress. I might not be staying, but I'm not about to show up to a town party in raggedy leggings and a stained shirt. Probably didn't need to wear an apron, but whatever. Old habits die slow, or whatever they say.

When I emerge from my bedroom, Slade's nowhere to be found. Apparently he didn't want to go with. I don't blame him. I wouldn't want to go either if I had a choice. Naomi offered to pick everything up and bring it to the party, but I wasn't going to make her do that. She lives out in the country on the other side of town.

I grab a box from the counter and heft it onto my hip. A sharp pain ricochets down my leg, and I suck in a quick breath. It recedes enough for me to shuffle my way to the front door that's hanging open. I spin around and use my elbow to hit the screen door latch.

"Shit," I squeak when I almost run into Slade.

"Caught you," he grumbles, snatching the box from me. "Go get the truck, Scarlett."

The rest of the cakes are stacked neatly on the porch. I wrinkle my nose, then decide against arguing and head for the trees. I didn't want Slade to know about my other vehicle, but I'm not putting the desserts into the bed of my truck. The dust alone would make them inedible. I pull out of the woods, keeping my gaze on the porch. He'll probably think I charmed the salesperson to get this car. It's too fancy for a town like this.

I climb out and finally look at Slade. He's focused on the car, though.

"Beautiful, don't take this the wrong way, but you're a puzzle I desperately want to put together."

I wasn't about to push my luck and ask Scarlett if I could drive, but I really wanted to. I've ridden in a few classic cars over the years. This one takes the cake.

"So, what year is this?" I ask, trying to sound casual.

"Sixty-nine," she mutters. I can barely hear her over the engine.

"I'm not a huge car person, but this is a classic, right?"

She sighs heavily as she inches along the gravel. "Yes, it's a classic. No, I didn't con anyone out of it. Yes, I own it. No, you can't drive it."

"Didn't think you conned anyone and wasn't asking if I could drive it."

She clears her throat and shifts gears as we hit the pavement. "It was my father's. My mother tried to give it to Holden, who told her to give it to me instead since he doesn't know the first thing about cars. He wasn't interested in learning. I was."

"So, your parents gave it to you? That was nice."

"No, they didn't. She still signed it over to Holden after our father said he was worried I'd sell it. I don't know why he'd think that since I helped rebuild this thing. I suppose he didn't know about that, though. My parents were pretty hands-off when it came to me. They didn't know how to handle my issues.

The mechanic in town was our neighbor and didn't care if I came around. Anyways, Holden signed it over to me, and we just didn't tell our parents."

She grips the steering wheel, and her knuckles turn white. I've spent enough time around her to know she's riding the edge of anxiety. If I keep pushing, she'll crash out, then feel guilty about it.

I hang my hand out the window and let the air cool my skin. I'm careful not to rest my fingernails on the black paint. She'd somehow know and I'd get an earful.

"How many people are going to be there tonight?"

"With the kids? Probably a hundred. Maybe more. I don't know. It's hard for me to estimate like that. Give me flour and I can figure out the grams by sight. People? Nope." She pops the P, and I breathe a sigh of relief. Maybe she'll relax more by the time we get there.

"What about distances?" I ask, a note of concern in my voice.

"Not great. Why?"

I tense as I stare at the stop sign we're rapidly approaching. "Because you're not slowing down."

My foot slams onto the invisible brake as her laugh bounces around me. She doesn't screech to a stop, but it's close enough. I didn't peg her as a speed demon. It only makes me want to delve deeper into who she is. I'm still not entirely sure what that means. We don't really have a future. The urge to find out everything about her eats away at me, though.

"You're a little controlling, aren't you?" She eases through the town, only the rumble of the engine echoing off the buildings.

"Not really," I murmur, glancing around. "Where is everyone? This place is a ghost town."

"At the party. Told you everyone goes to the Tates' party." She's back to gripping the steering wheel, and I keep my mouth shut.

The rest of the miles pass in silence. I hear the thud of the music before we take the curve, revealing a wooden fence bracketing a long driveway. She pulls onto the gravel and inches her way down the long lane. Trees block wherever this ends.

When the scene opens up, a large house with a wrap-around porch and flower boxes lining almost all the windows appears. It's idyllic in an elitist way, like something straight out of a magazine.

Scarlett doesn't stop in front, instead swinging to the right and taking another road toward the back. The car bumps along, and I wince at each one. She doesn't seem concerned, which freaks me out even more, though it should do the opposite.

"What the fuck is that?" I ask, gazing up at the large building in front of us.

"Technically it's a pole barn, but they don't use it for anything other than parties. They don't have crops or animals or anything. Just a shit ton of money and time. They like being the most powerful people in the room."

She delivers her statements with no emotion, no inflection. Just cold, hard facts. A mask has slipped over her features, cutting off the world from her inner thoughts. I hate it.

People spill out of the large open overhead doors, laughing and drinking. Instead of parking next to the other cars lined up in a temporary parking lot to the right, Scarlett heads behind the structure. A few box trucks with logos stamped on the sides are what finally gets through to me. This isn't a neighborhood barbecue or a small-town celebration. It's nothing like my parent's parties for the shifters in Moon Cove. Gunner catered this shit.

"I thought you were kidding when you said they might have fireworks," I mutter.

She shrugs, then hurries out of the car. "You don't have to help. You can stay here or you can go around to the front. Either way, doesn't matter to me."

Methodically, she grabs the boxes, attempting to stack them on top of one another. By the time I make it around the trunk, she's struggling to lift them all.

"Get out of the way." I hip check her and grab the boxes as she scowls as she. "Lead the way, beautiful."

"Don't call me that," she snaps, then whispers, "not here."

I nod sharply and follow her through the back door. No one notices our presence. Then again, we're in a kitchen—a full-ass commercial kitchen. I whistle, my gaze skipping around, and Scarlett shushes me. Workers rush back and forth preparing trays of food. Scarlett leads me through the throng, artfully dodging them. It's as if they instinctually move out of her way, but she's making a show of stepping to the side.

She must be using a bit of her power, though I have no idea how it works for lorelei. The only thing I can compare it to is when shifters are able to partially shift. I don't have that ability. Sensing other shifters is enough, according to the goddess.

I've never met anyone who has more than one extra ability, and over the years, even those have diminished. Dad said it had to do with shifters being with humans. I don't know how much I believe that, but I'm not knowledgeable enough to dispute him. Next time I visit Moon Cove, I'm going to have to ask him more about it.

Scarlett breezes out the double swinging doors, then holds one open for me. Getting through isn't easy with the boxes, but I refuse to make Scarlett help. She's already in pain with all the work she did today. There's a tightness around her eyes and stiffness to her movements. No one else would probably notice.

She gestures me toward a table off to the side. Music makes it impossible for us to talk. Add in the many voices of partygoers and I can barely think. I resign myself to merely handing her cakes and letting her arrange them. Her mask is firmly in place while she works, yet her eyes dart around as if searching for a threat.

I don't know why she wouldn't want to join in. Sure, no one greeted us, but we did sneak in through the back. I don't want to question her experiences. Except things aren't adding up. Bernice saunters up while Scarlett's back is turned, and I try to position myself between them.

"Well, isn't this cute," Bernice says as she gazes at the cakes. "Did you make them differently? They don't look the same as usual."

"They're exactly the same, Bernice. The same as the ones you buy to serve at the cafe. The same ones you ask Naomi to order more of so you can bring some home. The same as I brought last year." She states all of it while she continues to dish the whipped cream into a bowl sitting in ice.

"I don't know what you're talking about," Bernice hisses, then glances around. "Just hurry up and get out of here before Gunner comes around."

"Well, he has to pay me still, so I think I'll stick around until then. As I always do." She gives Bernice a deadpan stare until the woman pivots and disappears into the crowd.

I sidle closer to her and mutter out of the corner of my mouth, "Now I get why you don't like her."

Scarlett turns her head slowly and studies my face. I smirk, my fingers brushing hers. She jerks away and I sigh, shaking my head.

"Slade, you don't want to be associated with me. I promise you'll thank me later." She rubs her palms on her dress. "I'm going to find Gunner. Go get some food or something. I think they're about to start circulating."

I glance behind me at the kitchen doors. She's right, a barrage of waiters in jeans and flannel shirts are streaming out with trays in their hands.

"This party is weird," I mumble, but when I turn around, she's gone.

I didn't want to let her out of my sight, and if she thinks I'm staying without her...

My head throbs along with the beat of the music as I get closer to the speakers. Several heads swivel around as I pass. I smile and give a couple nods, but I don't stop. Not that they seem like they want me to. I make my way toward the large doors, searching for Scarlett. She couldn't have gone far.

A hand grabs my arm, and my first instinct is to rip it away. I whip around as the nails dig into my skin. Naomi, concern stamped on her face, tugs me toward the side of the room. She finds a pocket of space in the corner and shoves me into it.

"Where is she?" Naomi hisses.

"Uh, I don't know. I was trying to find her. She went to look for Gunner so he could pay her." I strain to search over her head, and she smacks me. "What?"

"You have to get her out of here. They're planning something. I don't know what, but it wasn't good. Gunner kept joking around, saying it would be the night's entertainment." She wrings her hands and bounces from one foot to the other.

It takes me a beat to realize what she's saying. Flashbacks to my childhood have me pushing past her and rushing through the crowd. I'm kicking myself for not grabbing my phone. Right now, I can't even remember if I have her number or not. I haven't needed it since we've been together every day. She hasn't left her property without me.

Naomi calls after me as I shove past people. I don't stop. If Gunner has something planned, it can't be good. I might have failed my sister, but I can't let it happen again.

I spot her blonde hair standing outside, talking to someone I'm assuming is Gunner Tates. He has a shit-eating grin on his very punchable face. A group passes in front of me and blocks my view. When I finally make my way around them, Gunner has his hand wrapped around Scarlett's upper arm and he's leading her away.

My wolf rears up, a force in my chest making it hard to breathe. I shove him down. The last thing I need is to shift right now in this crowd. This isn't Moon Cove or any of the other shifter communities I've been to. I'd incite a stampede, blow Scarlett's cover, and scare innocent people.

My wolf didn't seem to care much about her being around before. He's always more concerned with protecting me. Why he cares now, I don't know. Maybe it's my own distress infecting him.

Once I'm close enough, I grab Scarlett's hand and tug her to a stop. The relief on her face when she glances at me over her shoulder is enough for me to know I did the right thing. Gunner hasn't seemed to notice my presence as he keeps trying to pull her away. I drop her hand and wrap my arm around her waist. It's probably a mistake to have her so close—to claim her so publicly. We'll just have to deal with the fallout later.

"Sorry, but I'm going to have to steal her away. We have an issue with the ice." It's a weak excuse. It's the best I can come up with on the spot.

"I'm sure there's someone else who can deal with it," Gunner says with a smile that doesn't reach his blue eyes. "Who are you, anyways? I don't think you were invited."

"I'm Scarlett's assistant. We'll be out of your hair soon so you can enjoy your…party." I spin us around, then guide her back into the throng. Heads swivel toward us, their gazes following us as we head for the back of the barn. It's probably not everyone, but it feels like it.

Scarlett's nostrils flare, the only indication of how she's feeling. Whether she's pissed at me or the people around us, I'll just have to wait and see. Her hands tremble as she reaches for the empty boxes, and I move her out of the way.

"Stop it," she hisses.

Ignoring her, I grab everything, then bump her toward the kitchen. I don't stop until we're out the back door. I toss the boxes into the back and open the driver's door. She won't let me drive so I don't even ask, no matter how much I want to. The faster we get away from here, the better.

As she pulls around the building, I catch Gunner tracking us from the edge of the crowd. He narrows his eyes, pure venom etched in the lines of his face. I watch him in the side mirror until there's a turn in the road and blocks my view.

"What in the hell was that?" Scarlett spits out. Her knuckles are back to being white.

"Ran into Naomi. She said they were planning something. I had to get you out of there. I wasn't about to let it happen again."

*I can't let it happen again.*

# Chapter 18

## Scarlett

Slade refuses to say anything else about what happened. I didn't want to go with Gunner, anyway. I just wanted to get paid, and now I probably won't. The money would have been nice to buy more supplies.

My savings aren't doing well and won't be until I get the next dividend check from the few investments I have left. I glance at Slade from the corner of my eye and press my lips together. He hasn't asked me how I'm funding this whole thing. Yet.

*I* would be questioning how someone could live off selling some bakery items in a small-ass town like Hart's Hallow. It's fishy on the surface even with my house not being in the best of shape. Add in the land around my place and it's definitely suspicious. I could probably be on one of those shows of people buying tiny houses.

I pull in front of the house and grip the steering wheel. "Do not get out of this car."

His hand drops from the handle, and he exhales heavily. "I'll make sure you get paid."

"That's the least of my fucking worries. By the goddess..." I tip my head back. "Start explaining. Now."

"Naomi came up to me and said they were planning something."

"Yeah, but what were they planning?"

He shrugs, glancing out the side window. "Didn't wait to find out."

"Because of what happened before."

His jaw tightens and he gives a sharp nod. "Yup."

I wait for him to continue, but he doesn't. I swear he's more frustrating than usual. While I don't want to pry into his personal business, I need some explanations. I doubt Gunner would have done anything extreme. Not in front of all those people. Slade probably misunderstood Naomi or whatever Gunner was going to do wouldn't have been that bad. Maybe they finally would have accepted me. Not that I want that, but it would make life easier.

"*What* happened before, Slade?" I ask through gritted teeth.

He huffs and digs his nails into his jean-covered thighs. "My sister was set up in high school, shortly after her first shift. Our other sister wanted a boy…it was a whole thing. A bunch of kids from her school threw things at her. See, Moon Cove is a shifter community and on the circuit for supernatural shows. We lean into it. She was supposed to shift and was late. Fuck, I'm not explaining this well. Just suffice it to say, it wasn't a good situation and I didn't help."

"Did you know it was happening?" I may not know Slade well, but he doesn't seem the type to be a shithead to his sister. Or anyone, for that matter.

"Not until it was too late. Still, I should have known. Alissa had been acting weird for a while. I should have—"

"Read her mind? Confronted a teenage girl? Do you honestly think she would have told you what she was going to do?"

"No, but—"

"But nothing. Does your other sister blame you? The one who got pranked?"

He shakes his head. "You don't understand."

"Maybe not your family dynamics, but I do understand teenage girls. I was one at some point in my life. And I may not have grown up in a shifter community, but I have spent time around shifters. When they want to hide things, it's pretty frickin' easy for them." I sigh, wondering how my life got here—comforting a man in front of my house after I've sworn off people. "Listen, I don't know what they were going to do tonight. It could have been harmless or not. Unless Naomi figures it out, we'll probably never know. I *do* know I have to live with the consequences of *your* actions."

"I understand that," he mutters. "I just didn't know what else to do. I'll make sure to get your money."

"It's not about the money, Slade." I shove out of the car and slam the door shut before he can respond.

It's a little about the money. Most of mine is tied up in the cars and my house. I bought it outright after selling off lots of different things. I refuse to get rid of my vehicles, but I might have to think about it if something else breaks. Admitting that would be embarrassing at this point.

Besides, it's more about him not thinking things through. I have to live in this town after he leaves. I swear he broke one of the rules, though I don't know which one. Maybe the one about not being an asshole. Then again, he was trying to save me and that's not really an asshole move.

"You can't just walk away every time the conversation doesn't go your way, Scarlett," he calls after me.

"Watch me."

The screen door slams behind me, rattling on its hinges. I should fix the thing, but I don't know how to do it. Tightening a few screws shouldn't be hard. Except I have no idea where my screwdriver is. Or which one I need. I pivot, intent on checking when Slade crashes into the room. I scowl, crossing my arms.

"Don't break my house," I snap.

"I'll fix the damn door like I'm fixing everything else," he snarls, and a pang hits me in the chest. "Now, if it's not about the money, then what is it? Because I embarrassed you? Around a bunch of people you don't give a shit about?"

*Fixing everything else.* As if he didn't insist on staying. As if he didn't pretend like this was what he wanted to do. As if I wasn't a burden.

"You have no right to lecture me. You also don't have the right to judge my life or my relationships. Everything you know I've told you, so you actually have no clue how they feel about me. Or what they were planning."

I don't want to have this conversation. Not now or later. Especially since he doesn't want to be here. Holden forced him by calling in a favor—a life debt he couldn't refuse. I wouldn't expect him to choose the consequences. A whole year shifted probably isn't fun or healthy. Except he's fulfilled his promise. I even made it a damn rule, and I broke it as soon as Holden dropped off the face of the planet.

All the fight leaves me, and I drop my hands to my sides. "I'm going to clean the kitchen, then take a shower. Do whatever you want, but don't touch my car."

He doesn't follow as I stomp off, which is a good thing for him. If we kept talking, I'd either end up punching him or crying. Neither would be a good look for me. I want to tell him to go home. The longer he's here, the more of a mess my life becomes. The screen door rattles once more, and I blink away tears.

Why did I think he'd come after me? Why do I care? The ache in my chest won't go away, no matter how much I rub it. Standing in the kitchen, I realize I don't want to clean up. Not that there's much to do. I clean as I go when I'm baking. If I stack all the work at the beginning, I don't run out of steam afterward.

I wander into my bedroom and pull off my clothes. A hot

shower won't magically fix everything, but it'll help. I'm halfway through washing my hair when my arms get heavy. It takes me twice as long as usual to finish, and the water's gone cold by the time I step out. I need to eat. The thought of actually cooking might send me into a tailspin, though. Or I might pass out.

I peek out the door and search the area for signs of life. Nothing moves other than the hand on the grandfather clock in the living room. It ticks away merrily, unbothered by the tension still permeating the space. The ache in my chest grows, and I struggle to pull in a full breath. I stumble into the kitchen and catch myself on the island.

A steaming cup of tea sits on the counter. I narrow my eyes, then glance around at the silence. I fall onto the stool and wrap my hands around the mug, letting the warmth seep into my clammy skin. The first sip of tonic slides down my throat, heating me from the inside out. The second eases the ache in my muscles. By the time half the drink is gone, I have enough strength to fix the screen door or clean the kitchen. I probably won't be able to do both.

"Kitchen it is," I murmur.

I start with the island, then move to the counters. Putting things away and wiping down the surfaces shouldn't be this tiring. I let out a curse under my breath when I spot the unfed sourdough starter. In the rush to finish the cakes and get them to the party, I forgot I was going to do it afterward.

"Sit down, Scarlett," Slade says, though the bite is gone from his tone. I glance at him as he steps closer. He must have snuck in the back.

"I have to finish this or I'll be behind. You don't have to stay." Thunder rumbles outside, and I glance out the window.

"Doubt they'll be having the fireworks tonight." Slade smirks. "Doubt they'll be able to fit everyone in that warehouse."

"It's a pole barn. Retrofitted, but still a pole barn."

"Does it matter?"

I shrug as I set out the flour, water, and scale. As I reach for the jars, Slade beats me to it. He sets them on the island, then guides me back to my seat. I swear I only close my eyes for a second, but when I open them, my mug is full and he's muttering under his breath.

"What exactly do I do?"

I almost laugh at the lost look in his dark eyes. "Take the cloth off the tops and set them on the scale, then press the button. After that, you'll fill it with water. Mix in the water, then put it back on the scale. You'll have to—"

"Wait...go slower. My mom made bread, but this looks like pancake batter and I don't know what I'm doing."

I sigh and slide off the stool. "It'll be easier to do it myself."

"Oh no you don't. I'm perfectly capable of figuring this out." He puts the jar on the scale and pulls off the top. "How much water?"

"Thirty-nine grams."

He gives me a look, but pours some from the bottle. It's so slow, I'm pretty sure this will take all night. For complaining I was going too fast, he certainly listened well enough. I don't know how to feel about him doing my job for me. This is how I make an income. Besides that, it's almost like these starters are my pets. My nose wrinkles involuntarily. Even in my head, it sounds weird.

"Okay, what now?"

"Back on the scale and clear it out. Then fifty grams of the flour. Make sure you don't let the flour stick to the sides. I have to clean the jars more often then."

He nods, a look of concentration on his face while he follows my directions. He's starting the next jar when he clears his throat. I glance at him, waiting for him to address the elephant in the room. Maybe he's waiting for me to say something. He'll be sorely disappointed if that's the case. I'm too tired to get into the multitude of things between us.

Lightning flashes outside when he finally speaks. "I'm sorry. I get why you're upset. Not trying to excuse my behavior, but I thought I was doing the right thing. I don't always think through decisions. I'm much more of an ask-for-forgiveness kind of guy."

"Is this you asking for forgiveness?"

He snorts, his gaze flashing to mine, then back down. "Not yet. I haven't fixed anything. I am sorry, though. The shit with my sister kind of scarred me. Add in all the shit that went down right before I got here, and I've been a bit on edge."

"Do you want to talk about the shit from right before?" As soon as the words are out, I wish I could stuff them back in. I don't pry into people's lives. I don't ask them personal questions. Except I want to know more about Slade, which is seeming less dangerous the longer he's here.

"No, but if you see any weird figures looming about, maybe let me know." He says it with a laugh, but there's no humor behind the sound.

Something in my mind clicks into place, and I sit up straighter. There's no way I'm right. He probably won't even know what I'm talking about. I need to know, though.

"Slade, do you mean dark watchers? Are they following you?"

His gaze snaps to mine, panic clear on his face. "What?"

I drop my head to my hands. "Fuck me."

# Chapter 19
## Slade

Scarlett can't know about dark watchers. They're elusive and barely spoken about. No one outside my community even knows the lore behind them. By the way she's muttering, though, she does.

"How do you know about dark watchers?" I ask more harshly than I intend.

She waves her hand, dismissing my words. "That's not the important part. Why do you think they're following you?"

"They just seem to show up wherever I go. They showed up in a town I was in, then followed me to Moon Cove. On my way down here, they were dogging my every step."

She snorts, and I scowl at her. "Sorry. Dogging got me. Plus, I'm real tired. This ain't the time for deep talks. Dark watchers don't follow people. They pop up, rile shit up, then disappear."

"Well, they've widened their scope then. Because they are definitely following me."

I scrape the sides of the jar carefully, though I can't get all the gunk off. When I glance up, Scarlett's eyes are closed and her chin dips to her chest. Shaking my head, I set everything down and round the island. Hopefully there's nothing else for her to tell me. She jumps when I touch her lower back.

"Sorry. I'll finish these," she mumbles.

"No, you won't. You're going to go to bed." I nudge her toward her bedroom, but she doesn't move.

"The starter—"

"Will be perfectly fine." I ease her off the stool and guide her through the kitchen.

"It's only like seven."

"You're slurring your words and can barely keep your eyes open. You need sleep." Thunder crashes overhead, and we both jolt. "And I need to finish this up so I can get back before the rain starts."

She mumbles something I can't understand, then falls into bed. I can't stop my smile as she flops around trying to tug the comforter up. I attempt to help, but she bats my hands away.

Light flashes in the window, and I cross the room to shut the curtains. The rain hasn't started yet. When it does, it'll be a downpour. Hopefully, the roof of the shed doesn't leak. I'm pretty sure I spotted a few buckets in the corner of my room, though.

Scarlett's settled down with her lashes fluttering against her cheeks. I stare at her, noticing things I've missed before. A small smattering of freckles brushes across her nose. Her eyebrows are a little darker than her blonde hair, and her ears are slightly pointed at the tip. Despite spending so much time in the sun, she doesn't have even a trace of a tan.

I lean down and brush my lips over her forehead, then snap upright. I have no idea why I did it. Before she wakes up and catches me, I hustle from the room. When I reach the back room, my feet stutter to a stop. The kitchen won't clean itself, and if I leave it for Scarlett, she'll never let me in again.

My phone buzzes and I roll my eyes when my sister's name pops up. "What do you need, Kira?"

"Have you talked to Dad? He won't answer my calls, and Mom is dodging me."

I'm not surprised she doesn't greet me or ask where I am.

She's always straight to the point, especially when I start the call how I did. For the last ten years, she's been basically monotone on the phone. And in person, now that I think of it. With the panic in her voice, I'm no longer pissed she called me.

"What do you mean, dodging your calls?" I ask softly, glancing toward Scarlett's door.

"Why the hell are you whispering? Whatever. Every time I call her, she distracts me with questions, then guilts me about coming home, and before I know it she's rushing off the phone because of some imagined issue she has to immediately deal with." She huffs as if I'm being ridiculous or she thinks Mom is.

"Kira, she's busy. Everyone's scattered and she's dealing with the general store. I'm sure there's some producers in town or something. Plus, they're already gearing up for Samhain. You know it's always a big production."

"I know, I know. I just hate being so far away. We're so out of the loop, and I didn't expect it."

I put my phone on speaker so I can work while we're talking. This doesn't seem like it'll be a short conversation like normal.

"You didn't think moving across the country on a moment's notice would put you on the outside? Come on, Kira."

"Don't be an asshole, Slade," she snaps, then breathes an apology.

"Nope, you're right. It's rule number one." I clear my throat as I put the covers on the jars. "Listen, Dad wasn't feeling well when I left. He just said it was the changing of the seasons. And I'm sure Mom's just stressed about everything. You know how she tries to take on everything herself. Kind of like *someone* I know."

She snorts, and I picture the look on her face. Kira and I might have gone through some rough times lately, but I finally feel like we're repairing things. Or rather, *I'm* repairing what I broke. It seems like that's the theme of my life lately. Break shit, get defensive, grovel for forgiveness, then fix things. I need to find a better way or I'm going to end up shattering something I can't put back together.

"Do you think Mom hates me?" she whispers.

"No. Never. None of us do. Mom doesn't have the ability to hate."

She's silent, and I struggle with what more I could say. She's never confided in me about the things she's dealing with. Mostly, I leave it up to Alissa to talk her through things. I'm out of my depth and wildly unprepared.

"Kira," I breathe.

"No, you're right. I just had a moment. I know this type of thing freaks you out."

I make a noise of protest. "You can talk to me, you know. I'm pretty smart if you give me a shot."

I don't know why I said that. Scarlett's words from our earlier conversation might have impacted me more than I thought. My siblings, at least the ones younger than me, call me for the practical things. I'm their getaway driver, their call in the middle of the night, their savior from a bad situation. Feelings? Emotions? They turn to each other. I didn't think it bothered me before. Now, I'm not so sure.

"I know you're smart, Slade," Kira says, breaking me from my thoughts. "I just don't want to burden you."

"You're not a burden. Never were. Pissed me off more than once, but never a burden. Have you talked to Chase?"

"Yes. No. Kind of. Doesn't matter. This doesn't have anything to do with him. It has to do with our family."

"Uh, Kira, I don't know if you noticed, but he's your family, too. He's your mate."

There's a slam of a screen door on her end, and sounds from the night around Whispering Pines echo down the line. It's not all that different from Hart's Hollow. Moon Cove doesn't get quiet unless you run into the woods. With production crews coming in every few months and tourists flooding the town from spring to fall, it's even harder to live there. It's part of the reason I left. The center of town might be magicked off to anyone not part of the shifter community, but that doesn't mean much in the grand scheme of things. I always felt like I was one wrong move away from being exposed.

"Chase is still adjusting. Not to being mates, obviously. Being a shifter isn't easy in the first place. Since he didn't shift until he was older, it's hard on him. Add in he's a sliver cat and it's just... we're working on it. I don't want to add more stress to his world. I'm supposed to—"

"Lean on him. You're supposed to lean on him. Sorry to break it to you, but if you don't talk to him, he's going to feel like you don't trust him. He won't see your stress the same as his own. Probably be good for him to focus on something other than himself." I glance toward Scarlett's door again, though I haven't heard anything. I give the counter one more wipe down, then grab my phone and the spatulas to wash them off.

When I turn on the water, Kira huffs. "If you were busy, you could have just said so."

"Not busy. Just rinsing something."

"Where the hell are you, anyway? I thought you would be in Moon Cove."

"I, uh, had to help a friend," I mumble.

It's not that I don't want to tell her. Admitting I'm helping a woman would only send Kira down a path. She'd call Gemma to spill the beans, and before I know it, Jake and Chase will be up my ass wanting gossip. I'm glad Kira and Gemma are closer now, but if they start in on me, shit will go sideways. They'll have questions I can't answer since I'm not about to tell them Scarlett's a lorelei or about her illness.

"Okay. Keep your secrets. Can you just try to call our parents?"

"Yeah, I'll do it tomorrow. Listen, it's starting to storm here so I gotta go." I take the phone off speaker and press it to my ear in time to hear her sigh.

"Don't forget. And call me afterward. I want to know what's going on."

"Will do. Love you."

She hesitates for a beat, then murmurs, "Love you, too."

I hang up just as a crash of thunder rips through the air. Tonight isn't going to be fun, especially in that flimsy shed. I peek into Scarlett's room and find her still sound asleep. At least one of us will be rested tomorrow. I doubt I'll do anything other than jump every time there's a flash or a rumble.

As I hurry through the back room, my eyes catch on all the projects I've left half-done. Tomorrow will be slow going, and I doubt I'll be able to finish anything. I wanted to start on the bathroom, but that'll have to wait. Scarlett's list sits on a windowsill, and I stutter to a stop. I add fixing the screen door to the bottom. I feel like I've added more than I've finished. I could spend a year here and never get to everything. Not what Scarlett's asked of me, but all the things I've noticed.

The first pattering of rain hits the window, breaking me from my thoughts. Thankfully, I'm not soaked by the time I make it to the shed. I rip off my clothes until I'm in my boxer briefs and a chill rolls through me. Wind batters the small space and finds every little crack. My wolf howls in my head, and I grit my teeth. Usually, he doesn't give two shits about a storm. For some reason, he wants to run back to the house.

"Scaredy-cat," I mutter. "Nothing's leaking, and we've got blankets. You'll be fine."

He whimpers, crowding into the corner of my mind. I huff, realizing there's nothing more I can do other than go to sleep. Hopefully, there'll be a lull and I'll be able to drift off. As I crawl under the covers, more thunder crashes above me. Lightning splits the sky, and I squeeze my eyes shut. It doesn't help.

After who knows how long, I give up. I didn't think I'd be

able to hear the creaking over the wind and rain. Staring at the ceiling, I contemplate whether or not I should shift. I'm sure my wolf will just take off for the house. Scarlett wouldn't be happy with either of us. He'd probably cuddle right up next to her. Bastard doesn't understand boundaries. He just wants to be close to humans. Since she's the only one around, he'll gravitate toward her.

When the wall next to my head groans, I sit up and glance around. I grab my phone and pull up the weather app. Alerts pop up, one after another.

*High winds. Flash floods. Take shelter now.*

"Well, this isn't good," I mumble.

I swing my feet over the side and slip them into my boots. Going outside would be a death wish, but I don't want to cut my foot on a nail or something. I check the windows first and find water streaming from the frame. The door isn't faring much better. My hand hits the wooden beams holding the walls up, and it wobbles. As the wind batters the worn boards, I realize I don't have a lot of time before this thing is going to come down.

I snatch up my bag and hightail it out the door as the whole shed leans. Cold icicles hit my bare skin, though I barely feel it. I'm too busy glancing over my shoulder at the falling structure.

My body slams into something soft, and I tumble to the ground. Instinctively, my arms wrap around Scarlett. Because of course it's Scarlett out in the middle of a thunderstorm. I twist around, and my back crunches into the wet gravel, her on top of me. My groans mix with her shrieks, and I wish I had enough breath to tell her to stop.

"Goddess save me," I wheeze. At least my wolf will get what he wants now.

# Chapter 20

## Scarlett

I toss a towel at Slade, desperately trying to keep my eyes off the bulge in his underwear. I'm too afraid to ask why he's almost naked. Does he sleep like that? Even in this weather?

"Storm wake you up?" he asks as he wraps the fabric around his waist. If he takes off his boxers underneath it, my cheeks might go up in flames.

"Something like that," I mutter. I'm not about to tell him the goddess nudged me awake.

I disappear under my towel on the pretense of drying my hair. Not that I'm hiding from him and his very naked chest. I swallow a groan when I realize his room is gone. Right before we raced inside, the whole thing came down.

Hopefully he didn't have anything important left inside. He can't sleep on the hard floor in the living room, and clearly the couch is still out unless he shrunk in the last week.

"I'll get some blankets for you," I mumble, still hiding.

"No," he growls, and I peek at him. His nostrils flare, and he tugs my towel away. "You're going back to bed. I'm going to make sure the house doesn't fall down around us."

He snatches up his bag and pushes past me. The fabric around his waist drops as he steps over the threshold. I expect him to stop and wrap himself up again. Instead, he merely bends over and grabs it, then continues on. I couldn't pull my gaze away if I wanted to. His muscles ripple, though I didn't think that was a thing. A thin scar wraps around each shoulder blade as if he once had wings.

A sharp crack of thunder punches through my ogling, and I drop my eyes to the towel he left at my feet. By the time I look up, Slade has disappeared into the house. For the first time, I wish this place was bigger. Then I could tuck myself away in some random room where he couldn't find me.

I can't make him sleep on the floor again. He probably thinks I didn't notice his bones creaking or how stiff he was after the last time. Jokes on him, I've been hyperaware of him every time he's in the vicinity.

I shuffle after him, wondering if I can slip into my bedroom without him seeing. He's nowhere to be found, though I'm not searching very hard. When I step into my room, I find him running his hands around my window. At least he put on some shorts, though they do little to hide his body. I'm kicking myself for being so enamored with his back. It's just skin and bones…and muscles flexing as he reaches for the top of the frame.

"Rule number three," I mutter, and he grunts.

"Better to break a rule than have it flood in here."

"Whatever." I pivot and make my way to the closet. He won't be able to object to my taking the couch if I'm already sleeping.

I'm just tucking myself in when he stomps into the living room. I close my eyes, pretending I've already drifted off to dreamland. He sighs heavily as I even out my breathing and try to keep my eyes from fluttering.

I've never been good at bluffing, which is ironic considering my entire existence is basically lying to others. I can manipulate people to do whatever I want. When I was younger, my greatest fear was doing it unintentionally. These days it's clear I'm not deceiving anyone unless it's keeping them away from me.

"You can stop, Scarlett," he growls, his voice mixing with the thunder rolling overhead.

"I'm trying to sleep," I whisper. "Would be easier without you banging around."

I peek at him from under my lashes. He's moved on to the other windows, checking them for leaks. When he moves to the front door, I sit up, huffing.

He glances over his shoulder. "Did you forget about the massive storm wailing around us? Or the fact the damn shed blew away? I'm trying to save your damn house."

"Why are you yelling at me? I didn't huff and puff and blow your shed down. I didn't make the storm happen. And I didn't ask you to save my house from an imagined threat. This isn't the first gale we've had, and it won't be the last. Just wait a minute and the weather'll probably change." I tip my head back against the couch and pretend to close my eyes while still peering at him.

He gives me a look I can't decipher, then prowls toward me. It takes everything in me not to react. I fail when he plants his hands on either side of my head and leans in close. Our gazes collide, and my heart stutters.

"First of all, I wasn't yelling. Second, I'm not blaming you for anything except maybe for running out into the storm to do what? Prevent the shed from leaving this plane of existence?" His eyebrow pops up, and I swallow hard. "None of which matters because my goal here is to keep you safe, and I can't do that if you're constantly throwing yourself straight into danger's path."

"I don't do that. I'm the most introverted person in this town. And this isn't the first time I've run out into a storm. Probably won't be the last."

His jaw tics, and I have the irrational urge to press my lips to his skin. I bite my cheek to stop myself. By the narrowing of his eyes, I wonder if he knows. If he doesn't back up soon, I'll end up doing something we both will regret. Not right away. Later, though. Tomorrow in the harsh light of day I'll be kicking myself for giving in to my baser needs. I snort at the thought, then catch the smirk on his lips.

"You're not sleeping on the couch. Go to bed." He pushes upright and makes his way back to the front door.

"No." The word slips out, and I hold my breath as he freezes.

Slowly, he turns around and narrows his eyes at me. "What was that?"

I shouldn't push him. I don't even know why I am. Maybe I just want to see how far I can go before he breaks. Not lashes out in defense like I've seen. I want to know what happens when he loses control. It's thrilling and terrifying and foolish. If he lets out his wolf, things could go very wrong. He must be able to deal with his shifter side after so many years.

"I said no. Do you need me to elaborate?" I grip the blanket, hiding my hands from him.

"Oh, no. I think I've got it." He crosses his arms over his bare chest.

I swear I can feel the heat rippling off of him. Between his presence and the storm raging around us, it feels like we're cut off from the world. As if whatever happens right now won't impact the future. Throwing caution to the wind might be just what I need. I don't know whether I'm convincing myself to jump his bones or talking myself out of it.

He takes a step toward me, then another and stops. "You're not sleeping on the couch. Go. Now."

My stomach flips and I'm about to swallow my tongue, yet still I whisper, "Make me."

Something akin to desire flashes in his dark eyes, and before I know it, he's tipping me over his shoulder. I don't make a sound or fight him. I'm done resisting the desire I feel for him, the one I've studiously pretended didn't exist. Fear has ruled my life for so long, I don't know how to function without it.

Maybe I'm manipulating him. Maybe I've woven tendrils of magic around him. Maybe I'm using him to bury my weaknesses. Or maybe it's none of those things and I'm finally letting myself do something *I* want to do.

As his arm holds my thighs in place and he marches off to my bedroom, I realize I'm getting ahead of myself. While I've been having this grand revelation of self-discovery, he's probably thinking this is just fun. A little frivolity after a stressful night. Slade said himself he's personable, which probably means he's a flirt. None of it actually translates to anything deeper. It certainly doesn't mean he wants to sleep with me. Based on how I've acted since he got here, he'll probably put me to bed, tuck me in tight, then flit off to the couch. If he pats me on the head, I might lose it.

I tense as we enter my dark bedroom. He flips me around and a gasp leaves me. Bastard is going to slam me onto the bed, and my body will feel it for days to come. Instead, he swings me into his arms and sets me gently on top of the comforter. His fingers dig into my skin for a second before he straightens. I'm desperately trying to control my face and probably failing.

He tilts his head as he studies me. "Are you going to be a good girl and stay?"

*What. The. Fuck.* Good goddess, he's going to be the death of me if he keeps talking like that. I don't even know how to respond without giving away how much I want him. Panic swamps me the longer the silence stretches between us. His face gives nothing away. No twitch of the lips or narrowing of the eyes. He could be a statue for all he's moving.

"You can't sleep on the couch," I whisper.

Finally he cracks as he smirks. "Is that an invitation?"

A peal of thunder splinters through the air, and I jolt upright. Even if we weren't in the middle of a muddled mess of half-truths and almost confessions, I wouldn't want him to leave. While storms don't scare me, this one doesn't seem like it'll be slowing down anytime soon. Maybe it's the whistles from the other night or Slade talking about dark watchers or the shed crumpling under the weight of the wind. My independence might have gone with it.

"I'm going to check the house one last time," he mutters, unable to meet my eyes before stalking from the room.

Guilt, shame, and disappointment wash over me as he leaves, closing the door softly behind him. I shouldn't have flirted with him. We were bound to hit a wall. Or perhaps a cliff. We came right to the edge, neither of us willing to jump.

The more I think about it, the more I realize he was only playing along. The rollercoaster tonight hasn't helped me one bit, and he wasn't even on the ride with me. I talked myself into some fantasy where he wanted to sleep with me. I convinced myself to take a risk instead of seeing the situation for what it was—harmless fun.

And I can't even blame him.

I've been a bitch to him, pushed him away, and probably manipulated him. I cried and he offered to stay. If that's not manipulation, I don't know what is. While I haven't felt the tell-tale sign of warmth in my gut or tingle in my chest that tells me I've used my magic, it doesn't mean I haven't been. I've spent most of my life ignoring the fact I'm a lorelei. I've hidden that part of myself away—buried it so deep I barely recognize myself anymore.

I crawl under the covers and close my eyes. Still, the lightning flashes behind my lids, and I roll onto my side. It doesn't help since there are windows on both sides of my bed. I don't want to get up and close the curtains. Then I won't know what's going on outside, and I won't be able to see Slade when he comes in. *If* he comes in. He's probably already scrunched up on the couch, cursing his fortune.

Tomorrow. As long as the storm hasn't brought down trees or flooded the roads, I'll fix his car tomorrow. Then he can decide if he really wants to stay or go. I keep trying to get ahold of Holden, but he never answers. He changed his voicemail, informing everyone he'd be out of touch for the foreseeable future.

The familiar feelings of panic and loneliness hit me, making it hard to breathe. I shove them down deep next to all the other feelings I've buried. No reason to fear what I don't know. It never does any good. The only reason I'm thinking of him now is because of Slade, anyway.

It's my way of avoiding Slade's rejection. Not that I made it very clear what I wanted. He put it right out there, and all I had to do was seize the opportunity. Instead, I let the silence stretch until it was taunt, a steady vibration traveling the thread between us.

"Head out of the clouds," I whisper. "Eyes forward. Keep it in check. Don't engage."

It's probably not the healthiest advice my father gave me, but it's all I have. If anything, it keeps me firmly rooted in reality. Which seems ridiculous, given what I am. My entire existence, and really shifters in general, feels like something out of a fairy-tale. According to humans, we're not supposed to exist. We're the stuff of legends and mythology.

Sometimes I wonder if it'd be easier if that's all I was—a fairy tale.

# Chapter 21
## Slade

Nervous energy races through my veins, and my hands tremble as I fumble with the screwdriver. I wanted to check on the house one last time and give Scarlett a moment to make up her mind.

Then the screen door started banging against the siding, and I knew I had to fix it now. If I don't, it'll end up blowing away in this wind. What I didn't anticipate was how hard and cold the rain would be.

The drops are like pellets as they pierce my back. I'm kicking myself for not grabbing a shirt. I swipe the water from my face with my bicep and line up with the screw once more. Just a few more turns and it should be good. Then I can go inside and crawl in next to her. If she shoves me onto the floor, so be it.

"What in the hell are you doing?" Scarlett snaps from behind me.

"Making sure your door doesn't end up on the roof," I growl, then drop the screwdriver again.

Scarlett grabs my arm and attempts to haul me inside. I glance up at her, the rain pelting me in the back of my head. She glares at me as she tugs, though it's not doing anything.

"Would you get in here? You're going to get sick."

Sighing, I stand, then kick the tool aside. I'll pick it up later.

Right now, I'm too busy fixating on her bare legs. When I put her over my shoulder, I was trying so hard not to think about her soft skin under my palm. It's probably why I said the things I did. That, and I didn't want to let the opportunity slip away again. I swear if we can stop bickering long enough, we'll be able to find common ground…or at least a common bed.

"Shifters don't get sick, Scarlett," I say with a smirk. My face drops when hurt flashes in her eyes. "I meant like colds. Besides, I'm pretty sure that's an old wives' tale."

"Whatever. Doesn't mean you should be fixing a fucking door in the middle of all this." She gestures toward the window being lashed with rain. She presses her lips together, tension clear in every line of her body. "I'm going to—"

She spins and her shoulders droop as she makes her way back to her bedroom. I flip the lock and end up grabbing the pillow off the couch, then follow her. If she closes the door, I'll turn right around and crash on the floor instead.

I slow, then stop and wait until the creak from the hinges quiets. There's a sliver of darkness escaping, and hope curls in my gut. Or maybe it's my wolf. He's been hyperaware of where she is, constantly trying to get closer to her. It's as if he wants to protect the only other human around in this weather. I'm not about to admit it's anything more than that.

I gently push on the wood, and for once, the hinges are on my side. They stay silent as I slip into the room and again when I close the door behind me. I can just make out her form tucked under the covers. She huffs and mutters something under her breath.

"What was that, beautiful?" I murmur as my knees brush the mattress.

She flops onto her back, and I catch her glare in a flash of lightning. If it doesn't stop soon, we're going to have problems with the river. Scarlett said something about flash floods, and

I'm reminded of rule number two. As if I'd be foolish enough to go swimming after all this.

"I'm just thinking about how you're probably tracking water across my carpets. Thanks for that."

"Sarcasm is a bit unnecessary," I mutter. "You still pissed at me about the party? Is that what this is?"

Her mouth parts, and the denial on her tongue is practically begging to be released. I brace myself for her rejection. I wouldn't blame her.

"I...I didn't think you were going to..." She pulls her knees up and inhales deeply. "Where do you want to sleep?"

I point at the space next to her. She shouldn't look so surprised. I followed her shapely ass in here. I flirted pretty obviously with her. I stuck around when I could have left after a week. No one in their right mind would think I want anything other than to share a bed with her.

Then again, we have been butting heads almost every day. I took most of it as banter, but maybe she thinks I really don't want to be here. It'll take more than a couple lines to break down her walls. One good conversation will go a long way. Except then she'll have to admit she wants me. I don't know if she'd be that honest with me. I haven't really given her a reason to trust me.

Her throat bobs, and she flips the blanket over, leaving me a space to slide in. I hesitate a few seconds before shoving my shorts down. She doesn't say anything—doesn't make a sound. If she protested, I'd have to go digging for more shorts in my bag and hope they weren't soaked from the rain. There's no way I'd be able to wear pants in here with the heat billowing off me. I flick the curtains closed, then round the bed to do the same to the other window.

My wolf whimpers in my head, and I shush him. I'm doing what he wants, yet he still won't shut up.

"Did you just shush me?" she whispers as I climb in and pull the covers over me.

"Definitely not," I whisper back. "My wolf doesn't like storms."

Her arm presses against mine, and I dig my nails into my thighs. Anything to stop myself from reaching for her. If she wants me, she'll have to speak up. I doubt she will. Lying next to her will have to be enough.

"Do you need to shift?" Scarlett's voice holds none of the fear I expected.

"No. I wouldn't do that to you, anyway. I remember the rules, Scarlett."

More thunder cracks through the air and she jolts, her fingers lacing with mine. I swear the noise shakes the house much longer than normal. Scarlett trembles beside me, and I squeeze her hand. She must take it as a sign. She rolls toward me and throws her leg between mine. When she tucks herself close, her hair spreading across my chest, my breath catches in my throat.

I untangle our fingers and slip my arm around her. She mumbles something, and I glance down at the top of her head. I shouldn't, but I press my lips to the silky strands. I tense and glare at the ceiling, then clear my throat.

"What was that?" I ask.

"I don't like storms either. Maybe your wolf and I can cower together." She lets out a humorless laugh, and I tug her closer.

"I mean, if you'd rather cuddle with him, I suppose I could oblige."

She snorts, shaking her head. "And deal with the fur? No, thanks. Is he still worried?"

"Totally. Though he's better now."

"Oh, yeah. Because of the bed."

I can't tell if she's deliberately being obtuse or actually thinks I care about the fucking bed. "Doubt it's the bed, beautiful."

She's silent, though her fingers brush across my bare chest. We're in a silent standoff, neither willing to take that final leap. I could get up right now and retreat to the couch.

We'd pretend this never happened, wade through the awkwardness, and eventually I'd leave. Or I could roll her onto her back, cover her with my body, and kiss the shit out of her. Maybe we don't need words to figure things out between us.

When her nail flicks across my nipple, a growl leaves me. I flip her on her back and settle between her legs. She doesn't squeal, doesn't stop me. Instead, she gazes up at me, desire dripping from her eyes. I can barely make out her features in the darkness, but it's enough.

I slant my mouth over hers, swallowing her gasps as she grips my sides. I don't know what I expected, but it wasn't an explosion of colors behind my lids. It's as if the storm pauses while we crash together. I've been fighting this for too long, and I need to slow down to either savor her or give her a chance to stop this.

I pull back, and our heavy breaths fill the space between us. "I need to know—"

"I want this," she gasps, her nails raking across my shoulders to my neck.

At the slightest tug from her, I'm capturing her lips once more. This could be a very bad idea. Between my relationship with her brother and her being a lorelei, things could go very wrong. I don't want to hurt her. Yet she doesn't seem to care about those things right now. With the way she's squirming beneath me and her tongue sliding along mine, she's clearly not conflicted about this decision. I rip my mouth from hers and run my lips to her jaw.

"I've dreamt about this," I murmur into her velvet skin.

"The bed?" she asks with a breathless laugh.

I chuckle, then sink my teeth into the soft spot behind her ear. "Yes, the bed. With you in it. Naked and writhing underneath me." I latch onto the lobe, and her hips grind against my cock. "Just like that, beautiful."

I reach over and flick on the lamp, needing to see more than just an outline of her. She blinks, turning away at the sudden light. I seize the opening and nip at her collarbone. A soft moan leaves her as I suck and lick as far as her shirt will let me.

"Too many clothes," she whines as she tries to get her hands between our bodies.

I slide my knees to either side of her, then grab her wrists and lift them over her head. "I'll deal with this, thank you very much."

"I can undress myself."

"Well aware, beautiful." I don't tell her I want to unwrap her like a present. My own personal gift, complete with a bow on the front of her panties.

I release her wrists and drag my palms down her arms, then her sides. She shudders under my touch, and my cock hardens. I run my finger along the waistband of her underwear, barely skimming her skin, and her muscles jump. Her chest heaves under her heavy breaths, pushing her breasts practically in my face. I wanted to tease her more. My wolf whines in my head, adding to the urgency building within me.

"Do you like this shirt?" I murmur, toying with the hem.

Her gaze snaps to me, desire making her irises a deep blue. "No, why?"

I grin as I rip the shirt straight down the middle. Goosebumps scatter across her iridescent skin. I don't know if it's the lamp or part of being a lorelei, but I'm pretty sure she's sparkling. Or maybe it's just how I see her.

I brush the fabric aside, revealing her perfect body. My mouth waters as I gaze at her. When I duck my head to see all of her, she blocks my view. Her hands cover her hips, and her elbows jut out awkwardly.

"Scarlett," I say with a warning lilt.

Her cheeks redden, and she glances away. "If you stop, we're going to have a problem."

"We're going to have a problem if you keep hiding your body from me," I growl. Gently, I pull her hands away. I don't know why she wants to cover her hips.

She pushes onto her elbows and glares at me. "Either kiss me again or put your pants back on. Those are your options, sir."

Heat licks through my veins at her challenge and her calling me sir. I push onto my knees and rest my hands on her knees. She narrows her gaze, daring me to deny her.

"While I would love to do whatever you want me to do, I need to know what you're hiding from."

Her nostrils flare, and she stares at the ceiling as her finger traces her hip. I squint, trying to figure out what she's doing. Slight depressions in her skin appear. Or maybe I just noticed them. I brush her hand away and trace the marks myself. I swear they shimmer in the soft light. When I skip to the next one, she grabs my wrist and I glance up.

"I...You don't..." She swallows hard.

I hum, continuing on my quest to find every single one. There are more lines stretching up to her stomach and a few on her inner thighs.

"Are you done?" she snarls, and her legs tremble like she wants to close them.

"Not quite," I murmur, dipping my head to her skin.

She gasps, her fingers spearing into my hair, whether to pull me closer or push me away, I'm not sure she even knows.

"What are you—" Her words turn to moans when I reach her inner thigh. Her knees fall open, giving me even more access.

I shouldn't ask what happened. Having sisters, I realize what the stripes are and right now is definitely not the time to talk about it. The fact she thinks I'd care about them makes me irrationally angry.

When she moans my name, my head snaps up. A flush

spreads across her cheeks, and I can't help but grin. She gasps when I slide her panties down her legs. I toss them aside, then deal with my own.

I skim my palms along her calves. When I reach her waist, she pushes her hips toward me, silently begging for more. Her fingers flutter over my skin as if she's not quite sure where to go. As I dip my head between her legs, she grabs the back of my neck and yanks me toward her. I crawl up her body and seal my lips to hers.

Her skin against mine has fire racing through my veins. I fought against this desire yet couldn't stop dreaming of this for weeks. My arms tremble as I hold myself above her. I grunt when she winds her legs around my waist.

"Scarlett..."

She smirks at the warning in my tone, then digs her heels into my ass until I drop. A groan leaves me when my length slides along her wetness. I bury my face into her neck, and her nails run along my sides. A shudder rolls through me, and my arms tremble as I barely hover over her. After everything that's happened tonight, I'm almost waiting for her to change her mind.

When I can't hold myself up anymore, I flip us over and settle her onto my lap. Her palms slap against my chest, and her flushed face gazes down at me. Her tongue darts out to wet her bottom lip, and I grip her waist tighter. I know I'm in trouble when a smirk tips the corner of her mouth and she grinds into me.

She pushes up and raises her eyebrow, a question and invitation in the gesture. After a nod, I glance between us, and she wraps her hand around my shaft. I suck in a sharp breath, then grunt as she squeezes me. Before I can recover, she lines her core with my tip and sinks onto my cock. She throws her head back, and her hair cascades down her back and over my knees.

She lifts again, then drops onto my cock, a noise from the

back of her throat erupting from her. When she pulls the same move again, I thrust into her hard, just to hear the sound once more. It fills the hole in my soul, satiating me in a way I wasn't anticipating.

"More," she gasps, leaning back on my bent knees. Her nails dig into my thighs, and my wolf howls in my head. I'm not the only one reveling in the sensations she's evoking within me.

She's mesmerizing as she rides me, completely immersed in our joining. I can practically see the pleasure dripping down her body. I surge into her again and again, relishing the moans tumbling from her lips. A needy noise escapes me, and her gaze snaps to mine, a grin stretching across her face.

She leans over me, her nails digging into my chest as she rolls her hips. The move forces a groan from me. She could do this all night long and I wouldn't complain.

She dips her head close to my ear and murmurs, "Do you like that, sir?"

I growl, flipping her onto her back, and she gasps. "I warned you about calling me sir, beautiful."

I plunge into her, and she arches her back. It doesn't take long before she spasms around me and I follow her over the edge. Thunder rumbles overhead, mixing with our gasping breaths. I slip from her and roll off, then tuck her into my side. She hums, her body still trembling against me.

When I glance at her, I'm caught by the glow emanating from her. I swear her skin soaks in the soft light from the lamp. I sigh, a peace stealing over me. This is the first time in a long while I've felt this fulfilled. Whether it's because of her or being here, I don't know. Right now, with her in my arms, I'm not going to examine things too closely.

As her breathing evens out, I close my eyes. I'm going to enjoy every minute we have together. We'll figure everything else out later.

# Chapter 22
## Scarlett

I've made a lot of mistakes in my life. I can't bring myself to add last night to the list. Nor can I bring myself to pull away from his warmth. The storm has passed, yet the sky's still grey outside. I should get up and check the damage before it starts raining again. Except then I'd have to leave my bed and I'm exceptionally comfortable.

Slade's hand runs up my back, then to my waist again. I suppress a shiver, and my stomach flips. He's probably not awake and doesn't know what he's doing. He probably doesn't even realize I'm here.

The thought doesn't sit right in my head. It bounces around, invading all the memories from last night. It would probably be better if I wasn't here when he woke up. Then he could make up his mind about how he wanted to act. And we could avoid a lot of awkwardness.

I still don't think it was a mistake to sleep with him, but in the light of day, things feel different. We were in our own little world last night—cut off from everyone else. As if nothing else mattered other than the two of us.

With the rising of the sun, I'm forced to face the fact that we're not the only two people left on earth. I'll have to interact with the townsfolk after he made that scene at the party. He'll have to go back to his family. I'll have to deal with Holden and his questions. He'll have to…do nothing. He won't be impacted by his leaving. This is probably just a little fun for him.

*Fuck.* I squeeze my eyes shut, soaking up the last little bit of his warmth, then ease from his arms. His fingers flex against my skin. I freeze, but he doesn't wake, and I roll off the bed. Maybe the goddess is on my side for once. Bitch owes me for everything she's put me through in my years on this earth.

I stumble out the door and wince as I pull it shut. No noise comes from the other side, and I breathe a sigh of relief. I end up in the small laundry room tucked away behind the kitchen, digging for clothes through the dryer I never emptied.

Slade shredded my shirt and underwear, but I left my shorts next to the bed. I find a wrinkled sundress and tug it on. I can't find any panties, but it's not like anyone will be around other than Slade.

Humidity hits me as I slip out the front door. Grey clouds hang low in the sky, and the world seems muted. Even the birds are subdued. I should have grabbed my phone and checked the weather.

I scan the area, a nervous energy buzzing through the air. Glancing back at the house, I search for any sign of Slade. It's probably best he isn't out here. He'd probably make the situation worse.

"Oh my goddess," I wheeze as I round the house.

The roar from the river pierces the muffled world. I barely make it to the tree line before I'm met with raging rapids spinning their way downstream. My chest tightens and my vision blurs while I stare at the whirlpools forming on the surface. Debris floats by, seemingly oblivious to the destruction of the water as it erodes away the dirt on the banks. A gust of wind whips through the leaves hanging from the boughs overhead, and my hair billows around my head.

A voice yells at me to get away from the bank. I can't seem to move, though. My body sways as if I don't have control of myself. I never should have come out here.

If I fall in, I'll survive, but it won't be fun. And if someone finds me, I'll be too disoriented to keep myself in check. They'll fall under my spell, and who knows what I'll make them do. Because it won't just be a suggestion at that point. If I fall into the water, I'll become something else completely. At least, that's what I've been told.

"Just a dip, nothing more," I whisper, the words of my mother ringing in my head like an alarm.

She barks my name, and I struggle to listen—to break free of the pull from the water. Her voice morphs, becoming deep. The tone resonates in my chest. A strong arm wraps around my waist and suddenly I can breathe again. I slam my eyes shut when the world around me spins. Nausea bubbles up my throat, and I clamp my lips together.

"Breathe." Slade's command comes out harsh and demanding.

I curl over Slade's arm and concentrate on the air shifting around us. The screen door squeaking is my only under-standing of where we are. As soon as we're inside, thunder rolls overhead and the skies open up. A few more seconds and we would have been caught in a torrential downpour.

Slade drops me on the couch, and I track him from under my lashes as he stalks back to the front door. Apparently he didn't have time to put on clothes when he came searching for me. His muscles bunch as he shoves the wood in place and flips the lock. My mouth waters when he turns, completely unfazed by his lack of underwear. Or shorts. Or shirt.

"Want to explain all that to me? Or should I just jump right into scolding you?" he snarls, planting his fists on his hips.

My gaze pops up, meeting his eyes, and I swallow a nervous giggle. It would be wholly inappropriate to stare at his cock while he's upset. Except it's right there. It's hard enough to keep myself from ogling him when he's not wearing a shirt. Now that I know how he feels…intimately, I doubt I'll be able to keep from fantasizing about him for months.

Does he really expect me to have this conversation while he looks like he's posing as a nude model? Apparently so, given the way he's glaring at me.

"Rule number two," I croak out, then press my lips together.

If I say anything more, I'll embarrass myself. I might even resort to begging, and while it might be a good distraction from his lecture, it wouldn't be for my self-esteem. Especially since I don't know what last night was. Is this a one-time thing? A summer fling? The start of something more? I'm too much of a coward to ask right now.

"What the fuck does no swimming have to do with you trying to fling yourself into the river while it's flooding?" His nostrils flare and his eyes flash yellow. All the desire I felt moments ago fizzles out.

"I wasn't trying to…listen, it's a whole thing. Okay?" I don't really want to get into the specifics of the draw lorelei have to water.

"Is this a lorelei thing?"

Well, so much for hiding that. I exhale heavily and push to my feet. At least the nausea and dizziness have disappeared. The pitter-patter of rain hits the windows, and I focus on the droplets sliding down the glass while I get my thoughts in order.

"So I've been told. Water…rejuvenates us. But it can also lead to more destructive things. When the river runs like that, it sounds like the murmuring from our ancestors or something. It lures us in, just like we do people. Problem is, I can't control my powers when I'm pulled in like that. So, if you start forgetting chunks of time or don't know why you're doing something, you should tell me. Or just run."

I run my hand through my snarled hair and wrinkle my nose. I need a shower and some time alone. He's looking at me like I've grown a second head, and I don't like it.

"I'm not running from you, Scarlett. Why didn't you wake me?"

"Because you were sleeping. It's fine."

"It's not fucking fine," he explodes, throwing his hands up. He grips the back of his neck and tips his head back. "Sorry. Don't do that again. Stay away from the river and don't go wandering around after a thunderstorm. Got it?"

I roll my eyes, not that he notices. "Yeah, sure. For the next couple days, I'll wake you up before I go outside."

When I spin around, my dress billows up. I dig my nails into my palms, hoping I didn't just show him my whole ass. I'm trying to make an exit here. He probably didn't even notice, too busy being all pissy and gesturing wildly. As if any of that helps the situation. If he's a typical man, he most likely thinks I was serious. He didn't hear the passive aggressiveness in my tone.

He also didn't correct me when I implied he wouldn't be here for more than a couple days. Maybe he didn't catch it, but my brain doesn't care. It latches onto that one irrational idea and refuses to let go. I'll wash it away in the shower.

I close the bathroom door quietly behind me. I concentrate on calming my racing heart. The last twenty-four hours haven't been kind to my emotions. If I could just open my mouth and tell him what I want, my mind would settle. My feelings would level out. I could let go and have fun.

I strip down and step into the shower before turning on the water. Cold icicles hit my skin and make me shiver. A memory of advice hits me about not bathing during a thunderstorm. Still, I stand under the spray and let it freeze me from the outside in. Maybe it'll numb me enough to have a conversation with him without hurting my own feelings.

"Scarlett?" Slade calls as he knocks on the door.

He doesn't wait for me to respond before barging in. I can barely make out his form through the wavy glass. The room isn't big enough for him to hide in a random corner. I cover my snort with a cough when he sits on the toilet. If I wasn't so off-kilter, I'd tell him there's another bathroom in the house if he has to pee.

"You going to pretend I'm not in here? Doesn't seem like the best plan, but okay."

I wipe my face, then lather up my hair before responding. "I'm not pretending. You busted in here. Up to you to speak."

"You walked away in the middle of a conversation."

"And you tried to have one when you were naked. How about we call it even?"

I rinse the shampoo from my hair, letting the warm water wash away the excess energy still clinging to my skin. As soon as Slade grabbed me, the pull from the water vanished. Only the aftermath remained. Taking a shower helps feed the beast within me that wants to drown myself in the river and strips away anything else. Slade won't understand any of that. He might be a shifter, but I'm something outside of them.

He flings the door open and I jump, my shoulder hitting the wall. My eyes widen as I scan his still very naked body. Apparently we're having this conversation while we're both naked.

"I'd say my eyes are up here, but I understand the appeal," he murmurs, and I realize he's staring at my boobs. I resist the urge to cover up.

Sighing, I get some conditioner and do my best to ignore him. If he wants to sit there and stare at me, so be it. I can't lie, it's nice to be ogled by him. Better than what I usually get when I walk into town. Slade doesn't want to ignore me at all costs. He doesn't cross the street when he sees me coming. He slept with me, for goddess' sake. He clearly didn't have any reservations about that.

"I need to know what we're doing here," I finally say before ducking my head under the water.

"Right now? Right now I'm trying to decide whether to join you or scold you some more. I could do both at the same time, but I'm pretty sure I'd get distracted." He traces a line along the curve of my breast, then pulls back once more.

"I don't need to be scolded. I'm a grown-ass woman."

"Damn right you are," he murmurs.

"And I wasn't talking about right now." This is as close as I'm going to get to asking him what he wants. "Whatever you're about to say, remember I'm still pissed at you for interfering at the party."

He chuckles softly. "Duly noted. I don't know what you want me to tell you, Scarlett."

"I don't *want* you to tell me anything." I turn off the water and squeeze out my hair. "I just need to know where we stand."

He hums, then hands me a towel. Part of me wanted him to join me, to push me against the wall and show me he wanted me still. The other part is making fun of me for even considering he'd want something more than one night.

I really need to get my shit together. I'm not bad at sex. He seemed to have had a perfectly good time last night. Doesn't mean he wants a repeat. I'm still not sure we should do this, anyway. I'm still a lorelei. He's still a shifter. Same world yet separate.

"You want me to say I want to sleep with you again? Because I do. You'd know that if you actually looked at me. You want me to say I'm worried you'll get attached to me? Because I am. I'm willing to pretend we're just having a little fun if that's what you want. Or we could just see where this goes."

*See where this goes.* Is that all I'm good for? I have no idea what he means by pretending. If he hadn't said anything else, I would assume he wants to do something else. Something like date.

"Sounds like you want a summer fling." I wrap the towel around me and finally meet his gaze.

He grins, a mischievous glint in his eyes. "Whatever you want, beautiful. As long as you keep calling me sir."

# Chapter 23
## Slade

I hate this.

I hate telling her this was merely fun. I hate that she's waiting for me to run away. I hate how I'm still not sure what I want.

Whatever it is, it isn't this. She's tiptoeing around me, barely smiling. She hesitates every time she opens her mouth as if I'll attack her if she says the wrong word. I played this whole thing badly.

I could blame my missteps on outside influences, but it's my own cowardice. I don't want to scare her off or push too hard. Do I know what I want? Not really. It might sound cliche, but she's not like other girls. Even in my head it sounds ridiculous. For some reason, I can't put her in the same category as my other flings, and it terrifies me.

"What do you want me to do about Gunner?" I ask, glancing out the small window above the sink in the kitchen. Rain pours from the sky, a constant drum against the roof.

"I'll deal with it." She doesn't look at me, keeping her gaze on her bread.

"Fine. I'm going to get some of the staining done." I shove off the stool, a nervous energy overriding my senses. I need somewhere for it all to go.

"Can you do that when it's raining?"

"I'll figure it out."

When I get to the back room, though, I know doing anything in here will be a disaster. I don't know if I can stain, but it's tedious work. My eyes catch on the sledgehammer I left in the corner.

After sliding on my boots, I grab it and march back to the tiny bathroom. This project was at the bottom of the list. I don't really care. If she kicks me out, she'll be without an extra toilet, and she'll have to call someone else in to fix the mess.

Still, I slip on safety glasses and gloves. The first swing is as satisfying as I imagined. The vanity counter cracks, then slides off its base. If everything falls apart as easily, this won't take me long at all. My brain shuts down as I demolish the space. No worries about my family. No fear of the dark watchers following me. No indecision about Scarlett. Only the blessed silence permeating the corners of my mind.

I'm wheezing by the time I'm done. Shards of porcelain litter the space, and all that remains is the mirror. Being a shifter makes me hesitate with other superstitions. I'm not tempting the goddess or fate by breaking it. I drop the sledgehammer in the mess. As soon as I do, the thoughts rush back in.

I can't fix shit with my family. Not while I'm here. The dark watchers might freak me out, but they won't attack me. The only thing I can deal with is Scarlett. Except I still don't know what that looks like. Do I want to stay here? Could I live in the middle of nowhere and spend my days falling in love with her?

"Fuck," I breathe.

Love isn't on my radar. I'm a fucking mess of a shifter. I gave up on finding my fated mate when I was a teenager. It doesn't happen as often as I thought when I was a kid.

My parents touted it as an inevitability—special, but inevitable. They were mates, finding each other when they were teenagers, having seven children, running a successful business, and living happily ever after. They're the couple every shifter within the community looks up to. They might not have said outright a love like theirs was in our future, but we assumed that was what our future held.

I gave up that foolish notion and decided to live my life however the goddess gave it to me. And it worked. For thirty some-odd years, everything was fine. Then I had to stick my nose into Gemma's business and she fell into her mate's hands. My one decision to meddle started a chain reaction with Kira meeting Chase.

I'm sure Alissa will be next. She'll find some mountain man in the woods she ran off to. I'll find out about it in six months or some shit. Eli could be next, catching the eye of someone at college. I wouldn't be surprised if Sloane has already found her fated mate and is keeping it from us. She'll show up to Samhain one year, dragging them behind her. Or maybe it'll be Alister falling overboard while he's on the high seas and a mermaid will rescue him.

A snort leaves me and I shake my head. I don't think mermaids exist, but if they do, Alister would be the one to find them. Their lives have nothing to do with me, though. If they find their fated mates, so be it. I'll be happy for them, especially after how I dealt with Kira's relationship. Neither Kira nor Gemma told me they'd found their fated mates. Not that I expected them to. They knew and that was enough.

If Scarlett were my mate, I'd know. I'm not surprised. Maybe a little disappointed. Doesn't mean we couldn't find something more.

More than one night. More than dancing around each other. More than the banter followed by the silence.

She doesn't seem to want any of it. May have taken me a minute to figure it out, but she never told me what *she* wanted. She made demands about what I was thinking, where we stood, if I wanted her still. She never said where she wanted this to go. And I didn't say a damn word.

I shake my head and sigh, focusing on the problem in front of me rather than whatever's happening with Scarlett. The medicine cabinet won't be hard to remove once I've detached the front. The lights will have to wait until I can find an electrician to deal with them. I won't fuck with something that can burn down her house.

I reach for a screwdriver to remove the ugly thing and remember I only grabbed the hammer. It wouldn't take long for me to get my drill. It's just another thing in a long line of shit going wrong.

Fury flares to life within me. I latch onto the rage and grip the mirror of the cabinet. It takes almost nothing to rip it from its hinges. I grit my teeth, resisting the urge to throw the thing against the wall. Not only will it be a bitch to clean up, but I'll have a curse on my back. Seven years of bad luck or bad sex or bad relationships. Whatever the cost, I'd rather not pay it.

A soft sigh has me freezing, then slowly glancing at the door. Scarlett, arms wrapped around her waist, leaning against the wall, stares at me. She presses her lips together as if holding back a lecture or a snide remark. Whatever it is, I wish she'd just spit it out. She's always holding back, and I fucking hate it.

"So, the staining was a bust?" she asks softly.

"Tedious." It's not much of an explanation, and I set the mirror down. "This needed to get done."

She nods, her bottom lip slipping between her teeth. "Except it didn't. I mean, eventually, sure. Not yet, though. I could have hired—"

"No one else is setting foot in this house. Not while I'm here," I snap.

Her eyebrows shoot up. "You realize this is *my* house, right? I own it. So, if I need to hire someone to finish what you started, then I can."

I prowl toward her, and my hands land on either side of her. I lean closer and her mouth parts. Desire blazes in her blue eyes. My body responds, despite the conflicted feelings battling inside me.

"Your house. My reno. Besides, if another man steps in here, I'll end up ripping off his arms and beating him with them."

She glances away and mutters something that suspiciously sounds like *possessive bastard.* I don't know what's wrong with that. She doesn't want anyone in here anymore than I do.

"How do you know it'd be a man? Maybe I'll hire a woman? Or someone else?" She smirks as if she's won something.

"Don't fucking care. I promised to renovate your house, and I always keep my promises."

"Except you've broken most of the rules I gave you." She lifts onto her toes and peeks over my shoulder. "And my toilet. You realize you could've just taken it out, you know."

"Wouldn't have been as fun, though."

She scoffs. "That was you having fun?"

"Made me feel better." It's a lie. We both know it. Whether or not she calls me on it remains to be seen.

"Seems like it wasn't enough."

I lean closer, my lips brushing the shell of her ear, and I whisper, "I could think of something that would push me over the edge."

Her knees buckle, and I press my hips into her. She lets out a soft *oh,* and I loop an arm around her waist. We should talk, figure out what we're doing. Except with our bodies pressed together and an echo of rage still swirling inside of me, it doesn't matter. I can't bring myself to care about anything other than her and seeing her body again.

"Are you going to run?" I murmur, then nip at her earlobe.

"No," she breathes and buries her face in my neck.

I let out a light chuckle, then lift her. She winds her arms around my neck and clings to me. I'll drown out the voices in my head with her pleasure. She winds her legs around my waist and molds her mouth to mine. I make my way toward the bedroom, though I don't know if we'll make it. I stumble when her tongue licks across my bottom lip.

I swing us into the kitchen and set her on the counter. My palms skim up her thighs under her dress. When I reach her hips, I groan into her mouth and pull back.

"Still no panties? It's like you knew exactly what I've been fantasizing about."

"Stop talking and take off your pants." Her fingers fumble with my belt, and another chuckle leaves me.

I grab her wrists and force her hands behind her. She huffs, digging her heels into my ass. I take my time slipping off the leather, then drop it on the floor. When I unbutton and slip my pants down to my hips, she licks her lips.

I've never done a striptease for someone, but I now understand the appeal. With the way she's looking at me, I'll be lucky to get my clothes all the way off before she jumps me.

She sucks in a shaky breath when I reach for the hem of my shirt and tug it over my head. I drop it next to my belt.

"You're going to have to move if you want—" An unexpected laugh bubbles from me as she kicks her feet out. She scowls, yet she's fighting a smile.

Slowly, I push my pants down, then kick them off. I turn around and glance over my shoulder as I hook my thumbs in the waistband of my underwear. Mirth dances in her eyes and her mouth twitches. When our gazes collide, she raises an eyebrow.

"You're a tease, Mr. Livia."

I wiggle my hips in response. She laughs, tipping her head back. I'm sure I look ridiculous, but I'd make a fool out of myself every day if I get to hear her laugh like that. It's carefree in a way I haven't seen her before. It's as if all her stress and anxiety have vanished in the wake of my antics.

I shake my hips once more, then slide the fabric down, making sure to arch my back as I bend over. She grabs my ass and I yelp, jumping away.

"Ticklish, sir?" she says, amusement dripping from her voice.

A growl leaves me, and I'm not sure if it's from me or my wolf. He seems to have woken up somewhere between the hallway and the kitchen. He's been content to sit in the corner of my mind and salivate over her. Now, he's pushing at the barriers keeping me from shifting as if he needs to be closer. No amount of scolding will get him to pipe down.

I face her once more and step between her legs. She's still resting on her palms, lounging while I put on my little show. She doesn't move until I grab her hips and force her to the edge of the counter. Her hands land on my shoulders, and she digs her fingers into my skin.

"Do you have the gift of premonition?" I rest my forehead on hers.

She rears back, searching my face. "What? No. Why?"

"Because I'm pretty sure you picked out this island especially for me." I push the hem of her dress up. "Legs around my waist, beautiful."

Her brows pull low, still trying to work out what I'm talking about. She doesn't seem to notice when I line myself up with her core. I loop my hand around the back of her neck and kiss her hard as I push into her. She gasps into my mouth, a full-bodied shudder running through her. When I'm fully seated, her head tips back and I run my lips down her throat.

"Again," she breathes.

I pause, then roll my hips. "What was that?"

"Please, sir," she whimpers.

Heat flashes through my body, and I pull out slowly, then thrust back in. A whimper leaves her, and I do it once more.

The strap of her dress slips to her shoulder, and I seize the opportunity. It's not hard to expose her breast with the low neckline. Everything about her dress was an invitation. I swear she did it on purpose to drive me to the brink.

She lands on her palms once more, and I wrap my lips around her nipple. She arches her back, making that sound in the back of her throat I'm quickly beginning to love.

I glance down and revel in the sight of my cock disappearing into her. She squeezes my shaft, and I swear I grow harder. She drives me to the brink of ecstasy every time. Being with her is like nothing else I've ever experienced.

It's too soon to think of the future, but I can't help it. When we sip from our mugs in the morning or eat dinner on the porch or lie next to each other at night, I'm bombarded with the what-ifs.

What if I stayed? What if we did this forever? What if this is exactly where I'm meant to be?

Scarlett cups my cheeks and forces my head up. I thrust into her harder as she stares into my eyes. She spasms around me and her mouth parts. I'm caught in her gaze as she tumbles into oblivion. She throws her head back, still holding my face. I stiffen and shudder out my release. As my eyes flutter shut, I swear her skin glows. I'm too far gone to fully comprehend what's happening.

"Fuck," I breathe.

She drapes her arms around my shoulders and tucks her face into the crook of my neck. "You should do more stripteases."

Her giggles fill the room as I hold her close. Yeah, I could definitely get used to this.

# Chapter 24
## Scarlett

Three days.

Three whole days of getting used to Slade being fully in my space. It's surprisingly easier than I imagined. It might have something to do with him not being able to keep his hands to himself.

When he said he wanted to see where things go, I didn't expect this. He's never far from my sight. I thought the hovering would eventually piss me off. It hasn't. Part of me keeps waiting for the other shoe to drop.

"You know what I miss?" Slade calls from the living room. The last time I checked, he was reading a book Holden left behind.

"What's that?" I ask as I reach for some plates.

"The sun. Then again, if it was out, I'm pretty sure you'd make a mad dash for the river. The chase would be fun, but not the anxiety." He laughs at his own joke while I roll my eyes. Not that he can see me.

"Well, if I jumped in the river and turned into a demonic lorelei, maybe I could curse the Tates. And convince someone to fix your car."

"Don't need a car if I'm not going anywhere, beautiful."

He's been saying things like that a lot. I don't know if it's his subtle way of asking to stay longer. Or maybe it's just a reminder he's sticking around for now. I wasn't very good at figuring out if I wanted him to stay or go.

Every time I tried to push him away, I ended up reeling him back in. I'm still not totally convinced I didn't use my powers on him. It would make sense why he stuck around and took things to the next level. It certainly wasn't my sunny disposition.

Heat gathers in my gut a second before Slade's arms wrap around my waist and he presses his lips to my temple. I may not have heard him coming, but I seem to be hyperaware of his presence. I'd think it was the goddess at work if I didn't know any better. I've heard of shifters having fated mates. Apparently, the goddess didn't extend that particular trait to include lorelei. I'm pretty sure if I had one, it'd be Slade since he's the only person I've gotten close to in years.

"Whatcha making?" he murmurs.

"Beef Bolognese. Naomi gave me a tomato plant at the beginning of summer. I doubt they survived after the storm."

He hums, his hands running up and down my side. His lips brush my neck, and I suppress a shiver. I don't want to burn this meal because he distracted me. It wouldn't be the first time we'd been forced to eat cold food. He's just too hard to resist. Is it healthy? Probably not. If this is a summer fling, though, I want to create as many memories as possible. I've decided to let go and enjoy what he's offering. And I am definitely enjoying it.

"You haven't made your tea in a while. Do you need me to do it?"

I shake my head, my body tensing despite trying to stay calm. I don't want him to move, but I also don't want to kill the mood completely.

"It's a tonic. I only need it during flareups. The rain actually helps. Which is why I never complain about the weather."

He probably doesn't understand. Still, I hope he drops it. He's been trying to start conversations about a whole slew of things I don't know if I want to talk about. Not yet. It feels like if we do, the spell will be broken. We'll be forced to face the reality of our limited time together.

"I know it's a tonic. I also know the rain helps you. I just don't know *how*. Makes sense a lorelei would be attracted to water…and sexy wolf shifters…" He chuckles, and I can't help but smile.

"Well, if you find any sexy wolf shifters, send them my way."

He growls in my ear, then sinks his teeth into my neck. My eyes flutter closed, and I tip my head back to rest on his shoulder. He nibbles his way across my skin. I turn my head, and he captures my mouth in a bruising kiss.

"Keep it up and I'll have to punish you."

"Oh no, please, no," I say mockingly. His punishments usually involve burying his face between my legs. Hardly the consequences I want to avoid.

"Scarlett," he murmurs, and I hum. "Your sauce is smoking."

"Shit." I jab him in the stomach with my elbow. He grunts, dropping his hold on me, and huffs out a laugh.

I flip off the burner and stir the sauce, hoping I didn't actually burn it. When I turn to grab the plates, though, Slade's there holding out a bowl.

"I got plates."

He smirks. "Yes, but bowls will work better for Bolognese. Don't give me that look. It's not like I asked you to eat it with a spoon."

"Why the hell would you eat it with a spoon?"

He just laughs as he grabs both the bowls and sets them at our seats at the island. My smile drops when I realize we have assigned seats. It wasn't intentional. Neither one of us sat down and said *this is mine*. And it happened long before we started sleeping together. We fell into an easy rhythm without me noticing. I made space for him, and he didn't hesitate to fill it.

Slade's head pops up. "You good?"

I nod and force a smile back to my face. "Yeah. Yeah, I'm fine."

Hours later, I'm still thinking about my revelation. Three days. Not all of it happened in three days, but close enough. I'd blame the rain and being stuck inside. Except usually I get snippy when I'm forced into someone's company. I suspect most people do.

A little space never hurt anyone. Maybe this thing between us is too new. We're still in that golden zone, the time when everything feels fresh and new. Eventually things will fall apart. I'll have to figure that out when the time comes.

I glance at Slade. He's absorbed in his book once more. I'm supposed to be crocheting, but I keep miscounting so I've given up. The humidity has finally broken, the rain has stopped, and we're hanging out on my little front porch. It's a weird sensation, and I don't know how to deal with it—the contentment of this moment.

"You know, we could extend this porch," he says, breaking me from my disjointed thoughts. "There's enough land to push it out, then swing it around this side. Opening up the kitchen would be a whole thing, but you could build a deck off the space. It would be closer to the river. You'd have to close the curtains when it rained. Still, it could work."

"Sounds like a big commitment."

"I mean, you're not wrong. Maybe I just really like big porches." He chuckles, shaking his head.

I narrow my eyes and wait for him to continue. Instead, he goes back to his book. I open my mouth to ask him more about the porch or what his book is about. I don't know how to keep the conversation going, though. Dropping my chin to my chest, I struggle to focus on the yarn. The loops blur together, and I huff.

"Why are you knitting?" he murmurs, flipping to a new page.

"I'm crocheting. It's relaxing," I huff as I unravel a few stitches.

"Looks like it."

I inhale sharply and glare at him. "It is. And when you get done, you have something you can say you made."

"Do you *use* the things you make?"

I glance at the leaves shivering through the trees. "Been a while since I've finished anything. I used the bag I made once when I was living in the city."

"You lived in the city?"

I nod, slipping my crochet hook back into the hole. "Back when Holden was convinced I'd get lost in the woods if I didn't live with him. It was…noisy." I peek at him when he hums. "How did you and Holden meet?"

"He never told you? It's a funny story, actually. About five years ago, I was on my way back from visiting my sister Gemma."

"The one who lives north of here now?"

"One and the same. She also lived in the city then. Thought she could make it in the corporate world even though she hated it." He waves his hand away as if it's too much to explain. "Anyways, I was on my way back to Moon Cove and was driving at night. Took a wrong turn and ended up on gravel. Holden's car had broken down on the side of the road, and I stopped."

"Why in the sweet goddess would you stop?" Anyone else would think it was a trap. I'd never pull over for a broken-down car, especially at night. You call someone and let them deal with it.

He shrugs and gives me a soft smile. "I like to help. Besides, he wasn't in the car. He'd taken off into the woods. Found out later he hadn't shifted in a while and it was close to the new moon. You know, he never did tell me whether he was forced to shift or just decided that was the perfect opportunity."

"Knowing Holden, he was forced. He used to put it off until the last minute. Old habits die hard with him," I whisper.

I'm the reason he developed that particular habit. He was always terrified of leaving me on my own. I probably didn't help matters since I was scared I'd lose it if he wasn't around to keep me in line. I lived most of my childhood and early years being afraid of my own powers. It took my brother a long time to recognize I'd grown since those days of cowering under the covers when other kids would knock on the door to play.

"Either way, I was checking out the car when he came back. I swear he was about to hit me until I shifted." He chuckles as if being attacked is a normal experience for people. "I, uh, can tell if someone else is a shifter. Told you that, I suppose. Anyways, we figured out neither of us knew what was wrong with his car—"

"No shit," I mumble.

He keeps talking like I never interrupted. "So I offered to drive us to the nearest place to stay. We had to stay in that shithole an entire week until the local mechanic in some podunk town could fix it. Spent a good amount of time exploring the area. There was this cave they kept cheese in. We tried to get in, but they wouldn't let us. Almost got arrested. It was a good time. We always said we'd go back and do a bunch of cave tours all over the state. Never got around to it, though."

"Why not?"

He shrugs, yet there's an emotion in his dark eyes I can't identify. "Life just got in the way, I suppose. He did say he was visiting his sister." He smirks at me, then runs his gaze down my body. "I probably should have tagged along a lot sooner."

I roll my eyes, though butterflies erupt in my stomach. "I would have thrown you in the river."

"Pretty sure you wanted to when I first showed up."

"Still might," I mutter, picking up my project once more.

"You do that a lot, don't you? Randomly meet people and befriend them?"

"Yeah, kind of my thing. Like I said, I enjoy helping others. Traveling around, meeting people, finding new places. Especially when you find those little hole-in-the-wall ones that have the best fucking food or some random gem? Yeah, I like it."

I force a smile to my face. I don't know how to respond. Everything he's said is fine. Better than fine. He seems to have found exactly what he wants from life. Jealousy burns within me. Acknowledging the feeling might help in the long run, but right now it's hot and painful. The sensation rips through me, flaying me alive as all my insecurities tumble from the pit I've shoved them into.

I want to know what my purpose is in life. I want to know what makes me content. Not a fleeting happiness or a resigned silence. I want to know what it's like to be satisfied with who I am.

Before Slade bulldozed his way into my life, I thought I was comfortable. I spent so much time convincing myself I was fulfilled. Finding out I was merely lying to myself isn't an easy pill to swallow. I accepted I wasn't meant for anything more than what the goddess deemed good enough. Somewhere deep down, I mourn the ignorant peace I waded through without a thought.

I'll deal with it tomorrow. Or the next day. Or the day after that. I may not be able to go back and forget my revelations, but I can enjoy these moments while they last. It's the only way I'll be able to survive without completely falling apart.

So when Slade grins at me, I return the gesture. When he grabs my things and tosses them on the small table, I let him. And when he kisses me, I kiss him back.

# Chapter 25

## Slade

As days stretch into weeks, we fall into an easy cadence. It's exactly what I imagined back when I was sure pursuing Scarlett would be a mistake. It might still be, but I'm not going to change anything. Sometimes, she gets a look in her eyes—wariness or indecision. By the time I fully look at her, it's gone. More than once I've opened my mouth to question her. Opening that can of worms seems…ill-advised.

I swipe the sweat from my brow and lean on the broom I was just using. The back room is finally finished. I've been pushing myself to complete it. In these quiet moments, though, my thoughts go wild. Which is why I usually don't stop. Filling my days with the renovation and spending time with Scarlett. When I'm with her, she takes my entire attention.

Except she's not here right now. She went into town and insisted I stay home. I don't like it. As she reminded me, though, she's a grown-ass woman capable of going into a tiny village she's been to a thousand times before on her own. I didn't have an argument for that.

I rub my chest as my wolf batters against the bonds keeping me from shifting. He whines and I sigh.

"We can't go running after her," I mutter. "She's perfectly

fine on her own. In fact, by the time we get there, she'd probably be home. So settle the fuck down."

He whimpers in response, then rams my chest again. I swear he's gotten worse since we moved into the house. I need to shift soon before he forces the issue. If I did it right now, though, he'd take off after Scarlett. She probably wouldn't be happy if a wolf showed up in the middle of the cafe and followed her around.

I wander into the demoed bathroom and shake my head. I haven't touched it since I destroyed the place. Scarlett hasn't said a word about it. Or about how I basically ripped the medicine cabinet off the wall. It hangs awkwardly, and I sigh before grabbing hold of it. The screws give easily, but apparently they glued the back to the wallpaper. I drop it next to the shattered toilet, then immediately scoop it up again. Might as well get going on cleaning up my mess.

"Quit your bitching," I mutter to my wolf as he whines in my head. "She'll appreciate not living with this when we're finished."

I'm walking around in search of a shovel when my phone buzzes. After Kira called, I expected her to keep bombarding me with messages. Instead, it's been silence from all my siblings. I texted our mom, just like Kira asked me to. Nothing came from it really. Mom brushed me off and said Kira was just struggling with guilt at leaving. It makes sense, but still.

Holden's name flashes across the screen, and I answer, a tremble in my hands. "Holden?"

The line crackles, and I hold my breath as I strain to hear. "Slade?"

"Yeah, you're cutting out a lot. Are you okay?"

There's a pause and when he speaks again, it's disjointed and sounds like he's in a tunnel. "Fine…Tell Scarlett I'm…Gonna be a…Trip."

"Dude, I can't hear you. Can you text me?"

The line drops, and I pull my phone away to stare at the

screen. I don't know where Holden went or what he's doing. Hopefully, he'll be able to send a message, but I'm not counting on it. Scarlett would freak out if I told her. Then again, if I keep this from her and she found out later, she'd be pissed.

The last few weeks, we've been living in a cocoon. Holden's call feels like the needle that's been hanging over us. Our little bubble will pop, and I don't know where we'll go from there. She could insist I leave or demand I go find him. Wouldn't matter since I wouldn't even know where to start. Holden and I might be friends, but we're not besties. If he didn't tell his sister, he wasn't going to open up to me.

My screen goes black, and I slip it into my pocket. I'll deal with it later. Holden's a big boy. He can handle himself.

The last thing I want to do now is clean up. I don't have much else to do when it comes to renovations. Scarlett refuses to tell me what else she wants done. My phone buzzes again, and I almost drop it when I fish it out.

"Hello? Holden?" I yell.

"Um, no. Is this Slade?" a soft voice asks.

They sound familiar, yet when I check the number, I don't recognize it. "Yes? Who's this?"

"Sorry, this is Naomi. I own the—"

"I remember you, Naomi." I'm being rude, but I'm too wound up to care.

"Oh, that's…new. Okay, I got your number from Scarlett."

"Where is she?" I'm already moving, kicking debris aside.

She hums and there's a jingle on her end. "So, she came into town to drop off some bread. She mentioned going to the general store next. Except I saw Gunner go in there a minute ago. It could be nothing, but—"

"I'll be right there." I hang up and take off down the porch stairs.

My car sits in the driveway where I left it, covered in dirt. I doubt it will start, but I try anyway. Of course it doesn't. My wolf strains against the bonds, and I dash for the tree line. Between one step and the next, my wolf bursts through.

I hide in the back of my mind, allowing him to take over completely. He'll find her much faster than I could. Besides, I'll have to shift back when I get there. Thank fuck the goddess had the good sense to allow our clothes to shift with us, otherwise this would be one of those awkward situations.

Our paws hit the ground hard as we dodge trunks and jump over fallen trees. In less than half the time it usually would, the outskirts of town come into view. It takes everything in me to force my wolf to stop in the bushes behind someone's house.

He fights me as I shift back, leaving me woozy and disoriented. I barely felt the magic, which is never a good sign. If I keep pushing myself, I'll end up crashing.

I prowl through the streets, searching for Scarlett. Naomi said she was at the general store. Gunner might have tried to grab her, though. If he hurts her, I'm going to bury him so deep in the woods no one will be able to find him. If he makes her cry, I'll return the favor. It doesn't even matter what Scarlett says. I'm not about to let anyone hurt her.

As I pass Naomi's bakery, she hurries outside. She wrings her hands as she falls into step next to me.

"You got here quick," she whispers, and I grunt. "He just was saying something a couple days ago at the cafe. I went in for lunch and was sitting—"

I halt, then spin toward her. "Naomi, I don't mean to be rude, but I need you to get to the fucking point. Because if she's in there"—I jab my finger at the store—"and he's laid a fucking finger on her, I'm going to burn this entire town to the ground."

She nods, wide eyes fixed on mine. "He said Scarlett should pay for the scene she caused. And spoiling the surprise. Also, he mentioned something about her making it storm and ruining the party. I believe the word 'witch' was thrown around. Which is ridiculous, but he's an asshole."

"Thank you. You should go back to your store. Accomplice and all that."

I march off, not bothering to see if she took my advice. It's ridiculous to think Gunner believes in witches. I don't even know if they exist, and I'm part of the supernatural. I'm sure there's all types of shifters I've never encountered before. Scarlett herself is proof of that. Doesn't mean Gunner is smart enough to know about witches while I'm in the dark.

The door slams open, practically ripping the bell off the wall. It clatters around, and six people swing their gazes toward me. The man behind the counter points to the back. I nod my thanks, then prowl through the aisles. It's not a large store, yet it takes longer than I'd like to find them.

Rage boils up in me when I spot them. Gunner has her cornered, blocking her exit. He doesn't see me as I sidle up next to them. Scarlett meets my gaze and widens her eyes. I'm not entirely sure what she's trying to tell me.

Doesn't matter since my fist is flying and he's falling and Scarlett's groaning. I gesture to her and grab her hand when she holds it out. Gunner's still writhing on the ground, cursing me out and clutching his cheek while blood drips from his nose. I don't give a fuck.

"Slade, that was—"

"Don't, Scarlett. I'm two seconds away from beating him with that bigfoot statue, and Jake would probably put his boot up my ass if he found out."

"But that was—"

I spin her around and trap her against the changing room door. I stare into her eyes, willing her to see how close to the edge I really am. My wolf hasn't stopped howling, and I'm barely holding on to my sanity. If she says anything to defend him, I'll shatter into a million pieces.

"Don't push me, Scarlett."

She bites her bottom lip, and I swear she's fighting a grin. "That was hot. Can you hit him again?"

"For fuck's sake," I growl.

I grab her hand again and pull her through the store to the stares of everyone. Apparently my little stunt attracted quite the crowd. Maybe they'll think twice about messing with her. I won't always be around to protect her. I glance at her when we reach the sidewalk and realize she's practically glowing. It's a far cry from how she acted at the party.

"What happened?" I snarl softly.

"We'll talk about it when we get home. Maybe…after other things, too." Her cheeks redden, and I suck in a sharp breath.

"We're kind of in the middle of town, beautiful. You'll have to wait longer for that."

"Oh, I can wait." She wiggles her eyebrows at me and skips down the sidewalk, still clinging to my hand. "How'd you know?"

"Naomi," I say as I kick my leg out to adjust myself. "She called. I came."

"Just like you will be later," she mutters, then giggles. "Did you see how he went down like a sack of potatoes? Goddess, that was glorious. I've wanted to do that for ages. Pompous asshole."

I glance around at the townspeople who've gathered outside the shops. "Maybe don't gloat so loud."

"Oh, whatever. Maybe they'll learn not to fuck with me. Wish I would have done it myself, honestly."

I tug her across the street, then between two buildings. We reach the gazebo I pulled her through weeks ago. We haven't talked about Naomi being a shifter yet, but that's the last thing on my mind. When we reach the trees, she grabs my ass and squeezes.

"Scarlett," I growl in warning and spin around to cage her against one of the trunks.

"What?" She blinks innocently at me.

"For someone who didn't even want to be seen with me a few weeks ago, you're awfully handsy. Not that I'm complaining." I smirk, raising an eyebrow.

She huffs out a laugh. "Can't a girl live a little? Not like I've had anyone rock someone's shit for me before. It was hot and I'm not going to apologize for thinking so."

She tips her chin up, and I shake my head, chuckling. She presses her lips together and drags her fingertip down my chest. I grab her wrist before she gets too far.

"If you keep it up, we won't get home before I'll be forced to do something about it."

"About what?"

I push my hips into hers, letting her feel how hard I am. My wolf howls in my head. He knows what he wants and he doesn't care whether we're in public or not. He wants to claim her, just like I do.

"You're playing with fire, beautiful."

She inhales shakily, then winds her arms around my neck. "I'd make some quippy joke about not being afraid of getting burned, but I doubt you'd appreciate that."

"Is that so?"

She smirks, digging her nails into my skin. "I will say, I can be quiet if you can."

# Chapter 26

## Scarlett

Slade glances around, then leans to peek behind the tree. He steps back and disappointment crashes through me. Still, I allow him to grab my hand. Desire swoops in my gut when he tugs me deeper into the trees. Maybe I jumped the gun.

The branches of the weeping willows sweep low, almost touching the ground. It's excellent coverage if someone followed us. I doubt anyone would, especially after Slade's display in the general store. I'm sure the news spread fast, and that's why there were more people than normal hanging out on the sidewalks.

Slade swings around, his eyes darting from one trunk to another. I bounce on the balls of my feet, waiting for him to pick a spot. If he takes too long, I just might have to take over. I'm suddenly very glad I chose a sundress today. Not only is it green, allowing me to blend into the trees, but I won't have to get completely naked on the outskirts of town.

My body trembles in anticipation when he tugs me toward him and kisses me hard. He softens slightly, then digs his fingers into my ass. A soft moan leaves me, and he slides his tongue along mine. I squeal when he picks me up and he chuckles. He presses my back into a trunk, the bark smoother than I expected.

He sinks his teeth into my neck, and I moan as I cling to him. His body practically vibrates as he slides his hands under my dress.

"No panties? Naughty girl," he whispers.

He glances between us as I run my fingers down his chest to his pants. It's not easy to unbutton them with the angle and one hand.

"A little help," I mutter.

"Both hands, beautiful. I won't let you fall."

I huff but drop my hold on him and work the metal through the hole. I make quick work of the zipper, then use my heels to shove his pants down a little.

"Your ass is too fluffy," I whine, and he shushes me.

"I don't want my ass hanging out, anyway. If someone comes up on us, I don't want to be mooning them."

I snort at the visual, and he digs his fingers into my skin. I slip my hand into his boxers and wrap my fingers around his shaft. He sucks in a sharp breath, and his throat bobs with the effort to stay silent. He's hard, more than ready, and I stroke him as best I can at this angle.

"Scarlett," he warns through gritted teeth. We don't have time for me to tease him, though I wish we did.

He grabs my wrist, but I don't let go. I smirk as he tugs until his length springs free. He moves his hand to my ass once more. He presses his hips closer, and I yelp as the bark digs into my back.

"How's this going to—" A moan cuts off the rest of my question as he lowers me onto his cock. I latch onto his shoulders and drop my face to my chest as he fills me completely. I tip my head up to gaze at him.

He rests his forehead against mine. "As much as I'd like to take my time, we don't have that luxury. And remember to be quiet."

"Yes, sir."

A growl erupts from him, and he pulls out, then slams back in. I lock my ankles behind his back and cling to him as he plunges into me, never slowing. He buries his face into my cleavage—I wonder if he'll suffocate in there. Heat sparks inside me and pleasure fans the flames. I urge him on as my orgasm builds.

My brain short-circuits as I crash over the edge. Slade follows, groaning my name. Birds take flight overhead. I bite his shoulder while my own shake as I try not to laugh.

"Never sent birds scattering when I've orgasmed before," he murmurs with a chuckle.

Something crashes through the underbrush to our right, and we both freeze. My wide eyes meet his, and he grimaces all while fighting back laughter.

For a full ten seconds, we stare at each other. When voices rise above the wind rustling through the leaves, he pulls out of me and I drop my legs. I smooth down my dress as he tucks himself away.

As the voices come closer, Slade grabs my hand and tugs me through the drooping branches. He shushes me as a giggle escapes me. He glances over his shoulder with a grin. Happiness bubbles within me, and it hits me—I could get used to this. I really want to get used to this.

Slade clears his throat, and I glance over my shoulder. I turn back to the shower and rinse off the suds left behind from my cleaner. From the look on his face, I'm not going to like this conversation.

"Something you needed?" I ask when he doesn't speak.

"I forgot to tell you something, but I need you to not freak out."

I drop the scrub brush and face him. "Not a great way to start."

He winces, and I wonder if he's about to get arrested or something. Maybe he has felonies in another state and the law is after him. Could be that he hurt his hand when he punched Gunner. Then again, he had no problem holding me up against the tree.

"Holden called me." He tenses as if I'll hit him or something.

I nod, waiting for him to say more. "And?"

He lets out a heavy sigh. "And I couldn't really hear him. He didn't have good reception, I don't think. He might have been saying he was going on a trip and wanted you to know."

"Okay."

He's waiting for me to blow up. For me to make a decision. Maybe demand he go and find my brother or do something rash like run off to find him myself. I'm sure my breakdown when Holden first disappeared hasn't helped Slade's perception of me. Doesn't help I didn't open up to him. I never told him how much I've been thinking of my brother.

While Holden doesn't disappear often, he's done it before. And I can't blame him. He's spent most of his life looking after me. First, because I was a lorelei and then because of my illness. He always thought he had an obligation to take care of me. It must be exhausting for him—always worrying. Always wondering when I'll crash again.

"Slade, I'm fine. You can relax. I've come to grips with the fact my brother is fine. And even if he's not, well, there's nothing I can do to change it. He told me he was going to be unreachable. It's not like he dropped off the face of the planet without a word. My getting worked up about it has more to do with me than him." I grab the brush again, intent on finishing cleaning the shower.

"You going to expand on that or should I just let it go?" He doesn't seem upset with either option.

"You're confusing. You know that, right?" I say with a laugh.

He leans against the door frame, his shirt stretching across his chest. "I think I'm a pretty open book."

"If I tell you to let it go, will you? I don't mean will you nod and walk away. I mean, will you honestly not bring it up later when we're bickering or early in the morning when we first wake up? Could you truly let it go and not worry about it?"

He presses his lips together and gazes at a spot above my head. "I could let it go, I think. I'd worry about *you*, but I wouldn't hold it against you. Because that's what I think you're actually asking. If you don't want to explain yourself, then that's your business. Might hurt, though."

"My not sharing with you would hurt?"

I'm still getting used to him actually caring. I convinced myself sleeping together was just a fling—something to pass the time while he worked on the house. He's been trying to get to know me since he got here. When we finally gave in and slept together, I told myself it was because he was trying to get in my pants. The last few weeks, though, I've realized he might actually care.

"Of course it would." He steps forward and cups my cheeks. "Turns out I actually kind of like you, beautiful. And your butt. I *really* like your butt."

I tamp down the anxiety his statement elicits. The longer he's here, the further I fall. Everything about this spells disaster. I still feel like I'm heading straight for heartbreak. It's not that I think he's lying. He probably does like me, care about me, but that's not enough to base anything on. A relationship needs to be built on more than *oh, he's cute and funny.* Communication, trust, common goals, all those important things are more important.

I smile, then pull from his grasp. I can't open up with him touching me. "There's never been a time Holden wasn't there for me. We may not live together or even be close to each other, really, but he's always been a phone call away. I think I relied on that too much. I've lived with this…illness for a long time, and I convinced myself I couldn't do it alone. So, when he said he was going silent, I panicked. There's also the fact he wouldn't tell me where he was or what he was doing. With him always hovering, I guess I was trying to repay him by worrying."

"How does your worrying repay him for being family?"

I shrug, glancing away. "We don't have a family like yours, Slade. Our parents were hands-off. We didn't get life advice or extra love. If we were fighting, we didn't have other siblings to go to. We only had each other. Plus, you grew up in a shifter community. Other people knew what you were. They probably supported you, guided you. Hell, you probably had classes like shifting one-oh-one or some shit."

His nose wrinkles. "We did, but we didn't call it that."

"See? That's what I mean. You're used to having all this support. You can just call up your dad for advice or pop by on a Sunday morning and your mom will feed you. I'm not saying you didn't have issues or problems. It's just a lot easier to get through those things when you have others to catch you."

He's nodding like he understands, but I doubt he can. Not fully, anyway. I doubt anyone could if they didn't grow up like I did. He can't grasp what it would be like not to have anyone to lean on.

"Are you still struggling then? Because it seems like his phone call hasn't had an impact on you at all."

"Nope. I'm good. Well, as good as I can be while I'm figuring things out. It'll be fine. I've leaned on him less and less these last couple years. I bought this house and started selling my baked goods. I've got everything I need right here."

His brows pull low, and I brace myself. "Except what happens when you need help?"

"I hire someone."

"And someone to talk to? A shoulder to cry on?" He presses

his lips together like he doesn't want to go on. "What happens if you get sick? If you have a particularly bad flareup and you need someone, who do you call?"

I open my mouth, then snap it shut again. I don't know who I'd call if my brother wasn't around. Slade may not know much about leplexia, but I do. If things progress, I could end up in a bad way.

"Even if that happened, which I doubt it will because it almost never does, it's not like they'd be able to help. They can't take me to a hospital or a doctor. I've never found anyone in the community who knows how to deal with this. It's been a series of trials and errors. It's all I have. So, I'd call no one, because no one can actually help." When I catch the devastation on his face, I tense. "I don't say that to sound pathetic. Or like I wouldn't do anything. This isn't me giving up. I'm just being realistic."

"That's...sad. Scarlett, you shouldn't have to live like that. You could at least have Naomi. She wants to be your friend. You just have to let her in."

I'm already shaking my head before he's finished. "You don't know what would happen then."

"Neither do you."

He presses a kiss to my forehead, then walks out, leaving me with his final words. My instinct is to go after him and make him understand. If I argue with him long enough, he'll finally get it.

And when I finally got through to him, I'd be wrong. Blissfully wrong. I don't know what would happen if I befriended Naomi. If I wasn't sick, it would be easier. If I wasn't a lorelei, I might not think twice about it.

Except I am sick and I'm not a regular human. I'm not even a regular shifter. Slade said something about cryptids, but I'm not really one of them either. Most shifters think we're a myth. When they do meet one of us, most of them think we're lying.

It's exhausting. I'm sure Naomi is too nice to do something like that. Doesn't mean something bad wouldn't happen.

It's another minute before I follow Slade. He's in the kitchen, wiping down the counters.

"Okay, I'm not saying you're wrong…"

He chuckles, shaking his head. "But I am, of course."

"No, you're not. I'm just saying I need to talk through this to see where it ends. And I need to do that out loud. Might as well talk at you rather than the shower door."

He points at the stool, and the tightness in my chest eases. "I'm loath to point this out, but you realize this is you opening up, right?"

"Yeah, yeah, yeah. Listen, I get that letting in some people wouldn't *seem* like a big deal. Obviously, I can make friends," I say, and he gives me a look. "I'm serious. I have to force myself to be a bitch to people. It goes against everything I am, being a lorelei. Which is the problem. I'm not a shifter, at least not a normal one like you."

He holds up a hand. "I object to the use of 'normal' since it suggests anyone else is abnormal."

"Okay, so, not normal. Typical. I'm not a typical shifter. Say I befriend Naomi. We hang out, eat scones, take walks—"

He busts out laughing, and I scowl. "What are you from, the Victorian era? You're not taking a turn about the promenade while discussing the upcoming Season where they'll present you as an eligible bride. For goddess sake, Scarlett. Do you not know what friends do?"

"It's not the important part of the hypothetical," I snap. "We become friends and do *friend* things. Then things start to morph. I'm asking her for help and she's obliging—"

"As friends do."

"And then suddenly she's cleaning my entire house and signing over her bakery to me because I inadvertently used my powers on her. And when I figure out what the fuck is going on, it's too late. Do you know how the victims feel? After I've sucked them of all their free will, do you know what they're like? Husks. Not literally. But they wander about with no purpose. Some of them don't know how to function anymore. They don't remember who they were before they became whatever *I* wanted them to be. Do you honestly think I should subject Naomi to that possible existence because I want a *friend*? That'd be selfish."

He leans over and props his arms on the counter. "So you think if you hang out with someone, you'll eventually corrupt them."

"Happened before," I mutter.

"To you?"

"Well, no, but—"

"How do you know that's what will happen?"

I grit my teeth, realizing I shouldn't have even brought this up. "Because that's what I've been told."

"Except it hasn't happened to me. I'm not being manipulated by you. There's something to be said for being under your spell, though."

"Slade," I groan. "I need you to be serious."

His grin fades. "I am. I'm just not good at showing it. I thought if I could make you laugh, you'd feel better. But you're right, this is a serious concern of yours."

I don't know what else to say. He's never going to understand the fear I live with every day. Letting him in was the hardest thing I've done in a long time. I can't remember the last time I threw caution to the wind.

"Yet," I whisper, and he raises an eyebrow. "I'm worried you'll—"

"You're not going to lure me to do something I don't want to do, Scarlett. Why is it so hard to think I genuinely enjoy spending time with you?"

I don't have an answer. Not one he'll be satisfied with. "I

know you do. I'm just worried about a day from now. Or a week from now. If I get too comfortable, anything could happen."

I'm not looking further into the future than a week. His car will be fixed by then and he'll no longer be stuck here. He may like spending time with me and fucking me, but that doesn't mean anything. Not long term. Asking him what his plans are isn't something I can do right now. I'm not ready for his answer. Until I am, I'm going to take his advice and just see where this thing goes. Just like he said.

Except I'm pretty sure I've already fallen for him.

# Chapter 27
## Slade

Scarlett lets out a frustrated cry and throws the wrench down. She wipes her greasy hands on a towel and glares at the engine of my car. I've stayed out of her way, mostly waiting for her to ask me to hold a flashlight. I only asked once if I could help and got a muttered curse in response.

I lean back on my hands, my palms sinking into the thick blanket, and cross my ankles. She stomps off toward the river, and I track her until she disappears around the side of the house.

Thankfully, I don't have to worry about her right now. She's already done this half a dozen times. In about ten minutes she'll come back, calmer and ready to try again. I told her I'd pay to have it towed, but I'm pretty sure this has become a pride thing for her now.

My mind skips back to the conversation we had a few days ago. We haven't discussed her fears again, but I know they still haunt her. I catch her watching me when she thinks I'm not looking. Convincing her I'm fine and making my own decisions will take time. With her, it could take years. The thought doesn't scare me as much as it once did.

I lie back and peer at the fluffy clouds overhead. This is usually the point where I'm ready to move on. More than a few months in a place and I get antsy. Not this time. I'd be content to stay here for a while, maybe forever. It might be too soon for those thoughts, though.

I keep waiting for the jittery feeling to hit me. Instead, I get anxiety when I think of leaving her. Not because she needs someone to take care of her or needs help. It's just her—spending time with her, sleeping next to her every night, getting to know her.

It's as if my eyes have been opened to something I never thought possible. Not for me. Falling for someone was everyone else's destiny. With Scarlett, the possibility is there, sitting just outside my reach. I just have to keep striving for it.

"Are you going to help me?" Scarlett snaps as she stomps back into view.

"Any time you want, beautiful."

She scowls, blowing the strands of hair out of her face. "Don't call me that when I look like this."

I jump to my feet and loop my arm around her waist when she tries to walk away. "You're beautiful when you're all greasy from being a badass mechanic. You're beautiful when you're floury and wearing an apron. You're beautiful when your hair's all staticky when you first wake up. You're beautiful when—"

"Stop," she says with a laugh, trying to escape my hold.

I press a kiss to her neck, then let her go. She scowls over her shoulder, but a smile breaks through. She mutters something about finishing the car, and I lie back down.

"Do you need a pillow, sir?"

"What'd I tell you about calling me sir? Don't think I won't bend you over the trunk, Scarlett."

She coughs, and I tuck my hands under my head, closing my eyes. I don't know how long I doze, but Scarlett's whoops have me shooting upright.

"Finally got it on. Go fire her up and see if it worked," she calls.

I push to my feet. Sliding into the driver's seat feels weird after not driving for so long. Half my adult life has been spent behind the wheel. Scarlett always drives when we go into town. Not that we've been doing that lately.

Naomi took it upon herself to pick up the orders since my display in the general store. Apparently, Bernice was shooting off her mouth all while wanting more cakes and breads. Both she and Naomi have been selling out much earlier than normal. I don't want to say it's because I put the town bully in his place, but I think it might be. Maybe Scarlett's not the only one who's had problems with the Tates.

She gives me a thumbs up, and I turn the key. The motor chugs, not fully turning over. I barely catch Scarlett's scowl before she disappears under the hood. A loud thwack reaches me, and the engine roars to life. I push out and can't help the smile on my face when I find her jumping up and down.

I pick her up and swing her around while she squeals. When I put her down, she grabs my face and kisses me soundly.

"I told you I could fix it," she says smugly.

"I had no doubt. Probably won't be driving it much, but you did a great job. Now will you show me how to bake the sourdough?"

She rolls her eyes. "Yes, fine, we can go bake now."

I pick her up and carry her inside. She takes off to shower, telling me to wait until she's there before touching anything. We already fed the starter this morning so it should be ready. At least, that's what she said. I end up puttering around the kitchen, grabbing the large glass bowl she usually uses and the ingredients on the recipe card.

"I told you not to touch anything," she scolds, and I grin.

"You know, my mom has recipe cards like this. No one else in the family likes to cook like she does. Pretty sure she cried one Yule because she thought no one would want them when she died." I laugh at the memory, and Scarlett hits me in the arm. "It's fine.

She'd just had a little too much wine. I promised her I'd take them. Then she pushed me in the lake later and said I wasn't allowed to touch them because I wouldn't appreciate them. When I tell her I successfully made sourdough, I'm hoping she'll change her mind."

"Well, she can give them to me. I'd appreciate them a lot more than you would."

She bustles around the kitchen, not realizing what she just said. She mustn't. I've never had someone want to meet my mom, much less promise to take care of her recipe cards. It's hard to think she's the same person who just days ago said I wouldn't stick around more than a week.

She sets the scale in front of me. "Okay, so first we're going to weigh the ingredients."

"Why do we weigh them? Isn't that what they invented measuring cups for?"

She shrugs and hands me a large cup. "You can, but this is more accurate. Baking is more of a science. If you're more precise, it'll turn out better. At least, for me. I know some people who can just toss things together and they have the best damn bread in the county. I'm not one of them. If I leave it a minute too long on the counter, it overproofs. It's a whole thing."

"Gonna be honest, that's terrifying. I don't want to fuck this up."

"First of all, I'm here, so you probably won't fuck it up. Second, if you do, well, that's the nice thing about sourdough."

"It's forgiving?"

"Nope. We always got more starter." She grins. I can't bring myself to return it. "Okay, to make you feel better, we'll measure everything out first."

She grabs more bowls and sets them out. It takes a lot longer for me to do this than her. Especially since the sunlight keeps catching her hair when she passes by the window. By the time I measure out the cocoa powder, I'm so distracted I end up practically filling the bowl. She just laughs, dumps it back into the container and tells me to do it again.

"This feels like a lot of ingredients," I mumble.

"It's only seven. You're fine, Slade. I promise if it sucks I'll still eat it, then set it on the windowsill and pretend a wild animal stole it in the night."

I lean my hip against the island and cross my arms. "Bold of you to assume a wild animal would eat it. Besides, isn't chocolate bad for most animals?"

Her eyes widen and her gaze meets mine. "Wait, are you allergic to chocolate?"

"What? No. Besides, I'm a wolf, not a dog. I'm pretty sure shifters aren't allergic to anything."

Her shoulders slump in relief, and another wave of peace washes over me. If someone had told me a year ago I'd be standing in a kitchen with a woman I'm falling for and making sourdough, I would have told them they were ridiculous. Even six months ago, I would have laughed. Now it's a regular Tuesday. Actually, I have no idea if it's Tuesday.

She grabs the bowl and hands me the cup. "Okay, water and starter in the bowl."

I glance at the other ingredients and reach for the sourdough starter. "Uh, Scarlett? Is that supposed to be smoking?"

"Wha—ahh!" She rushes over to the cocoa powder and knocks the whole thing off the counter.

I don't know whether to laugh or freak out. I round the island to help, not that she needs it. She's stomping on it with bare feet while she cusses. All she's accomplishing is causing dark powder to fly everywhere.

"I think it's good. At this point, you're just making a mess."

"The damn thing started on fire. Did you know that could happen?" She pants for breath, staring at me.

I scan her from head to toe. Her bare feet are completely

covered, and she smells like chocolate. "It wasn't actually on fire, but no. I'm not the baker here so I didn't know."

She picks up one foot as if she has plans to walk to the bathroom. "Um, a little help?"

I swing her into my arms and step over the mess. "Two showers in one day? Really breaking those rules, aren't you?"

"The ten-minute shower rule was so you didn't use all the hot water."

"I'll put in a bigger water heater. Then we'll be able to shower as long as we want."

She sighs, melting into me. I set her right in the shower and step back. When I reach for her waistband, she bats my hand away.

"Just go measure out some more cocoa."

I slowly pull the door closed, then peek through the gap I've left. She peels off her shirt and throws it at the door. She shakes her head, a smile playing on her face. When she turns around, I think she's trying to hide from me. Instead, she wiggles her hips as she pushes her leggings down. She bounces her ass a few times and I grin.

"Go bake," she shouts, then throws her pants toward me. I slam the door shut. I swear I haven't stopped smiling since we figured our shit out.

When I get back to the kitchen, I'm reminded of the mess. I have no idea how to clean up powder this fine. I'm sure if I use a wet washcloth, it'll clump together. If I sweep it up, I won't get everything. I opt for a combination of both. By the time the shower cuts off, I'm busy reading the recipe card and mixing everything together.

"What does it mean to rest?" I call, then jump when she appears next to me.

"Just cover it and let it sit. Like a steak. You're letting it rest. Does something with the gluten or yeast or something. I never can remember. You cleaned?"

"Of course. Wasn't about to leave it for you to do. You saved us from burning alive."

"Very true," she says seriously. "However will you repay me?"

I smirk as I grab her hips and force her to walk backward toward the bedroom. She stumbles, then finds her footing.

"We've got thirty minutes to kill. I can think of a couple ways."

For the first time in a long time, maybe forever, I think I'm exactly where I need to be.

# Chapter 28

## Scarlett

I can't seem to keep the smile from my face. It's a weird sensation, and I'm still not sure if I should trust it. I'm practically skipping down the aisles of the grocery store. Part of me wishes Slade had come with me. He's the first person I've ever wanted to spend *more* time with. I'm finally getting to the point where I'm envisioning a future with him. Something beyond next week.

I hum while I check off items from my list. Once I've gathered everything, paid for it, and bagged it all up, I finally make my way home. I usually enjoy the drive back. I don't leave my property often, and it's a nice time to unwind. The curves are predictable and comforting. With the sun shining overhead and a little music on, I can relax. Now, I'm practically bouncing in my seat and forcing myself to slow down.

Slade said he had a surprise for me when I got home. I don't know what he could possibly have done. It's not like he goes anywhere, and I'm pretty sure he doesn't know how to get mail delivered for himself. I wouldn't be surprised if it was just his body, naked and covered in whipped cream or something.

My chest twinges as I take another curve, and I wince. The longer I'm gone, the tighter my chest becomes. I could brush it off, chalk it up to being in the car for a few hours. Except that's never my luck. Add in the rash that appeared on my side this morning while I was in the shower, and I'm pretty sure I'm heading for another flare. Even after all these years, there was a little voice in the back of my mind whispering *maybe it's gone*. I know better. Yet I still fell for it. I've gone months without symptoms, and then I'm knocked down again.

At least I know how to deal with these episodes. Slade on the other hand…

Except he's been asking me what to do if I have a flare-up. He's been probing for more information about leplexia. I should have let him call his sister to learn more. He asked if he could, but I didn't want her to make the connection. My illness isn't exclusive to my being a lorelei, but close enough. Only a few types of shifters get leplexia.

As soon as Slade calls his sister, his whole family will know. I may not have grown up in a big family, but I've seen how they work. One little whispered comment and then his father would be calling him. Slade said he was the one to go to for advice. Wise and kind and all the things people say when there's a sage old man in the movies.

I'm pretty sure his very wise and kind father would worry about him associating with me. Then he'd warn Slade about being with someone with an illness like mine. It'll never go away, never get better. From the things Slade has said, his father wouldn't tell him what to do. He wouldn't scold him or force him home. Not like mine. He would plant the seeds, though. Add in that I'm a lorelei and everything would unravel.

I shake my head. Maybe I should tell him to call his family. If Slade doesn't have all the information, he shouldn't stay. I wouldn't *want* him to stay.

I realize I've been hiding him from the world, too afraid he'll run away if he hears other people's opinions. But if he was going to change his mind about me merely because of what other people think, do I really want him sticking around? My thoughts muddle together, and I'm not entirely sure what to think anymore. I don't even make sense in my own head.

"I'll just talk to him about it when I get home," I mutter.

Slade seems to ask the right questions and reorder everything so it clicks. Makes sense why his siblings call him to fix things for them. He's actually probably a lot more like his father than he thinks. The conversation will have to wait until after his surprise, though. I'm not about to ruin anything for him.

As I crest a hill, a dark shadow flashes in the corner of my eye. I swing my head around, searching the tree line for the animal. Except nothing is there.

I slow down, not wanting to hit something. If I end up in the ditch, it won't be pretty. It occurs to me I don't have Slade's number. In the beginning, I didn't want to have any ties to him. Then I forgot because he was always there. When I was cornered by Gunner, calling him didn't even cross my mind. I make a note to ask him for it when I get back.

I swing around another curve and let out a yelp as another shadow flies across the road. I slam on the brakes and search for wherever it came from. It wasn't distinct enough to be an animal.

The leaves shiver through the trees, though there's no wind. I don't know what in the goddess is going on, but I'm not about to stick around to find out. Slade might know what's happening.

My eyes skip back and forth as I drive, searching for a silhouette to form and rush me. It's as if there's a thread tied around my heart, tugging tighter as the miles pass. It takes me twice as long to make it the rest of the way. My muscles relax when my house finally comes into view.

It's not until I'm climbing from the car that I spot another shade lurking between the trunks. I'm kicking myself for not coming in through the front of the house. It would have taken me another five minutes, though, and I didn't want to extend this trip any longer than need be.

I squint into the gloom, but the shadow vanishes. No fanfare, no zipping through the trees, just poof, it's gone.

Maybe it's just another symptom I haven't experienced yet from my illness. I'll have to call Holden—

My feet stutter to a stop and I sigh. Now I'm really going to tell Slade to call his sister. She might know how leplexia works and be able to help. I'd rather not be running from shadows my mind conjures. A tonic and some rest wouldn't be bad either.

I gather all the bags, looping everything on my arms. I should take two trips, but I won't. Especially with my eyes playing tricks on me. Next thing I know, I'll be stumbling into the river or something. I wish I could harness the giddiness I had while I was at the store, though seeing Slade will help.

I struggle my way to the house and huff when I reach the stairs. Once I'm up, I try three times to open the back door.

"Slade," I bellow, kicking at the wood.

Nothing. I grit my teeth and kick again. I press my ear to the window and strain to hear him coming. Finally, I give up and drop a few of the bags and turn the handle. It's twice as hard to grab everything again, but I manage, barely. I end up shuffling sideways down the hallway.

"Slade, where are you? I bought out half the grocery store, but we won't have to go out again for like a month." My skin burns as the plastic handles slide down my arm. "I did find some new pastries I want you to try. I might be able to recreate them."

I finally glance around the space. Nothing moves. Slade doesn't come bounding out like he usually does. My chest tightens, and I force myself to take even breaths. There's no reason to get freaked out. Yet.

"Slade?" I call tentatively as I wander around the island. "Where'd you go?"

The living room sits empty, Slade's book lying innocently on the side table with a bookmark still stuck between the pages. Despite knowing better, I search for signs of a struggle. Probably from the movie Slade made me watch last week. The bathroom door hangs open, so I know he's not there.

I don't have any luck in the bedroom either. No Slade. No nakedness. No whipped cream.

The longer I search, the higher my anxiety climbs. I didn't see him when I came in the back, yet I search there anyway. The bathroom is cleaned up, a shiny new toilet in its place. I barely glance at it. I don't have time to admire the job he did.

I slam out the back door and scan the area. The birds chirp, the wind rustles the leaves, and the creek babbles in the background. No shadows lurking about or distant shouts from an injured man.

"Maybe he had to shift," I breathe. "That's probably it. He waited too long, and he thought he'd get it over with while I was gone. There's no reason to freak out."

Slowly, I force myself to turn back to the house. Methodically, I put the groceries away. My eyes keep straying to the window. I don't have much to do now that I'm done, and I don't have it in me to relax.

I end up wandering around the rooms as if he'll magically appear. My joints ache and I make myself a cup of tea. The tonic doesn't do as much as it usually does, but that's not surprising.

As the sun marches across the sky, my nerves fray even more. I grab my phone and pull up Naomi's number. It takes me another ten minutes to finally call her. As it rings, I push out the front door.

"Hello, Scarlett," Naomi says by way of greeting. I barely hear her. There's a roaring in my ears. "Scarlett? Are you okay?"

I clear my throat. "Slade's car is gone. Is he in town?"

"Oh, not that I've seen. I've been at the bakery most of the day. Stopped by the general store and the cafe. I also got my hair cut at Lucy's. Not that I think he'd be there. Maybe he went to Belle Creek to get more lumber?"

"I, uh, just came from there. He wouldn't…It's fine. If you see him, will you give him my number? I don't think I did." I tug at the hem of my shirt, over and over. My vision blurs, but I refuse to cry.

"I'll go look for him," Naomi says, snapping me out of my spiral.

"Oh, no. You don't have to do that. I'm sure he'll be back soon and then I'll feel ridiculous for even calling you. I'm sorry. I shouldn't have bothered you." I press my lips together, desperately trying to keep my shit together.

I take measured steps down the stairs, concentrating on where his car has been parked for weeks. I just fixed it, got it running.

Was that what he was waiting for? Was he merely making the best of his time here, and as soon as it was possible, he left? Did he think it would be better to take off instead of talking to me? A cleaner break and all that. If this was his surprise, I don't want it.

"It's not a big deal. I don't mind helping. I was going to go for a walk, anyway. Bernice has been lurking about, and I wanted to be nosy—see what she's up to." From the sound of it, she's already making her way down the sidewalk. "I don't see his car. I mean, I don't see a car that I haven't seen before since I don't know what his looks like."

"It's yellow," I choke out. "Like, garishly yellow."

"Yeah, that thing would stick out like a sore thumb. I don't understand why everyone wants to buy a blue car. And why do they make so many white ones? It's like they don't expect dirt to be in, you know, on the earth. Doesn't earth *mean* dirt? I think I read that somewhere. I'd never buy a white vehicle if I could help it. Not that I have a car, but that's besides the point."

"Yeah, I don't know," I whisper as heartache wells up inside me.

I already know she won't find him. He left without a word,

leaving me with nothing but memories and a completed renovation.

Maybe that's what he meant when he said he had a surprise. Not just taking off, but being done with the projects I set out for him. Being done with me in the process.

"My rambling isn't helping you, is it? Do you need me to come out when I'm done? I don't mind."

"No, it's fine. If he doesn't want to be found, you being here won't change that."

She hums like she wants to disagree, then gasps. "You don't think he went out to the Tates' farm, do you?"

My knees almost give out. There's no reason he would need to go out there. Gunner hasn't bothered either of us since he got sucker-punched. The last time we were in town, the man practically ran the other way. Gone was his confident swagger and sardonic smirk. I never got paid for the cakes, but I didn't care. If Slade went out there, Gunner will only stir up more trouble. I stumble back up the stairs, intent on getting my keys.

"Naomi, do not go out there. I'll—" I freeze when I spot a piece of paper taped to the front door and fluttering in the breeze. My hand trembles as I catch the edge and scan the note. "I have to go. He's not at the Tates. He's fine. I have to go."

I hang up before she can question me. I read the letter again before tugging it off the door. The rest of the world falls away as I drop into the chair—*his chair*—on the porch.

His coffee cup from this morning sits empty on the table, like he didn't have enough time to take it inside when he was done. I swallow hard and read the note one more time.

SCARLETT,

SORRY I CAN'T WAIT FOR YOU TO GET BACK.
SOMETHING CAME UP AND I HAVE TO GO HOME. I
DON'T KNOW HOW LONG.
IT ISN'T YOU. IT WAS NEVER YOU.
SLADE

# Chapter 29
## Slade

"Slade? Slade." My mother's voice floats to me into the depths of my numbness.

I shake my head and focus my blurry eyes on her. "Hey, Mom. What do you need me to do?"

She gives me a sad smile and grips my hand. I squeeze her fingers, just enough to let her know I'm here. A shout from downstairs is quickly shushed. Mom glances toward the stairs and pulls in a shaky breath.

"They're not doing well," she whispers.

"None of us are. What can I do to help?"

That's all I've said the last week. *What can I do? How can I help? What do you need?* When I told Scarlett I was the fixer, I wasn't joking. It's all I know how to do for the family. It's been my role for as long as I can remember.

Except now I have no idea how to fill that role.

I'm just as lost as the rest of them. Mom's the only one holding up. I'm not entirely convinced she hasn't been keeping things to herself for months. When I asked her why, she just shook her head. I'm sure she didn't want to bother us. Except now we're all reeling and none of us knows how to deal.

"We need to set the tables out. Maybe Chase can help you?

Or Jake. Alister and Sloane went for a run, and Eli isn't holding up very well."

I bite back my reply. Telling her none of us are holding up will only hurt her. She doesn't deserve the extra guilt.

"Yeah, I can do that. In the back garden?"

"Yes. Oh, and don't let Kira help. Last time she did, her and Chase almost fell down the stairs. I'm surprised they found their way to each other with all the bickering they did." She laughs lightly, but the sound is hollow.

She squeezes my hand one last time and walks out of my childhood bedroom.

I glance around the space. Remnants of my youth, mixed with some trinkets from my travels, take up most of the shelves. I always felt oddly nostalgic yet nervous when I slept in here as an adult. Like I didn't quite fit here anymore. It's the reason I kept running. Each time, I was pulled back, though. Now, it just feels empty—a feeling I can't quite name and can't get back.

I rub my chest at the ache, then turn toward the door. Jake and Chase linger just outside, giving me the space they think I need. Jake gives me a nod, and we head across the hall.

"Gladys said people will be dropping off food soon," Jake says gruffly as he grabs a table.

"Don't know why we need more. People have been coming by for days with random dishes." Chase runs his hand through his hair as he glances around the bedroom.

"It's what people do when someone dies," I say, then press my lips together. I shove the grief away, forcing myself to keep my shit together.

Jake's hand lands on my shoulder and he squeezes. It's probably the most comfort I'll get from him. Actually, it's probably exactly what I need. Anything more and I'll shatter. He turns back to the task at hand, leaving me to rein in my emotions.

"You seen the dark watchers lately?" Chase asks. I know he's trying to distract me, and I could hug him for it.

"No. Chased me all the way to—" I clear my throat. "They disappeared once I got where I was going. Thought they'd show up once I left, but they didn't. Maybe they were just haunting me as punishment for being an asshole to you and Kira."

"Doubt it. They would have left you alone once we got everything figured out. Unless you're harboring some resentment toward me." Chase shoots me a grin, but I can't return it.

"No. I definitely am not."

Footsteps pound up the stairs, and I glance over my shoulder. My younger brother Eli flies by, and I go to follow him. Jake grabs my arm and stops me.

"Choose your words wisely. He's fragile."

"He's twenty-two, Jake. Of course he's fragile."

Sympathy swims in his eyes, and he wipes his hand over his beard. "He's not the only one."

I don't have it in me to deny it. Of course we're all hurting. If I can help Eli, though, I will. It's the only thing I know how to do right now. I trudge after my brother and hesitate when I reach his bedroom. When I knock, he doesn't answer. I crack open the door and hear his quiet sniffles.

"Eli? Can I come in?" I call softly.

"Whatever," he snaps, and I push inside, shutting the door quietly behind me.

His room isn't the time capsule mine is. Just a year ago he was still coming home for every holiday from college. His place is lived in and comfortable. No dust on the desk or emptiness in the closet. His bedsheets are mussed, though it might have been from scrambling onto the bed when he came in here.

"Might as well sit down instead of hovering by the door like you'll need to flee from my wrath," Eli says bitterly as he leans against his headboard.

I snort, the first genuine smile I've had since I got the news lifting my lips. "As if I'd be afraid of your wrath. What are you going to do? Pummel me with your noodle arms?"

He rolls his eyes. Mostly because he's not even close to having skinny arms. He's built exactly like Dad—tall and thick with the same wavy hair.

"I could take you now. You're getting old and decrepit." He sobers and tucks his chin to his chest.

I drop onto the bed and lean against the wall. "What happened?"

His head snaps up and he glares at me. "What happened? Are you fucking kidding me? Our fucking dad died, asshole. Or did you not notice while you were catching up with your *friends?*" He spits the last word out like a curse.

I bite my tongue until he settles back once more. Apparently, Jake knew exactly what he was doing when he told me to choose my words wisely. My first instinct is to smack the shit out of him. A tear slips down his cheek, and he angrily swipes it away.

Resting my head back, I stare at the poster on the opposite wall. "I had this friend, Indigo—"

"What kind of name is Indigo?"

I could take offense at his question, but I know what he's actually asking. "Black swan shifter. Rare around here, but where they were from it was pretty common. At least in their family. Anyways, they were visiting the same campground I was. We knew some of the same people. We got to talking one night after everyone else went to sleep. One of our mutual friends had just lost his mate. I couldn't understand why he would go on the trip. Wouldn't he want to stay home? Mourn her loss?"

"It's what I would do," Eli whispers and swipes another tear away.

"I thought so, too. Indigo gave me some insight, though. See, our friend didn't have any family left. Not on his or his mate's side. They were the only ones left. He came on the trip because he *needed* companionship. Being alone in the house they shared, surrounded by her memories, would only drive him further into the darkness he was feeling inside. Indigo was the one who convinced him to come along. He needed to be around us to heal—to feel some semblance of normalcy."

"Sorry," he mutters.

"I don't need your apology, Eli. You need somewhere for the anger to go, and if it's straight at me, so be it. I can handle it. Don't take it out on the girls, though."

"That's why I came up here. I didn't want to blow up at Mom. She's acting like this isn't that big of a deal. While the rest of us are losing it, she's just calm. I don't understand it." He shoves the heels of his hands into his eyes, probably trying to stop from crying.

"Mom and Dad were mates. They lived and loved for years. She knew. Even if it wasn't consciously, she knew. At least, that's what I think. She's already grieved, probably with him while he was around. And we got to see him before he went."

He swallows hard. "I don't know what to do now."

I hold out my arm, and he crawls over to me. He curls into my side like he used to do when he was little. His soft sobs fill the air, and I just hold him. A numbness spreads through me as I try not to let his sadness infiltrate me.

If I break down, I can't help anyone. My siblings need someone to be strong. They won't turn to Mom, not wanting to add to her grief. Who else will make sure Kira doesn't spiral? Or make sure Alissa doesn't disappear farther into the woods? I'll wait to fall apart later. When I'm sure they won't do the same in my absence.

"Where were you?" he asks gruffly after a few minutes.

"I'll pretend that wasn't an insult," I mutter. "I was in Hart's Hollow. Was helping a…friend."

He pushes upright and leans against the wall next to me. "A friend?"

"A friend asked me to help his sister. I was doing some renovations on her house."

"What'd she say when you left?" His gaze burns into the side of my head, but I refuse to look at him.

"She wasn't there. I left her a note." I shove off the bed. "I'm going to go help Mom. When you're ready…"

He snorts as I reach the door. "Maybe you should fix that situation before you fix the rest of us."

I grit my teeth as I walk away. Jake and Chase finished the job while I was with Eli, and now I don't know what to do. I'm sure they took the tables and the chairs out to the back garden already.

As I make my way downstairs, I listen for my siblings in the kitchen. I should help them, but I can't bring myself to. I wander out the back door and along the path toward the patio where we usually have parties.

An hour later, the space is filled with sympathetic community members. The entirety of Moon Cove shut down. All the tourists were shuffled out, citing a gas leak. With the town split into the tourist side and the shifter side, it wasn't so hard.

Magic keeps humans out of Moon Cove proper, anyway. I almost feel bad the businesses will be losing money. It's the way this place stays alive. Apparently, with my parent's large general store being closed for now, every other store closed, too. Whether out of respect or lack of customers, I don't know.

"I'd say it's good to see you, Slade, but not like this," Vince says as he shakes my hand. He's probably the closest thing Kira has to a best friend. He's grown out his light brown hair, making him look older somehow.

"Yeah," I murmur, not sure how to respond. "Did you see Kira?"

He nods, glancing around. "And Chase. He still seems wary with me, but I think he's coming around. You think I could steal him away from her?"

My lips twitch like they want to smile yet can't. "Doubt it. Mates and all that. If anyone could, I'd put my money on you."

He narrows his gaze. "You don't have to force it, Slade."

"Force what?"

He grips my shoulder. "Being okay."

He walks away, disappearing into the crowd. Usually, these occasions are punctuated with laughter and joy and excitement. I barely get done with one conversation before I'm being pulled into another.

Tonight, nothing is normal. Nothing is usual. Nothing is the same. It's subdued and quiet and sorrowful. And I'm hiding in the corner like a scared pup, not sure where to go or what to do.

"Dad would have hated this," Alissa mumbles as she drops into the chair next to me. "He'd hate everyone crying over him." She hands me a drink and takes a sip of her own.

"Remember when Old Man Harrison died? I was like fifteen, and we had the reception here. No one knew what to do since he was always around. Then Dad brought out those old speakers he kept in the basement and started blasting eighties hairbands?" I stare at the crowd gathered, then glance away when I notice their tears.

"Did he headbang, too? I feel like I remember that."

I smile, shaking my head. "Yeah, he did. Pretty sure Mom made him stop when he broke the table."

"Wait, I don't remember that part."

"He was dancing on it, playing air guitar. One of the table legs snapped and Mom freaked out on him, saying he was going to break his hip."

She snorts, rolling her eyes. "Yes, that thirty-six hours it would have taken to heal would have been devastating."

I watch our mom greeting others. Gracious, smiling, and elegant. She's usually more…vibrant. It's like Dad took her glow with him when he died.

"Slade," Alissa whispers, and I turn toward her. "Did they tell you how he died? Because no one will tell me."

"Because you'd drive yourself into a hole trying to research it. You'd think you could have prevented it, even though we all know you couldn't."

"But if I—"

"No one could have stopped it, Alissa. You saw him. He was too far gone, and it doesn't matter what ultimately took him out. It's no one's fault. No one's to blame. It's just part of life. You know that. The goddess decides. We just let the moon guide us."

She scowls and slumps down in her seat. "I hate that epitaph. It's ridiculous. *Let the moon guide you.* As if the moon ever sent us somewhere good."

"Bet if you asked Gemma or Kira, they'd tell you all the good things that came from letting the moon guide them."

She turns toward me and I meet her gaze. Her eyes are so similar to mine, it's like looking in a mirror. I never gave much thought to how alike the Livia siblings are, yet so different.

I wonder if Dad wondered about these things, too. Probably, but I never took the time to ask. Regret slams into me, making it hard to breathe.

"Did Dad tell you to look after us? Is that why you're trying to be all wise? You can't take his place, Slade," she mutters.

I shake my head. "No, he didn't."

She doesn't press further, thankfully. I'm not ready to talk to her or anyone about our last conversations. Mostly, it was him repeating the advice he's always said. *Let the moon guide you. Don't run under the full moon. Live life as the goddess intends.* There were no grand declarations or sage words of wisdom I haven't heard before.

"It wasn't your fault either," she whispers. "You know that, right?"

"Mhm." It's not that I think I could have saved him. The guilt still eats at me.

"Slade, I'm serious."

"I just wish I would have been here more. I was always chasing another adventure instead of—"

"You were living your life, Slade. Just like I was when I moved into the woods. And Gemma when she went to college. And Kira when she moved to Whispering Pines. And Alister when he fucked off to the high seas. Dad wouldn't have wanted you to put everything on hold just to be near them." She shakes her head, and her nostrils flare as she fights back tears. "I just don't know what Mom's going to do now."

"I can—"

"You can't fix this, Slade. No one can fix this. Like you said, this is part of life. You can't fix us."

She pushes to her feet and wanders off, leaving me to sit with everything. She doesn't realize how hard it is for me to accept I can't fix this. It's all I know how to do.

I make my way toward the beverages. I don't remember finishing the drink Alissa gave me, but apparently I did.

Pushing through the sea of black isn't easy. Doesn't help I hate we wear black to these types of things. Fadings, Joinings, First shifts—we wear black like the new moon to signify the new beginning. I always thought white was more appropriate when someone faded to be with the goddess.

As I'm filling my glass, someone bursts out laughing and I glance up, then freeze.

"Scarlett?"

I *shouldn't be here.*

Slade stares at me like I grew two heads. Or rather like I busted into a private family gathering. A fading, if I'm not mistaken. I've never been to one, but it's pretty much the same as a funeral, and I've gone to a couple of those.

Behind the shock, Slade looks like a shell of himself. I wish I would have succeeded in talking myself out of this foolish trip. This is the last place I should be.

"What are you doing here?" he asks, and I rip my gaze away from his.

"I'm sorry," I breathe and spin around. Of course I run straight into someone else.

"Whoa there. You okay?" the man asks, his hands gripping my arms to keep me from falling.

"I'm fine," I gasp and attempt to step back.

"Hey, it's okay." He reaches for me, his light hair flopping over his forehead.

Naturally, I run right into the table Slade was standing at. A stack of cups tumbles to the ground and I wince, hoping I didn't take out the entire drink dispenser. I don't want any more attention on me. And I certainly don't want to cause a scene.

"Fuck, fuck, fuck," I whisper, tears filling my eyes as I scramble to get the cups.

"Stop," Slade hisses. "Shit, just stand up. Hey, Mom."

I jump to my feet, staring at the ground as I set the cups on the table. When I try to slink away, the man from before blocks my way with an apologetic look.

"Hi, honey. Who's this?"

I glance at the older woman with grey-streaked hair. She's smiling at me, and I panic. "No one. I'm no one. I'm sorry for barging in. I'm going to—"

"Nonsense, dear. Did you know Bennie?" She's still smiling, and it's starting to freak me out.

Panicked, I glance at Slade. He won't meet my gaze, instead staring off over my shoulder. I don't know who Bennie is or who he was to this woman or to Slade.

"Uh, no. I didn't have the chance. I'm, um, sorry for your loss. Again, I'm sorry for…everything." I shuffle back, running into the tall blond man.

"Chase, would you be a dear and get Kira? I need her to save Gemma from Crystal. We both know that woman will run when she sees Kira coming." She sighs as he walks away. "Now, I'd really like to know your name."

"Scarlett," I whisper. "I'm—"

She holds up her hand, and I fall silent. "I've heard enough people apologize to me over the last week."

I nod like I understand. Actually, I do. No one was overly sad when my parents died. They were too busy in their lives to form any real connections. Holden and I weren't even going to have a funeral. Except then a lawyer stepped in and said we had to in order for Holden to get his inheritance. More people showed up than we were expecting, and they all said the same thing. "I'm sorry for your loss." I hated it.

"Sucks, doesn't it?" I finally say.

"Scarlett," Slade growls, and his mom shushes him.

"Yes, it certainly does. I'll leave you to deal with this one." She waves her hand at Slade, then fixates on me. "If you disappear without coming to find me, I'll be disappointed. Understood?"

She gives me a knowing smile, but I have no idea what I'm supposed to know. It's like we're in on a secret and she forgot to tell me what it was. Slade doesn't move as his mom kisses his cheek, then walks away. He's so still, his gaze a million miles away.

"Who's Bennie?" As soon as the question slips out, I want to stuff it back in. I should have just said I was sorry and walked away, too.

"My dad."

Two words, yet they hold the weight of his despair. His dad. The person he looked up to, admired. The one he strived to be, though he didn't say it out loud. I could tell every time he talked about the man.

And I just crashed into his grief, thinking I was going to do some grand gesture. "I didn't know. I thought it was...something else."

"Nope." He runs his hand through his hair and glances around. "What are you doing here, Scarlett?"

"I don't know."

His brows pull low, and I realize he still hasn't looked at me. "You don't know."

"I mean, I thought I did, but this isn't...I mean, I messed up. I shouldn't have come. I just—" I clear my throat when he tips his head back.

A woman slips next to him. "Slade, Gladys told me to ask you where more ice is. She said you'd know."

"Uh, yeah. I'll grab some. Mom doesn't want anyone in the house right now." He pivots as if he'll just walk away, then sighs and gestures for me to follow him. I don't want to. I want to just leave.

Following him to Moon Cove was a mistake. I should have let him go. Except I wasn't going to at first. I sat on that note, reading it over and over and agonizing whether or not I should come. I'd convinced myself the last couple lines meant something else.

*It isn't you. It was never you.*

At first, I thought he meant I wasn't meant for him. That I was never the one he would choose. After I was done with that spiral, I somehow persuaded myself to think it meant I was never the problem. I latched onto that thought.

Impulsively, I packed up my car and just drove. Several times I almost turned around. My memories with him were the only things that kept me going. Now I'm wishing I would have gone home. I wish I had never chased this ridiculous fantasy.

Despite the anxiety, I follow him into the house. He's already disappeared, yet I follow the path. It's like I know exactly where he is. I step through the back door and swing to the right into a small room. It's lined with freezers, and I find Slade digging in one. He pulls out a couple bags of ice. When he turns and spots me, he freezes, his gaze darting away from mine.

"I don't know why you followed me. I left a note," he says with no emotion in his voice.

"I read between the lines. I *thought* I was reading between the lines. It was a mistake, and I won't make it again." My chin trembles when he doesn't react. "I'm going to go. I'm sorry."

I can't stand here and have him look through me. He's grieving and I'm not about to add to it. If he wanted to talk to me, he would. He's making it pretty clear I shouldn't be here, despite what his mom said. Trying to force him to make a decision about us would be cruel. I turn around and head outside.

He doesn't stop me.

I thought I could just slip away, but of course I run into someone else. Someone whose eyes are exactly like Slade's. She narrows her gaze and scans me from head to toe.

"Oh, *you're* the one. Well, this should be interesting." She smirks, and once again I feel like I'm on the outside of a secret.

"I'm sorry?"

She waves her hand dismissively. "Don't mind me. I'm just enjoying the reprieve from my heart breaking. Mom, Gladys to you, wants to see you. Oh, and if she says some cryptic shit, just roll with it. She rarely reveals what she actually means. Usually right, though." She turns and flounces away, only to swing back a few steps later. "Oh, heads up, she's got a little bit of the extra juice. Can see mates and all that. Thought you oughta know."

I have no idea what she's talking about. In fact, I have no idea who she is.

"See you met my sister, Alissa," Slade says from behind me, and I wince. "She tell you anything insightful?"

"No. I'm going to—"

"Better go say something to Mom. She'll lay into me if you don't."

He pushes past me, careful not to actually touch me. I get he's hurting, but I can't help but feel like it's personal. His behavior doesn't surprise me. I read into things and thought he wanted a future. Something more than the summer, anyway. I should have kept my skepticism. Then I wouldn't be in this mess. At least if I cry, everyone will think it's because I'm mourning. The thought makes me feel like an asshole.

I stick to the fringes of the large crowd. It spills off the patio, practically all the way to a lake shimmering under the full moon. It's not hard to avoid everyone.

I spot Gladys patting someone's arm while tears stream down their face. I can't imagine comforting someone when your own heart is breaking. This woman lost her mate, and yet everyone seems to think their grief is more important. Or that she should share in their pain.

Interrupting would be an asshole move so I stand

awkwardly a few feet away next to a tree. A minute later, two women walk near the shore, their voices barely carrying to me.

"Did you see the blonde woman who almost knocked over the drink table? I swear Slade was about to throw her out," a dark-haired woman says with a laugh.

"He looked like a deer caught in headlights," the second woman says.

"Wonder who she is."

"No idea, but I overheard Alissa saying she was a lorelei. Like a legit lorelei. I don't know how Slade got caught up in her net, but her showing up here? Clearly she wanted to sink her claws into him further. Probably thinks he's getting a big inheritance or something."

"Poor Slade. He just lost his dad. I suppose the lorelei don't care about things like that, though, do they? They just take whatever they want without any remorse."

They wander off, their voices too muffled to hear any longer. My chin trembles and I struggle to keep my tears from falling. I should have known Slade would say something to his family. They probably know all about me. Or at least whatever Slade's told them, which obviously wasn't very flattering. It's my worst nightmare come to life. If I hadn't made up my mind to leave before, I would now. I can't be around these people a second more.

I hurry past the crowd and hear Gladys call out to me. She catches my arm when I've almost made it to the side of the house.

"What's wrong? Are you okay, dear?"

I bite my cheek until copper floods my mouth. It's the only way I'll be able to keep myself from breaking apart entirely.

"I'm fine. I just wanted to say goodbye. I'm sorry again about this."

"Oh, Scarlett," she murmurs.

"No, I'm okay. I just remembered I need to get back home. Tell Slade…just tell him I'm fine and I'm sorry."

I tug away from her hold and rush into the shadows. By the time I reach the driveway in the front, I'm running. I parked in front of the deserted general store, and I'm panting by the time I reach my car.

When I slide into the front seat, I lose it. Sobs wrack my body, and I rest my forehead on my steering wheel.

It's more than just the women's comments. It's more than the embarrassment of crashing a funeral. It's even more than Slade's rejection. It's everything. My entire life.

I was perfectly fine before he came into my life. He wormed his way in and planted seeds. He made me believe I could have something more than a solitary existence. I truly thought I was better than the world had made me to believe.

I never should have fallen for his ruse. Even if it wasn't on purpose doesn't matter. I'm worse off now because I'm aware of how alone I am. Of how much I've lost.

Holden's gone. Slade's gone. Letting Naomi in now would be a disaster. I can't do it. I just need to get to Hart's Hollow. If I can make it home, I can put my life back together. I cut myself off once before. I can do it again.

As soon as the pain stops, I can do it again.

# Chapter 31
## Slade

Hours after the reception started, most of the crowd has cleared out. I ran away almost an hour ago, though I'm still within shouting distance.

Dad and I used to sit here on the edge of the lake, hiding behind the small group of trees. My siblings weren't able to find us here, but I'm pretty sure Mom knew where we disappeared to. Still, she never bothered us, letting us keep our secret.

I lean against a trunk and stare out at the water lapping at the shore. My lip curls at the dark watchers lingering on the rock overhang across the way. Kira and I used to run there when things in the house got too chaotic. Now, those bastards are desecrating our hideout. It's as if as soon as Dad faded away, the entirety of Moon Cove fell apart.

The black figures aren't much to look at. They've never gotten close enough for me to see any details. Not that I want them to. Being omens of…something, doesn't make me want to go chasing after them. I hate how little we know about them. It sets me on edge. It's why I've been freaking out for the better part of a year while they follow me around the whole damn country. The only reprieve I had was with Scarlett.

Dad would know why. He'd know what to do. He'd give some sage advice I didn't understand until later. Or maybe for once, he'd give it to me straight. He'd tell me about the dark watchers and why they won't leave me alone. He'd tell me what I needed. Except I never told him about them. When I was here last year, I kept shit to myself for the most part. He knew something was up, but I played it off.

Numbness takes over, and Scarlett fades from my thoughts in the wake of my guilt. I'll deal with her sudden appearance later when I'm able to concentrate on anything other than keeping my family together. Alissa doesn't know what she's talking about. If I can just get my shit together, I *can* fix us. Not like Dad would, but enough to be able to function at least.

"Hiding?" Mom's voice floats to me, and I roll my head toward her. "Mind if I join you?"

"Not very comfortable sitting on the ground. Want me to get you a chair?" I'm already pushing to my feet, but she shoves me back down.

"I'm older, not old, Slade. I can handle being on the ground. Plus, I'm a shifter, same as you." She settles against the tree only a foot from me. Not Dad's tree, thankfully. I don't know if I'd be able to handle it, even if it is her.

"Everybody gone?" I ask after a few minutes of staring at the lake.

"No, but you know how they are. They'll hang around, afraid of what will happen when they're all alone in their houses. Your dad was a big part of this community. Turned the whole place around when we were almost a ghost town. I think a lot of people are feeling lost without him."

I grit my teeth, not wanting to complain to her. She taps the back of my hand and I sigh. It's been our thing since I was little. She taps my hand again, a demand for me to spill my secrets.

"I think I'd very much like to punch every single one of them in the face. Not one of them cared about anyone except themselves and their own feelings. They didn't give two shits that we lost him, only that *they* did. It's fucking disgusting." It's probably harsher than I'd usually be, but I don't give a shit. It's the truth, and sometimes the truth hurts.

She hums, nodding her head. "People need to share their hurt, otherwise it will consume them. It's why we do these things. It's not to say goodbye or ask the goddess to bless the shifter in their fading. It's because being alone when you're sad is worse than losing them in the first place."

"Still, he was your mate, and they don't seem to get that you're probably hurting more than they are."

"Some of them probably don't understand it. They've never had a mate and can't comprehend the pain that comes from this. Others, though…"

"What?" I snap, instantly regretting my tone. She merely grabs my hand and holds it between her palms in her lap.

"Others know I understand. They want someone who can relate to them. It's not perfect, but it's human."

I snort, fixing my gaze on the dark shadows across the lake. "We're not human."

"Of course we are. We're human and shifter and magic. That's the beauty of the gifts the goddess bestowed upon us. She allowed us all these extra abilities, yet still kept our humanity intact." A soft smile plays on her lips.

I open my mouth to ask how she can be so calm. How can she smile? How can she give all these people a pass? I know others who shift after they lose their mate. They spend years in their shifted form, completely abandoning their human life.

"How are you doing this?"

"One minute at a time, dear."

"But—" All it takes is a look and I snap my mouth shut.

"If you have children, you'll understand. Yes, he was my mate, but he was so much more than that." She huffs. "I want to know about Scarlett."

My chest tightens, and I curl my free hand into a fist. "What about her?"

"Well, from the way she was speaking, I don't think you invited her."

"Nope."

I don't want to talk about her. Not right now. I don't have enough room in my head to keep anything other than my memories of Dad alive. If I let anything else in, I'll forget. He'll fade away, just like his shifter form did. I don't have it in me to let him go.

"Perhaps you should have told her what was going on so she wouldn't have felt bad about crashing a fading."

"I left a note," I mutter.

She snorts. "Let me guess, it said something like, 'I have to go. My bad. Catch you later.' Am I close?"

"Not even a little. I just said I had to go home, and I was sorry I couldn't wait to tell her in person." I keep the rest to myself. My mom doesn't need to know I tried to assure her my decisions had nothing to do with her. She was never the problem, and she shouldn't blame herself.

"She's who you were staying with?"

"I really don't want to talk about it, Mom." I close my eyes, hoping she'll drop it.

"You can't put your life on hold because of this, Slade."

I shake my head, refusing to engage. When I steal a glance at her, she's staring at the outcropping. Dark watchers. At least a dozen of them now. Of course more of those fuckers turned up. I doubt they're there to pay their respects. Dad may have been important to us, to this community, but he always said the goddess doesn't play favorites. If she did, I'm sure he would have been one of them, though.

She clears her throat. "Perhaps they'd go away if you went after your mate."

Her words slice through the anger and the grief, stabbing at the ache in my chest dangerously close to my heart. "I don't care if they're around. They can haunt me the rest of my days for all I care."

"So you knew she was your mate?"

I exhale heavily. "Yeah. Figured it out when I left."

"And you left her behind? Slade, I raised you better than that," she scolds.

I dig my nails into my palms. "Mom, I really don't want to talk about it. Mates don't have to be together. Not all the time."

I tack the last words on so she doesn't give me shit. Except Scarlett being my mate doesn't change anything. Not right now. I didn't have enough time to process the news before I got here. I was too worried about Dad.

When I got to Moon Cove, I didn't have room for anything other than my family. I juggled my siblings' emotions, helped deal with people stopping by with food, and spent enough time with Dad before he faded away. I didn't have the extra strength to think about Scarlett being my mate. At least I was able to tell Dad about her before he died. Still, I don't have it in me to add my problems to hers. I doubt my mother will understand, though.

"You could have called her," she sniffs.

"No, I couldn't. I don't have her number," I say, and she mutters under her breath. "It never came up. Meant to get it, but we didn't get around to it. Mom, can we just drop this?"

"Can we? Yes. Will I? Maybe. Just tell me, does she know you're her mate?"

Pain stabs through my head. I just want a nap. Or food. Or a drink. "Unless she figured it out when I left, I don't think so."

"And you just let her walk out of Moon Cove? Honestly, Slade, I raised you better than that."

"You already used that line, Mom. Doesn't hold as much weight when—wait, what?" I whip my head toward her. "What do you mean she left Moon Cove?"

"Oh, now you want to talk about it." She gives me that look.

The one only a mother can. "I assume she left since the hotel is closed and her car is gone. Fancy car, by the way."

"Get on with it, Mom," I grit out.

She sighs and pushes to her feet. "She told me to tell you she's fine and she's sorry. I think you should go after her." She holds up her hand. "I understand you think you're not capable of doing everything. And you're right. You *can't* do everything. We don't need you to solve things here, Slade. You can't take away your siblings' grief. We just have to wade through it. Now, if you need to be around us to help you process, then fine. But I think you'll feel a lot better if you're with her."

She gives me another smile, then disappears into the night. I should follow her, make sure she gets home okay. It's not that far, but still. Except if I go back to the house, Alissa will question me about Scarlett. Eli will break down in my arms. Gemma will keep giving me those looks full of sympathy. Alister will corner me again and grill me on why I didn't do more, though more tactfully than that. Sloane will press her lips together and narrow her eyes. Kira will cling to Chase, refusing to talk to me about anything. Not that I blame her.

And Mom. Mom will pretend like she's fine.

I push to my feet, uneasiness filling my gut. Against my better judgment, I pull in the magic floating through the air and shift. My wolf takes over, seeming to know where he wants to go. I let him while my mind wanders to other things—mundane things. Except Scarlett keeps popping up.

It's like she's dogging my every step. I keep seeing her face when I asked her why she was in Moon Cove. Surprise, shame, panic, hope, confusion. She cycled through the emotions, then started over until she finally settled on defeat. It's not that I didn't want her here. I just can't help everyone...

*I can't help everyone.*

My wolf takes me around the lake, up the hill, and skids to a stop at the outcropping overlooking the water. Moon Cove glitters in the distance, reminding me of memories I wish I could forget. I spent so many years here. I grew up running those streets and exploring the woods around us. Going to dinner at the cafe with Mom on our specific days was a staple of my childhood. And hiding in the spot among the trees with Dad.

Even with all those memories, I still craved something more. When Gemma left for college, I went too—finding adventure wherever I could. I didn't think I'd find a place to settle down that wasn't here.

Then along came Scarlett and her grilled cheese and her yoga and her renovations. She took over my entire existence. I don't understand why it took me so long to figure out she was my mate.

When I tried to leave, though, a vise clamped around my heart. The thread tying us together, the one I mistook for lust or affection, tightened until I was sure it would snap. Except it never did. Even now it tugs me toward where I'm sure she is.

My wolf lets out a growl and crouches as we stare into the forest. It takes me a minute to see what he's seeing. A shadowy form floats between the trees. This close, I'd assume I'd be able to make out more than just dark mist, but I can't. My wolf leaps toward it before I can stop him. A snarl leaves us, and he snaps at the dark watcher.

"It's already gone," Kira calls from behind me, and I swing my head around. "I think I figured out why they appear randomly."

She drops onto the rock ledge, back facing me, and pats the spot next to her. I lope over, my senses still on high alert.

She sighs as she sits back on her palms with her feet dangling over the edge. "You think anyone else comes up here? Probably not, but I like to think Dad did after we grew up. He used to sneak me up here when I was little, like four or five. Some of my favorite memories."

She buries her fingers in my scruff, and I close my eyes. I

don't need to shift to be here for her. Eventually, she'll get to the point of what she wants to say. Or maybe this is what she wants —a walk down memory lane. Wasn't I essentially doing the same thing earlier?

"You know, when I got the call, Chase wasn't home. He was off in the woods with Jake trying to clear a path some trees fell across. I didn't want to wait for him, and he wasn't answering his phone. I wrote him a note, just like you, then threw some things in a bag and took off. I didn't want him to worry, but I also didn't want to ask him to come with me."

I swing my head toward her, and she huffs out a laugh. "Don't give me that look. I didn't want to be a burden. He was in the middle of helping with the summer camps and dealing with some things with his parents' estate. Adding to his stress wasn't something I wanted to do. Except my plan didn't work. That foolish bastard ran after me. Shifted and took off, trying to catch up to me. The only reason he caught me before I got too far was because I had to pull over I was sobbing so hard."

I shift and she yanks her hand away with a yelp. She mutters a curse and leans away from me while I settle next to her. We swing our feet in sync, and I finally look at her.

"Are you trying to make some comparison between your situation and mine? Because I don't think they're close enough for that."

She shrugs, then glances to her left. "He's out there. Not close enough to hear. He doesn't like being too far from me here. Probably thinks I'll be lured back to Moon Cove through nostalgia."

"Or he thinks I'll push you off the cliff." The joke rings hollow.

"Slade, as someone who fought against the mate bond, I'm not going to tell you to go after her. I am going to tell you to not let her think it's her fault."

"I told her it wasn't. In the note, I said it wasn't her."

Her gaze softens as she peers at me. "Does she know that?"

She pushes to her feet and shifts before vanishing into the night. She doesn't need my answer. I know she means well and is trying to help, just like Mom, but it doesn't change where I need to be.

Scarlett doesn't need me. My family does. I can't imagine being the only one who leaves while everyone else sticks around. I'd be abandoning them, pure and simple.

If I went after Scarlett right now, she'd get a shell of me. I'm in no condition to do anything for her. I'm barely holding shit together for everyone else, much less myself. A mad dash back to Hart's Hollow would drain the last bit of me. And the guilt over leaving so soon would eat me alive. I'd end up resenting her and blaming her for my choices.

No, I can't go right now. Scarlett will understand. She has to. Otherwise, I don't know her as well as I think I do. I'll explain why I stayed later, when I've dealt with things here. Hopefully, she'll actually listen.

# Chapter 32

## Scarlett

"Rule one, don't be an asshole. Broke that one several times over," I mutter to no one in particular. "Rule number two, no swimming."

I glance around at the water I'm soaking in and snort. Since I'm currently breaking that one, I might as well keep going. I flip onto my back and close my eyes as I float.

The small pool of water technically connects to the river, but not enough to pull me downstream. Time and flooding carved out the bank, leaving this area behind. It's one of my favorite places to come when my bones and joints start to ache. Something about floating helps.

"Rule three is no going in my bedroom." Since I've been sleeping on the couch for a week, I may have kept that one. Then again, I have been going in there for clothes. Maybe that doesn't count.

"Rule four," I sing, and birds rush from the trees, sending the leaves rustling. "No showers over ten minutes. Guess I broke that one a lot over the last few days." Crying in the shower has become somewhat of a pastime regardless of how cold the water runs.

"Let's see, is number five not eating or not doing laundry?" I ask the dark watcher skulking on the opposite bank. He's been the only companion I've had for a while. "Either way, doesn't really matter, does it? And then there's rule number seven. No fixing the car. Well, I suppose that would require me to have a broken-down car and since he's not here, it doesn't really count."

Maybe that's why he hasn't shown up, his car broke again. It was on its last legs when I fixed it up, anyway. I didn't hang around Moon Cove long enough to scope out the mechanic situation.

If he is going to slide back into my life, though, I doubt it would be now. I don't know how long it would take to work through that type of grief. I have no compass to guide me for something like this.

With the look on his face when I showed up, I don't know if it's entirely about him losing his dad. He kept asking why I was there. He wouldn't meet my gaze. He went to extreme lengths not to touch me even in the most mundane ways.

Adding in the things I overheard those women talking about makes me question everything. Slade may not have been gossiping about me, but his sister sure was. He must have told her I'm a lorelei and she spread it around, opening me up to criticism. I'm sure he didn't think it would be a big deal since I was never supposed to be in Moon Cove.

Can I live with everyone in his life hating me merely because of what the goddess made me? Slade wouldn't cut off his family, and I don't blame him for that. He'd be in an impossible situation, though. I'd never go back to Moon Cove. He wouldn't want to leave me behind. At least, I don't think he would. It's unsustainable. *We're* unsustainable.

I shake my head, sending ripples through the water. "Rule eight, one week. Can't break that rule. Today is the last day I'll wallow, then I'll get back to putting my life back together. Just one more day."

I don't want to wait. I've cried. I've raged. I've second-guessed. I've gone through all seventeen stages of heartbreak and, while I may not be ready for acceptance, I'm tired of not being okay.

"It was only a couple months, Scarlett, and half that time was spent snapping at each other. You can't be heartbroken. Heartbreak only comes if there was love, and there's no way you were in love." Except I'm pretty sure I was. Or am. "Can't make someone want to be with you."

A whistle rings out, deep within the woods, and I sigh. "Rule number nine. Not about to break that one." I'm not concerned with the sun high in the sky and the birds and insects keeping up their song. It's probably just some random asshat trying to scare someone. Besides, I have wallowing to do.

I float for who knows how long, cycling through arguments and reasonings. None of it changes things. Unless he's here, standing in front of me, everything will stay the same. I'll keep fixating on what I could have done differently. First thing I'd change is driving my ass up to Moon Cove.

Huffing, I flip onto my stomach and make my way toward the shore. I keep my eyes on the water. I'm not ready to encounter the dark watcher again. They're becoming an annoying addition to my life. I wish Slade had taken them with him when he left. I thought I saw them on my way out of Moon Cove, but it was late and dark despite the full moon marching its way across the night sky.

When I reach the bank, I pick my steps carefully on the rocks littered in the sand. Finally, I glance up, reaching for my towel, and a shriek leaves me. I stumble back into the water until I'm up to my knees.

"Thought we weren't supposed to go swimming?" Slade gazes at me, his dark hair ruffling in the breeze.

Gone is the animosity from a week ago, though some of the emptiness remains. He's plopped himself on the edge of the grass, his arms resting casually on his knees with his fingers laced together. Despite his relaxed position, tension lines his body.

"Were you sitting there the whole time?" I swear my entire body reddens from the embarrassment. "You're not supposed to eavesdrop on people. It's rude."

He glances off, frowning. "Wasn't eavesdropping, Scarlett. Just got here."

My mind blanks and I grasp for something to say. I thought if I ever saw him again, I'd do something other than stand here, slowly sinking into the wet sand. Yelling at him doesn't seem appropriate. Demanding answers won't get me anywhere. Breaking down would send me into another spiral.

So instead I settle for the same words he dropped at my feet a week ago. "What are you doing here, Slade?"

He shrugs, his knuckles turning white. "Mom said you seemed upset when you left Moon Cove."

I barely keep my mouth from dropping open, and I cross my arms. "So, you drove halfway across the country and snuck up on me because your mom wanted to know if I was okay? Bullshit. Why are you really here? Did Holden call you?"

He tips his chin up, and I huff. Of course that's what happened. I don't know how Holden knew I was wallowing or what happened between Slade and me. Actually, it doesn't make any sense unless Slade ratted me out. He's the type of guy who would tell my brother because of bro code or something ridiculous like that.

I stomp forward, flinging water as I go, and snatch up my towel. I wrap it around myself like a shield. Not that I'll be able to resist him in any way, shape, or form. Even now with a whole host of emotions swirling inside me, I feel the pull toward him. Whether it's magical or something else, I don't know.

"I'm perfectly fine. You can tell Holden that since he doesn't think it's necessary to call his sister." I march past him, then struggle to keep my anger up the incline.

"I didn't talk to Holden," he calls, and I spin around, almost sending myself tumbling. Bastard is sitting in the same position, gazing at the water.

"Well, then it must be the parental guilt your mother heaped upon you. Either way, I'm fine."

A humorless chuckle leaves me. "While my mother definitely knows how to slather on the guilt, she doesn't employ it very often. Especially not in this case. She's a little busy, anyways."

Shame slices through me, and I swallow hard. "I'm sorry."

"Don't be. You didn't mean anything by it. She wouldn't take it that way either."

I wait for him to say more, but of course he doesn't. "Okay, then," I mutter and spin around.

"I didn't know how to tell you," he says, and I freeze again. He could be talking about his dad dying or leaving without telling me or about what happened in Moon Cove. I don't know if I have it in me to ask.

"It's fine."

"It's not. I didn't…"

"You didn't have to come here. I mean, I don't need you to apologize or anything." I wince, realizing he probably wasn't saying he was sorry.

"Do you know?"

"Slade, I can't do this. I have no idea what you're talking about or what you're trying to say."

"I'm trying to communicate," he mutters, tucking his chin to his chest.

"You're not communicating. You're having half the conversation in your head and I'm fucking lost. So, just spit it out so I can get on with—"

He shoves to his feet and whips around. "Get on with your life? If you want me to leave, just say that, Scarlett."

"I just want you to tell me why you came back," I whisper.

"Why'd you follow me to Moon Cove?"

I clutch the towel tight and glance over his shoulder at the goddess's minion keeping watch. "Because I thought it was something else. I thought it was a sibling emergency you didn't want to ask me to go on. Or, I don't know, your mom needed help at your family's store. It wasn't like you were very forthcoming with your note. And I'll have you know, I agonized over whether or not I should go. When you wrote it wasn't me, I thought…a lot of different things. I just settled on the wrong answer."

"You thought I meant you weren't the one for me. And then when you showed up, I broke rule number one."

"You can't be an asshole when you're grieving," I mutter.

"I definitely can. As was pointed out by my mom, my sister, my other sister, my older brother, and my best friend." He glances everywhere but at me. "I told you we should see where things go. I lied."

"I know." I stare at my feet, hoping he doesn't notice the tears forming in my eyes.

"Don't think you do, actually. I knew back then what I wanted. I just didn't want to scare you away."

I swallow hard. "Yeah, I get that."

We were on such weird footing back then. I thought we'd gotten over it. I should have just said something later, when things had calmed down. When we were on the same page, planning for things in the future, and settling into a routine. I was too scared to say anything. I've lived my life being cautious of others, but this was just me shying away from possible rejection.

His knuckle brushes against my chin, and he tips my face up. His skin on mine sets my body on fire, and I struggle to stop myself from launching into his arms.

"Are you making assumptions again, beautiful?"

I bite my tongue and shake my head. If I open my mouth, either a love confession or a denial will fall out. Since I don't know what my brain will decide to do, I swallow down all the words struggling to escape.

"Yeah, that's what you're doing."

"No, I'm not. I get what you're saying," I snap as I lean away from him. He grips my chin, forcing me to stay.

"If I would have told you I wanted to stay with you, be with you, would you have let me in? Or would you have pushed me away like you're doing now?"

"I'm not pushing you away," I cry. "I'm literally standing in front of you."

He nods, then rests his forehead against mine. "I'm sorry I acted like I did in Moon Cove. I was numb and couldn't process anything. I was so focused on trying to fix everyone around me. I thought I had to be the strong one."

"I don't blame you," I breathe, closing my eyes. "I'm not upset with you. I crashed into your family's grief, then acted like a weirdo. Then you show up, and I yell at you."

He brushes his lips against mine, and I lean into him. We have so many things to discuss, but I yearn for him—for the closeness I've missed since he left.

"Did you figure it out? Did the goddess tell you?" he murmurs.

"Did she tell me what?"

He pulls back, then drops his hands to his sides. "Mates. I didn't want to tell you, to pressure you..." He runs his fingers through his hair and sighs.

"Lorelei don't have mates."

"Says who? Because I feel it here." His fist hits his chest. "Plus, I talked to Alissa, and she said—"

I hold up my hand. "I don't particularly want to know what she said. Even if we are, which makes sense with the way I've been feeling, it doesn't erase all the other things standing between us."

He crosses his arms like he's gearing up to prove me wrong. "Like what?"

"Like my illness."

"Not a problem for me. I like the idea of taking care of you for the rest of our lives."

I swallow hard. "My being a lorelei."

"Again, not a problem. I've got more than a couple cryptids in my life." He smirks, and I have the irrational urge to push him down the hill.

"For the record, I didn't want to do this." I wait until he nods, then suck in a deep breath. "Your family. Your friends. Your hometown."

"What about them?"

"Well, they know I'm a lorelei because of Alissa. I overheard a couple of women talking, and they...well, let's just say it wasn't very nice. I have a feeling your family—"

He holds up his hand. "First of all, I don't give a shit what some gossipy old biddies had to say about you. Like to know who it is, but their opinion doesn't matter. Second, Alissa doesn't care what your shifter side is, except for the fact she's now hyperfixated on finding every single thing there is to know about them. Expect a presentation when we visit Moon Cove next. Though that'll have to wait a bit."

"Why's that?"

"Oh, they're all pissed off at me because I waited until Gemma and Kira went back to Whispering Pines before coming here. If you lived closer, I would have just came and got you, but I needed to be there for my family. I was..." He clears his throat. "I was hoping you'd forgive me for not racing after your car. It's not that I didn't want to."

"Slade, I don't—"

"Don't tell me you don't know." He grabs my hands as if he thinks I'll run away. "Just tell me you want to make this work. That you're willing to try."

"Slade, I don't—"

"I need you, Scarlett." He drops to his knees, and I groan. "You're my solace. You're the thing I've been searching for. I kept skipping around, waiting to find a place to call home. And then I came here. It took me a minute to figure out it was real— that *you* were real. Once I did, though, I knew I couldn't let you go. I found home. If you don't want to stay here, fine. We'll go anywhere you want. Just don't tell me to go. Please."

"Get up. You're going to fall down the hill."

He smirks, glancing up at me through his lashes. "So, you don't want me to get hurt?"

I let out a breathless laugh. "No, I don't want you to get hurt. Who would extend my porch then? Or help me with my sourdough when I was sick? Or punch assholes who think they can do whatever they want?"

He scrambles to his feet and cups my cheeks. "Do you want me to drive over there and punch him again? Because I will."

"No, I want you to kiss me, then pretend I wasn't crying, then take me back to the house so I can shower."

He presses his lips to mine, and something clicks into place. This might not be perfect, *I* might not be perfect, but I'm willing to try. For him.

"Anywhere else we need to go after this?" I ask as Slade and I reach Naomi's bakery.

"Not that I can think of. Especially with us going up to Moon Cove in a couple days, we don't really want to stock the fridge or anything." He slips his arm around my waist and squeezes my hip.

"I was more thinking like getting dinner at the cafe or getting snacks for the road trip."

"Nah, I picked up the snacks yesterday. And before you ask, yes, I got you those weird pretzel things you like. Plus, I'm making dinner tonight, so as much as I'm sure you'd love to hang out with Bernice, it'll have to wait until—" He freezes and I jolt to a stop, glancing up at him. I follow his gaze to a guy a little older than us. The man paces back and forth in front of Naomi's, muttering to himself.

I jab Slade with my elbow, and he grunts. "Who's that?"

"Um, my brother," he mutters. "Alister?"

Alister whips his head around and visibly relaxes. "Slade, thank fuck. I've been wandering around this town for an hour trying to find you."

Slade tugs me forward, and I peer through the window to find Naomi. Her gaze darts between the floor and Alister. I wonder what happened before we got here to make them both so jumpy.

"You could have called," Slade says, pulling his older brother into a tight hug. "What do you need?"

"Phone died. Lost my charger. Barely figured out where this place was since it wasn't on the paper map I had." He shakes his head, and I catch a glint of red in his long hair. "Anyway, Mom gave me a care package to give to you since I was going this way. It's in the rental I parked in front of the general store."

"So you're not going to be home for Samhain?"

"Gotta get back out there. The ship won't sail itself, and we have to leave before the autumn gales set in."

Slade nods like he understands, but I can tell he doesn't. When Slade said his brother was sailing the high seas, I thought it was a metaphor. When I found out Alister was actually captaining a ship, I laughed. I'm just as baffled as the rest of his family.

"Okay, well, we have to drop these loaves off here, then we'll go back to the car with you."

Alister finally looks at me, and I swear his eyes narrow slightly. "So you're the new mate, huh?"

"Alister," Slade says, a warning in his voice.

"What? It's her fault."

I rear back like he slapped me and drop my hold on Slade's hand. "I didn't do anything."

"Oh ho, you certainly did. All Mom can talk about now is mates and when the rest of us are going to find ours. Three down and only four to go. Sloane left early just because she couldn't take it anymore. Still going back for Samhain. Traitor."

Slade bursts out laughing, and I nervously join him. Even if Alister's joking, he delivers everything so seriously I don't know how to take him. Slade doesn't seem offended, though, so that counts for something.

"Well, maybe my visit will make her think twice about

harping on the rest of you. I could do some freaky lorelei stuff or something," I say uncertainly.

"See that you do. It's a good thing I don't get reception on board. I'd never hear the end of it." He pivots sharply and yanks open the door to Naomi's bakery, then ushers us inside.

"Hey, Naomi," I call, and she appears from the swinging door to the back.

Her smile disappears as soon as her gaze alights on Alister. A deep flush takes over her face, and her eyes widen. I glance between them and find panic on Alister's face. Slade seems oblivious as he plops the box onto the counter.

"Fresh loaves. We tried a new one this week. It's got some random fruit in it I can't remember," Slade says cheerfully, woefully ignorant of the tension in the air.

"Dates." I slide next to Slade and rap my knuckles on the counter twice. Naomi's gaze snaps to me, and she swallows hard.

"We'll see how that goes. I've had about a dozen people try to put in orders in the last two days for your cheese bread. They were not happy."

"Do you need me to say something?"

"Oh no. I just told them to talk to Slade if they had a problem, and suddenly no one did." She forces a smile to her face.

Slade laughs and I force myself to join in again. We're going to have to have a talk about reading the room.

"Well, if you don't need anything else, we have to scoot," I murmur.

When I try to pull Slade away, though, he resists and gestures to Alister, who's still frozen by the door. "This is my brother Alister. And this is our friend Naomi."

Alister shakes off whatever stupor he was under and crosses the space in two strides. I scramble out of the way as he sticks his hand over the counter. Hesitantly, Naomi reaches out and they shake. I swear they both shudder and release each other much too quickly not to mean something. Whatever is happening between them isn't my business, but I'm nosy.

"Alright, we gotta get going. Still have to pack and all that. Thanks, Naomi. See you in a couple weeks." I grab Slade's arm and drag him away. Alister follows, glancing several times over his shoulder at the woman.

I'm practically bouncing by the time Alister drives off in his rental car. Slade keeps giving me concerned looks. If he doesn't get his butt in gear, I'm going to leave him and call Alissa instead. Or maybe Kira. She's always up for a juicy piece of speculation. Then again, I probably shouldn't be spreading things in Slade's family.

"Finally," I breathe when Slade climbs in the passenger seat. I take off before he can buckle.

"What's your hurry, beautiful? You got a hot date or something?"

"Well, yes, but also, did you notice?"

"Notice what?" His hand slams onto the dash as I take a turn. He's always so dramatic when I drive.

"Uh, your brother and Naomi? They were acting *extremely* weird with each other. If I didn't know any better, I'd say they'd met before." I'm not going to voice my other theory. I doubt Slade would take me seriously since I didn't really notice we were mates until months later.

He rolls his eyes. "Alister probably just thought she was pretty. Besides—"

His phone rings as we pull up to the house. He pulls it out and puts it on speaker. "Hey, Lissa, what's up? You in Moon Cove?"

"I'm always in Moon Cove. I don't have time for pleasantries, Slade. I need to know what physical symptoms you had when you knew Scarlett was your mate."

"Doing some research?"

"Something like that," she mutters, and I narrow my eyes.

Something is up with the Livia clan, and I'm not entirely sure if it's typical of them or not.

"Uh, I can text it to you. Kind of a long list. Plus, I don't know what was stress over Dad acting weird and what was the mating bond."

"You're no fucking help," she groans. "Fine. I'll figure this shit out on my own. Like usual."

The phone beeps, and Slade gives me a confused look. "The goddess must be up to something because this shit is getting weird. Sloane called me in the middle of the night last night and asked when the last time I saw a white feather was."

"Well, if she is up to something, we won't be able to do anything about it. You know they have to let the moon guide them just like it did us."

He sighs and pushes his door open. "Yeah, but you know how it is."

I follow him into the house and head straight for the kitchen. I'm still recovering from the last flare-up, and I don't want a repeat when we're in Moon Cove if I can help it.

"You know, I've been thinking…" I murmur as I set the kettle on the burner. "We should probably come up with some new rules."

"Is that so?" he asks, still staring at his screen. My words must process slowly since it's another minute before he sets his phone on the island.

I lean against the counter, and he boxes me in. "Rule number one—"

"I must kiss you at least once a day." He grins, then presses his lips to mine.

I pull back before I get lost in him. "Rule number two, don't keep things from each other. Even if we think it'll hurt."

His eyes soften and he kisses me lightly. "Rule number three, if you hear a whistle, no you didn't."

I give him a look, then take a deep breath to calm my nerves. "Rule number four, say *I love you* at least once a day."

He opens his mouth, probably to give the next rule, then snaps it shut. "Yeah, that's a good rule. Why don't you do that one first?" he breathes.

Sliding my hands behind his neck, I stand on my tiptoes and kiss him again. "I love you."

He doesn't say it back, and my stomach flips. Even though I know he loves me, I still need to hear him say it. I need the certainty those words bring.

When he reaches over and flips off the stove, my brows pull low. My stomach flips again when he tips me over his shoulder and makes a beeline for the bedroom. I'm laughing by the time he drops me gently on the bed.

He peels off my clothes in record time, and his lips skim across my body as he whispers something I can't hear over and over. I strain to hear him while still enjoying his touch. It isn't easy to concentrate when his fingers are slipping between my legs. He stands suddenly and rips off his shirt. Next his pants go flying across the room, and he crawls on top of me.

Cupping my face, he stares intently into my eyes. "I love you, Scarlett. My beautiful mate. My solace. My home. Never doubt that I love you.

Tears spring to my eyes, and he brushes them away with his thumbs. The rest of the world falls away as he shows me exactly how much I mean to him. We might not have everything figured out, but we have each other.

And that's more than enough for me.

# Thank You

Ready for another adventure?
Check out the other works available by Emilia Abraham.
If you'd like to hear about the other stories, sign up for my
newsletter (including extra scenes & epilogues), visit my website,
or follow me on social media visit:

emiliaabraham.com

## Special Thanks:

- K.B. Barrett Designs-Cover Artist and Formatter
- Dragon Smith Publishing, LLC-Emily Michel-Editor
- Erenee-Beta Reader
- Krysten-Omega Reader

# ALSO BY EMILIA ABRAHAM

Also by E. Abraham:

**Shadows of Synd:**

Under the Shadows-Book 1

Between the Shadows: Novella

Running From Shadows-Book 2

Becoming Shadows-Book 3

Shadows Within Us-Book 4

Beyond the Shadows-Book 5

**Ruins of Rima: Spin-off Series**

Chasing Darkness-Book 1

Charmed by Darkness-Book 2

**Havoc in Harris Duology:**

Phantom Betrayal

**Novella:**

Cadence of the Xylophone

**Available on Newsletter:**

Extra Scenes

Bridging Epilogues (Shadows of Synd-Book 1 & 2)

**Also by Emilia Abraham:**

Write on the Edge

What Not to do When Summoning a Demon

**The Cryptid Chronicles:**

Bewitched by Bigfoot

Seduced by the Sliver Cat

Lured by the Lorelei

# ABOUT THE AUTHOR

After many years of dreaming of becoming a full-time writer, Emilia Abraham took the leap, bringing her words to print. From sweet contemporary romance to spicy why choose and everything in between, she focuses on the happily ever after.

Emilia lives in the Upper Midwest with her husband (who's probably sick of listening to her expound on fictional men) and three kids (who try to steal her post-it notes). When she's not writing, she enjoys reading, playing video games, and consuming copious amounts of energy drinks.